Shenanigans

Shenanigans

BY

NOEL K HANNAN

INTRODUCTION
BY IAN WATSON

First published in 2000 by
Pendragon Press
Po Box 12, Maesteg, Mid Glamorgan
South Wales, CF34 0XG, United Kingdom

book design, typesetting and editing by
Christopher Teague

ISBN 0 9538598 0 0

printed and bound in the UK by
Antony Rowe Ltd, Wiltshire

Dedication

For my father
Peter Camillus Hannan
1930 – 1994

The rock on which I built my life

Contents

Author's Note

Should you require a soundtrack to the reading of this collection, I recommend *Dead Cities* by The Future Sound of London.

Introduction

BY

IAN WATSON

Welcome to the worlds of Noel Hannan -- gritty, passionate, painful, and lyrical. Welcome to his words which so vividly describe those worlds with such buoyant invention, energy, grim irony, and yes, evocative beauty too.

By his mid-thirties, Noel Hannan has packed in rather a lot of experience: apprentice printer and bookbinder, clerk at a rail depot, Territorial Army combat medic and armoured reconnaissance commander, martial artist, writer of numerous well-received comic publications, manager of a computer centre, and goodness knows what else -- and his short stories range expertly wide afield. Here are post-collapse Manchester, the slums of Caracas, a space habitat, an alien advent, the new wired Jerusalem, Europe and the Middle East torn by terrible techno wars, a literal Purgatory on Earth, the Irish tragedy mapped on to distant planets.

Violence threads through these stories of anguished survivors, and of others who fail to survive feral or fanatical or tyrannical surroundings; and the tools of violence as well as the technology of oppression or liberation (sometimes indistinguishable from one another) are spotlit with a hard-bitten precision of observation in vividly realised scenes. Many of Hannan's characters are miscreants, undesirables, social rejects in squalid barrios haunted by the dispossessed or by cyber-cowboys, and some are fools, but there are heroes and saints as well, although heroism is not always so laudable, nor rewarded. And there is love – bitter, doomed, yet also fulfilled (or at least promising) in the most unlikely of circumstances.

"The skinny kid who had once almost starved to death was now an enormous, malevolent, fifty-year old chocolate-smeared Buddha with the density of an imploding star..." "The sodium ghost of a city to the east..." Images to die for almost casually spice the feast of fast-paced events.

Hannan is a dab hand at thinking big. Tectonic warfare

swallows up small countries, scrunch. A political leader is assassinated and resurrected repeatedly while the human race mutates around him, until far in the future he seeks the ultimate escape of a black hole. I'm reminded here of vintage Van Vogt or Charles Harness, although other stories in this collection are much more in streetwise cyberpunk vein; or should I say post-cyberpunk? Hannan is quite a specialist in apocalypse now. His writing can be fairly hallucinatory, and I imagine his stories being written apace in a state of white-hot mental fire, yet always under control, carefully scripted, a difficult trick to pull off. The themes, too, can be hallucinatory – a shaman serving big living (and exquisite) pollutant-mutant fish in his third-world slum restaurant; sexy hockey-skaters gliding on a glassed-over toxic River Seine.

Noel Hannan has an enviable talent and a lot of momentum.

Ian Watson, Northamptonshire
February 2000.

(Ian Watson is the author of many successful and critically acclaimed science fiction novels, including "Lucky's Harvest", "Oracle" and "Hard Questions".)

<u>Seeds</u>

ILLUSTRATION BY RIK RAWLING

In the Year Zero, Professor Genesis trekked for three weeks across the harsh Crystal Desert, through the Black Mountain Pass where he sheltered against the incessant caustic rain under a plastic sheet for two days, until he reached the Wood.

The Wood was an incongruous name for a vast tract of primeval forest dominated by ancient oaks with trunks as big as giants' thighbones. The Professor set down his two bags in the clearing and threw back his head, taking in great lungfuls of clean air.

During Year One, Professor Genesis forsook the mighty branches of the oaks, preferring to forage on the forest floor for deadfall with which to make his cabin. He laboured long and hard, through day and night, until he could stand back and look at the three-roomed, verandahed, thatch-roofed house with pride.

He held out his hand, palm-up, as a chill breeze sent a shiver down his spine. A single snowflake settled on his palm.

Just in time.

Snowbound during that harsh winter of Year Two, the Professor again laboured long and hard in the largest room of the cabin, which he had designated his laboratory. He had diligently unpacked his two bags on to the oak lab table; one, containing the biomorphic lifeclay, the other, intricate, expensive tools, wiring and silicon. The long cold nights and blizzard-swept days were perfect conditions for undisturbed experimentation of the highest order.

As Year Three came around, and the snowmelt ran in great rivers throughout the clearing and drip drip drip came the Chinese Torture from the Wood, the Professor took off his intensifying goggles and looked upon Jason and Jessica with chest-bursting pride.

Jason was a cybernetic creation, lovingly crafted from alloy and silicon, a sleek chrome angel with angular features, graceful on his gas-absorbed suspension legs, towering over his creator with the dim red glow of gratitude in his photo-electric eyes.

"Thank you for making me."

Jessica was a biomorphic creature, grown mature and whole from the samples of lifeclay in the Professor's bag. She was short, plump and well-furred, with a pleasant bear-like face. Her flanks were spotted with many nipples to suckle non-existent young, and she gazed at the Professor with undiluted love in her great liquid brown eyes.

"Thank you, Professor Genesis, for making me."

The Professor set to the task of teaching his children with rare enthusiasm, and all was good and peaceful in the cabin as spring warmed into summer.

One balmy night in the summer of Year Four, the Professor was woken by mewling coming from the open door of the cabin. He struggled into his dressing gown and slippers and, followed silently and faithfully by Jason, padded out across the clearing to the edge of the forest canopy. There, huddled in the deep roots of an ageless oak, lay Jessica, with a litter of twenty young suckling noisily at her teats. There were furred ones and bald ones, ones with snouts and ones with pug noses, ones with claws and ones with paws. None bore anything but a passing resemblance to Jessica, but this did not seem to concern her as she cooed over them and nudged them gently around her furry flanks. She beamed at Professor Genesis as he bent and stroked the fur on her forehead, damp from the exertions of labour.

"You have done well, Jessica," he said. "What took me an age of labour to complete, you have done twenty times over in a single night."

"You are their Creator too, Professor," Jessica demurred. The pups mewled and cried.

That night the Professor spent an hour recording the events in his dusty logbooks. The experiment continued.

The following night, equally as balmy, and with Jessica and her brood safely in place in a nest of quilts in one of the cabin's rooms, the Professor was once again woken by noises in the dark. He stumbled blearily from bed to investigate, and was greeted by tiny flashes of light and sparks from his laboratory.

Jason sat in the Professor's chair, his chrome fingers working with incredible precision with the soldering iron and electric screwdrivers from the Professor's bag. Around his head orbited a dozen or so tiny machines, LED's blinking and synthesised voices chattering as they described a wide arc around Jason and peeled away to explore the room. The last one slipped out from beneath the tip of Jason's tool and took to the air, spinning and tumbling until it found its balance, and came to a halt a few inches from the Professor's face. Blinking lights and beeps constituted a greeting. The Professor extended a palm and the little machine landed on it.

"My children," Jason said. "Have I not done well, Professor?"

"Indeed," said Professor Genesis. "I am a very proud grandfather."

Once again the Professor spent an hour of the dark night updating his logbooks, then returned happily to bed.

By the time the summer of Year Four began to bronze and rust into autumn, Professor Genesis and his communities of morphs and netics had outgrown the confines of the cabin he had built in Year One. They worked hard together to build extensions on the north and south faces of the house before the winter once again extended its icy grip on the land. The morphs scavenged the forest for the season's deadfall, while the netics used their motorised cutters and aerial abilities to prepare and construct the extensions. Well before the first snows came, the cabin was twice its previous size and the Professor, the morphs and the netics lived in happy co-habitation. Segregation was unheard of - animals and machines huddled down in corners together, to the Professor's constant delight. The experiment, this diverse world in microcosm, was exceeding his wildest expectations. He recorded it all diligently in his great logbooks.

During that winter of Year Four, with snows drifting deep against the cabin and the inhabitants confined within, two young netics, fresh and sparkling from Jason's soldering iron, took it upon themselves to conduct an experiment of their own on one of Jessica's brood, a mature rodent-faced male from her second litter. In a remote and quiet corner of the cabin, the inquisitive netics stapled the protesting morph's limbs to the floorboards and dissected it with a flashing cutter wheel.

The wailing screams of the butchered creature brought the Professor and the rest of the community running to find the source of the terrible noise. By the time Jessica found her child, the creature was dead and the culprits had disappeared.

"Netics did this," Jessica spat from between sharp, gritted teeth. "See, steel staples and the mark of a cutter. What have you got to say, Jason."

Jason stood immobile and silent, his photoreceptors blinking, recording and replaying the scene. Netics clustered around his feet and circled his head. The morphs stayed clear, grouping behind Jessica's furry legs and peeking around the side. Imperceptibly, they were dividing into two camps.

They waited for a comment from Jason. Even the Professor seemed interested in what he was about to say.

"You have no proof, Jessica," Jason replied in even, measured tones. "Do not accuse us of such terrible crimes without good reason. Morph and Netic are friend in this house."

"Not any more." The attention switched back to a furious Jessica like a tennis match. She held out the tiny ruined body in her paw, brandishing it in Jason's face. It was already starting to putrefy, breaking back down into lifeclay.

"Netics did this," she repeated. She turned and stalked away. The Morphs followed her silently. Jason returned to his laboratory with his Netics in tow.

The Professor made urgent entries in his logbooks. He tried to keep his observations dry and scientific, but he had to admit that he was upset at the turn of events. To interfere at this stage, however, was unthinkable.

The Morphs braved the snows in the clearing to bury the dead child, in the shadow of the great oak where the first litter were born. There were no Netics present. Jessica used her big paws to scoop a shallow grave and gently laid her child to rest.

Jason and the Netics looked on from the window of their room in the cabin that had wordlessly become exclusive Netic territory ever since the killing of the Morph. Jason was sad for Jessica, but he had made no effort to punish the perpetrators of the crime. *After all, it was only a Morph.* Jessica could make some more - she had already produced five wildly diverse litters this year, and the Morph population was straining the confines of the cabin. Unconsciously, Jason had gone into overdrive at the Professor's bench, churning out Netics at the dead of night in an effort to keep the balance of forces in equilibrium. The battle lines were being drawn.

The Professor presided silently over the opposing

camps, now well entrenched in the north and south extensions. He did not speak to Jason and Jessica of the rift in the communities, but recorded all happenings studiously in his logbooks.

Shortly after the killing and the partitioning of the cabin, two young Morphs, muscular creatures from Jessica's latest litter, probed the security of the Netic camp at midnight and found a tiny machine floundering with a low battery in the Professor's workshop. Using tools in their opposing-thumb hands – the first so equipped from Jessica's womb – they dismantled the struggling Netic and carried the useful bits back to their lines – a cutting wheel, a propulsion unit, a needle laser. Quietly, the Morphs began to arm themselves.

The Morph raiders left no trace of their victim, and it was days before Jason reported the missing child to the Professor. Jessica was summoned, but she denied all knowledge of the Netic's disappearance.

"I have seen Morphs armed with metal things," Jason accused. "Cutters, lasers – your filthy clay brood are arming themselves with Netic dead. Cannibals!"

"Was it not you who castigated me for accusing without proper evidence, Jason?" Jessica replied sweetly, but the Professor was shocked by the venom in her voice.

As the winter of Year Four became the spring of Year Five, and the Wood sang with the fertile joys of the season, the Morph-Netic War intensified. Each and every night, raiders from both camps met on the battlefield of the Professor's laboratory, Netic lasers crackling and Morph catapults and cutters scything through the air. Each morning, the Morphs dragged Netic dead back into their territory to break down into weapons while Morph casualties, decomposing into lifeclay, were spirited into the Netic camp to be used as fuel in Jason's new breed of reactor-powered creations.

The Professor could stand it no longer. The experiment was spiralling out of control - the chaotic notations in his logbook were evidence enough of this. He had not had a decent night's sleep in months, and his laboratory was a free fire zone. He summoned Jason and Jessica. He told them to come alone.

It was the first time they had deliberately disobeyed him. Jessica arrived flanked by two gargantuan creatures, almost as big as she was, all talon and hard muscled flesh, the sole product of her last litter. Jessica looked old and tired. Her fur, once lustrous and thick, now looked grey and mottled.

Jason was accompanied by a squadron of tiny jets performing a perfect orbit around his head like a crown of thorns. The jets were shiny, stubby and noisy, and their minute wings were loaded with missiles and laser pods. They farted and belched black smoke as they held station. Jason, by comparison, had lost the mirrorshine from his alloy chassis, and appeared stooped and downcast.

"Respect to the Creator from the Democratic Republic of Morph," said one of the Morphs through incisor teeth.

"Respect to the Creator from the Free State of the Netic," burbled a jet.

The Professor sat down sadly at his desk. His logbooks were piled there, the hasp on the fore-edges sealed with tiny padlocks.

"The experiment is over," he said. "Netic and Morph must no longer make war on one another. You are both my creations. You must live in harmony as you once did."

The two sides mulled this over. There were hurried, mumbled negotiations.

"The Democratic Republic of Morph begs to differ with the Great Creator," said the second menacing Morph, "but the Morphs are the Creator's One True Living Creation. The Netics are merely mindless automatons. The Democratic

Forces will not cease hostilities until all Netics are banished from the cabin."

"Begging to differ with the Great Creator and the slime pup delegation from the Democratic Republic of Morph," sneered a jet, "but the Free State of the Netic is the Great Creator's One True Living Creation. The Morphs are nothing but circus tricks. The Free State Defence Forces will not rest until every Morph is repelled from the cabin."

The Professor gave the statements some thought.

"I have decided," he said at last, "to banish both the Morphs and the Netics to the Wood. There you will learn to live in harmony or perish by each others' hands."

The delegations gasped.

"Great Creator – !" Jason spat.

"No, this is not the way!" Jessica protested.

But the Professor had already turned away, storing his ledgers on the shelves with exaggerated precision. When he turned to face them again, they had gone.

For the rest of the spring of Year Five, the Professor was alone with his thoughts and logbooks in the cabin. He had lied to the Morphs and Netics - the experiment was far from over. He watched the woodline for days on end through a long brass telescope mounted on the veranda, scrutinising the Morphs constructing tree houses with neatly thatched roofs in the north end of the Wood, while the Netics built metal framed shelters in the south end. For a while, there was peace in the Wood and the only sounds that stirred the Professor from his sleep of a night were the sweet sounds of honest labour. The experiment was taking a turn for the better once again, and the Professor was content.

Professor Genesis's initial logbook entry for the summer of Year Five stated that he was preparing to allow the Netics and Morphs back into the cabin after several months of peaceful coexistence in the forest. However, the entry was unfinished. Even as the Professor's pen was scrolling across the page, the Wood erupted into chaos.

The Professor rushed to the veranda and jammed his eye against the brass telescope. In the hazy spring twilight, he could see wave upon wave of tiny Netic fighter-bombers sortieing against the Morph treetop positions, LED's twinkling and missiles exploding amongst the high branches. The battle appeared to be going the way of the Netics until the Professor trained the telescope at ground level and saw dozens of Morph fighters skirmishing through the deadfall at the woodline, heads bound in bandannas and Netic weapons remodelled for hands held at the ready, faces camouflaged and body outlines broken up by carefully applied twigs and leaves. Silently, they brought the fight to the heart of the Netic camp.

With a sad sigh, the Professor returned to the cabin for his logbooks. He deleted his previous entry with firm strokes of his pen, and began to record what he had seen.

The war raged for many months, throughout the summer. In the brief lulls between the fighting, the Professor witnessed through the brass telescope flashes of light from the Netic camp, as new machines were built or battle-damaged ones repaired. In the Morph encampment, the tree-houses destroyed by jet missiles were rebuilt and occasionally the sounds of young Morph fighters familiarising themselves with stolen Netic weapons could be heard.

The Professor recorded it all fastidiously and scientifically, though his sadness grew as the toll of slaughter and suffering became evident on the page. Finally, he could stand it no longer. He returned to his laboratory and once again laboured long and hard through several hot summer nights.

Dawn's early light presented him with a new Netic and a new Morph, very different from Jason and Jessica, patterned on the evolutionary improvements he had witnessed in their children. They would not look out of place in their respective camps. He whispered messages to them and sent them scurrying to the woodline.

The Morph returned first, early the next morning. She chirruped her message to the waiting Professor.

"The High General Jessica of the Democratic Forces thanks the Great Creator for his request. However, a meeting in the Morph camp is too dangerous now – Netic air attacks are a constant threat. To safeguard the welfare of the Great Creator, High General Jessica will come to the cabin at sundown."

The Netic messenger arrived shortly after midday.

"The Lord Lieutenant Jason of the Free State Forces extends respect and thanks to the Great Creator for his request. Unfortunately, Morph assassins make the Netic base unsafe for the Great Creator to visit. Lord Lieutenant Jason will come to the cabin at sundown."

Having delivered its message, the Netic turned and shot the Morph with weaponry that the Professor did not recall installing, and sped away into the woodline before it could be stopped.

A great battle raged all day in the Wood, but by sundown an uneasy truce was in place. The Professor dragged a rocking chair out on to the veranda and watched through the telescope. The acrid smell of battlesmoke assailed his nostrils, and he could see burning debris here and there in the trees. Occasionally a Netic would slip between the foliage, carrying Morph dead back for fuel, or Morph raiders would be seen mauling dismembered Netics to their own camp.

As the Professor watched the treeline in the dying light, two indistinct blobs emerged from opposite ends of the Wood and advanced across the clearing toward the cabin. Their features and details solidified as they neared him.

Jessica looked as tired and bedraggled as the day she had left the cabin. Her head was adorned with the multi-coloured plumage of some unfortunate bird, but the rest of her body was camouflaged with the tied-on twigs and leaves of the Morph raiders. She bowed stiffly at the waist.

"Respect to the Great Creator."

Jason's mirrorchrome skin had been anodised to a gritty matt black, swathed in frosted grey tiger stripes. His photoreceptors glowed dully. He looked like a fearsome urban war robot.

"Respect to the Great Creator."

The Professor rose to his feet. Jason and Jessica remained in front of the veranda, standing apart and not acknowledging each other's presence.

"Why must Morph make war on Netic?" Professor Genesis thundered into Jessica's face. His knuckles whitened on the veranda's handrail. Jessica took an involuntary step back.

"Why must Netic make war on Morph?" He turned his venom on Jason. Spittle flashed on Jason's black face.

"Answer me!" the Professor raged. "Night after night, day after day, Morph kills Netic and Netic slaughters Morph. Do you think I created you to destroy each other? Is that your idea of respect to your Great Creator? Hmmm?"

There was silence for a time. Then Jessica spoke.

"I have no power over the Morphs," she said. "The children of my litters who were born under the shadow of the Great Creator are all dead. Now, they are born to war with the Netic and know no better. I cannot stop the war." She bowed her head.

"I too am merely a figurehead among the people," said Jason, "and have none who remember the sweet life under the guidance of the Great Creator. Netic is now created only for war."

Jason's photoreceptors glimmered and faded.

"Help us, Great Creator," he said.

"Yes, help us," said Jessica.

Professor Genesis, his anger dulled by Jason and Jessica's submissive response to his outburst, slumped back into his rocking chair. He steepled his hands and looked at Jason and Jessica through the 'v'.

"Return to your camps," he said at last. "Return with your people to the clearing at first light, in two days time. I will show them how Morph and Netic can live in harmony. Tell them to come and keep their weapons sheathed. Do you have that much power over your forces?"

Jason and Jessica nodded and left. In seconds, they were Doppler shadows against the dark mass of the Wood.

The Professor returned immediately to his laboratory, and for what was to be the last time, laboured long and hard through the night.

At daybreak, two days later, the mighty armies of the Free State of the Netic and the Democratic Republic of Morph faced off from opposing sides of the clearing, with the Professor's cabin occupying No Man's Land. Netic jets flew sorties to buzz the forward enemy positions, and Morph raiders dug foxholes and growled at the nuisance attacks from behind camouflage sheaves of leaves and twigs.

Inside the cabin, Professor Genesis was aware of the tension and anticipation outside. As soon as he was satisfied that the forces of both sides were in position, he swung wide the cabin doors and stepped into the sunshine.

Silence descended over the assembled armies. Jessica and Jason fussed among their broods, pushing younger members to the ground in prostration.

"Do you not know who that is? Kiss the earth!"

"Show some respect for the Great Creator!"

They were, by and large, ignored.

Professor Genesis noted this and turned to say something to the interior of the cabin. He moved to one side as Kane stepped smoothly out, down the veranda steps and continuing out until he occupied the centre of No Man's Land. He turned to each side and spread his arms wide. The Professor glowed with pride.

For what a fine creation he was. Neither Netic or Morph, but a glorious melting pot of both. Fully three metres tall, a muscular figure of metallic flesh, intricate fractal patterns of circuits burning across his torso and chest, a writhing, living crown of thorns resting on his forehead. Thick and shiny hair flowed down his back. He smiled beatifically at each of the armies in turn. They looked on in wonder.

"What is it?"

"Is it Netic?"

"Is it Morph?"

"Is it neither?"

The Professor stepped from the veranda and began to circle Kane, who stood rigid, facing the Wood with subtle neutrality.

"See my greatest creation," the Professor orated. "His name is Kane. He is Morph –"

A great cry went up from the Morphs, followed by a metallic growl of discontent from the Netics. Weapons were loaded, jet engines gunned to screaming point.

"– and he is Netic!"

The Morphs howled and gnashed their teeth, and the weapons of the Netics were lowered in favour of a cacophony of beeping and flashing lights.

"He is both," Professor Genesis explained. "Lifeclay and cybernetics in perfect harmony. See, he is beautiful, peaceful and good. Morph and Netic, look upon my example and ask – 'Cannot we live in such peace?' "

There was silence for many minutes among the armies. Then murmured discussions were held which did not involved Jason and Jessica. Eventually, a young Morph strode forward, brandishing a needle laser, even as a half-squadron of Netic jets were preparing to take off on the opposite side.

"All respect to the Great Creator," the young Morph mumbled in an offhand way. It was a phrase he had been taught at birth, along with killing Netics with his needle laser, and he didn't understand a word of it. He understood killing Netics right enough though.

"The lifeclay has been contaminated, infected with Netic metal," he continued, bringing the laser up into the aim. "We will release this poor Morph from its life of eternal shame and damnation."

And he shot Kane through the right eye.

The half-squadron of Netic jets struck out from their lines. An amplified tinny voice announced their intentions.

"Respect to the Creator. Good Netic stock has been infiltrated by dirty Morph lifeclay. We will rid this abomination of its infestation. Mercy to the poor unfortunate Netic."

And a volley of missiles from wingtip pods ripped through Kane's chest. He cried out, a startling, chilling noise that combined a Morph's throaty death rattle with the high-pitched squeal of a defunct Netic, and fell to earth. Blood and hydraulic fluid leaked out into the ground.

Professor Genesis ran to Kane and cradled him in his arms even as the armies rolled over him, careful to keep him out of their battle, and the war resumed in earnest.

Later that night, as the battle returned to the Wood and flashed and grumbled sporadically through the darkness, Professor Genesis lay on his pallet in the cabin, moulding two simple, final messengers out of lifeclay and circuits, and sending them on their way. The he rolled over, and died.

Jason and Jessica came before dawn to bury the Professor. They found a piece of shrapnel imbedded in his chest, a fatal wound received while the battle had raged in the clearing. It was impossible to say whether a Netic jet or a Morph gun had done it, and it didn't really matter.

They buried the Professor in a shallow grave directly in front of the veranda. Jason marked it with an imposing chrome cross which Jessica draped with the multicoloured pelt of a dead Morph raider. Then they returned to their camps without exchanging a single word.

The war raged on through Years Six and Seven, territory changing hands in the space of hours, losses mounting on both sides, Jessica's womb and Jason's production line working at full capacity to keep the front line supplied with fresh superevolved warriors to take the fight to the enemy. The Morphs developed multi-armed, razor clawed predators to travel at high-speed over the forest tracks while Netics temporarily forsook air power to build vast batteries of tracked artillery that pounded the Morph treehouses to smithereens. And so the war raged on.

Before the end of the summer of Year Eight, Jessica slipped away from her camp and crossed the clearing to the cabin. She was not missed – old and grey, she was ignored by her warriors when not actively producing young, and all traces of the Great Creator had been removed from the Morph doctrine. She was not surprised to find Jason sat on the steps of the veranda, reading the Professor's logbooks. His battle-colours of black and grey were wearing off, and rusty swathes of chrome showed through. His once-smooth hydraulic joints creaked with lack of fluid as he rose to greet her. For the first time in years, they embraced.

"I'm glad you decided to come," Jason said. "I'm sure we can do it. Look, I have found a diagram in His book."

He indicated a cross-sectional illustration of the human system in the book. Jessica peered at it through rheumy eyes.

"Nerve systems, electricity," she said. "Much like a Netic."

"And blood and live tissue," Jason replied. "Much like a Morph."

With Jason's joints creaking and Jessica's old bones protesting arthritically, they began to exhume Professor Genesis.

The Professor sat sipping tea with Jason and Jessica on the veranda as the sun slipped into the Wood, igniting the trees with a fiery sunset. The Wood was silent except for the occasional clang from the Netic camp or squawk from the Morphs.

"An artillery barrage is planned for tonight," Jason said.

"A raid was scheduled for tonight too," said Jessica. "Two hundred Morph raiders, right into the heart of Netic territory."

The Professor poured more tea. He looked very healthy considering his corpse had still been in the ground no more than two hours since. His body flexed with the electricity that Jason had induced into him, and his heart beat strongly with the help of Jessica's lifeclay implant.

"And what now?" he asked of his two creations. "You have taken me from my grave, where I was warm and safe, and returned me to your forsaken war zone. I cannot stop the war – your warriors do not even know who I am anymore – and you cannot stop the war. What would you have me do?"

"Take us away from here," they said in unison.

"Find another Wood," Jason said.

"Build another cabin, before the winter's snow," said

Jessica.

"Start another experiment?" The Professor, ever the scientist, raised one inquisitive eyebrow.

"Complete the experiment," Jason said. "Prove that Morph and Netic *can* live in harmony."

"Leave these communities to burn each other out," Jessica said. "I feel no love for these children."

"Of course!" said the Professor. He rose and paced the veranda. "Why didn't I think of it before? Without the womb and the mechanic, the Netics and Morphs will war to oblivion. They will wipe each out! Of course!"

Professor Genesis raced into the cabin then returned moments later to stick his head around the door frame.

"What are you waiting for? We've got to pack."

Before dawn, the Professor, Jason and Jessica were tramping north through the Wood. Jason and Jessica each carried one of the Professor's large bags, and the old man set a cracking pace, his logbooks under his arm, his progress aided by a stout walking stick. As the deep blue sky brightened in the east, they caught sight of the Black Mountain Pass, and paused to savour the sight.

Behind them, the sounds of war reached their ears from the Wood. Artillery whumped and thumped, and the war-whoops of Morph raiders filtered through the trees.

"Witness the sounds of civilisation self-destructing," Professor Genesis said sadly. They began the long trek to the mountain pass.

Deep in the heart of the Morph camp, in the dark backroom of a treehouse, a Morph female wailed and bit her tongue and spat out a mewling pup from her loins. Another five followed in quick succession. A Morph male held a slimy pup up to the dim light of a Netic LED suspended from the roof. The pup bit his hand, drawing blood.

"A fine warrior," he said.

And in a steel Netic shelter, a dextrous machine with agile metal claws found Jason's abandoned tools, and within a few minutes had fashioned a crude armoured creature from scrap leftovers. It belched and revved and demanded to be let loose into battle.

Fine warriors all.

And the war raged on.

Saturday Nightshift

ILLUSTRATION BY JOHN WELDING

The alarm clock wakes me gently, just as I like it. It casts its watery hologram against the whitewashed far wall and murmurs with its insistent voice

Ninepmtimetogetupninepmtimetogetupninepm

I crawl out of bed and search for something fairly clean to wear among the jumble on the floor. I find a pair of graphite leggings and a black bra that don't smell too bad, so they'll do,

The pinkbluegreen neon slices in through the horizontal blinds. I pull the cord and the room is illuminated by the huge Sony graphicsboard mounted on the apartment block on the street corner. I've lived in this flat for two years and I've never owned a light bulb. Thank you, Sony.

I love to watch the city

(my city)

at night. It's raining, a mild drizzle that does little to dissipate the omnipresent heat but turns the landscape into an entertaining kaleidoscope. Neon and graphics reach up as far as the eye can see, climbing to heaven on the flanks of blind skyscrapers, then plunging down into the fathomless depths of Hell, all perspective lost in the mirrored, rain-slicked streets. Then oil mixes with water and turns the city

(my city)

into a bad hallucinogenic vision.

I've a little more than an hour to go before I have to be at work, but there's *always* time to watch some teevee. I switch on the Amstrad Multiscreen in the corner, a forty-inch beast that lets me watch eight channels simultaneously. I would've liked the sixteen-screen version but this was the best I could afford. It's still the most expensive thing I own. I sit and channel-flip for a while.

News on Channel Eighteen. The civil war rages in Europe. I take a mild interest as I'm due to be conscripted next year. It pays to know who it is you're supposed to be fighting. Apparently, Luxembourg has fallen to the Turko-Serbian-Slovak Alliance and there has been another nuclear attack on Athens. Elsewhere, the US shuttle Columbus is in orbit around Mars, preparing to send down the first manned exploration vessel. Good luck to 'em, I say.

I tire with current events pretty easily, so I look for some gameshows. *Russian Roulette* is on, my favourite, so I slip a blank disc into the recorder and set it going. I can watch it when I get back from work. In the corner of the screen, the home shopping channel intersperses its adverts for a fruit juice machine with shots of a hot summer beach, each one-tenth of a second and barely visible. But I know that they're there and I reckon you'd have to be brain dead not to see them. Prime time teevee for rehabilitating junkies. Who sunbathes these days anyway? No one, unless they want skin cancer. Come to think of it, I do feel kind of thirsty.

Time to go. Joe Takei won't be impressed if I'm late again, and I need the money from this job to keep the flat. I've no wish to be out on the streets again, no thank you.

As I struggle into my Gore-Tex smock and dig through discarded clothes for my cycling helmet and mask, something catches my eye through the window on the vast civic graphicsboard downtown, a blaze of colour and light that overwhelms even the Sony board no more than a street's width from me. The civic board, in an impressive scrolling array of animation, trumpets the start of the game playoffs, sponsored by Nintendo, for the World Supreme Champion. The contestants are Duane Kasparov (CSI) and Kylie Manatova (Australasia – Pacific Rim Conurb). The prize is a Caribbean island. Images of the game players appear on the screen – androgynous, withered things with bloated heads, bug eyes and overdeveloped hands. Kylie has had her eyelids removed so she doesn't need to blink. Her camp reckons this is a championship-winning strategy.

I'd love to be a World Supreme Champion, but to

sacrifice your body, even for a Caribbean island of your very own? No thanks. I like my body, and there are others who appreciate it too. Reminded of this, I do a few callisthenics to limber up. I add a couple of exercises for my game playing fingers too. Just in case.

I've got my helmet on now, and my mask hangs from it by a press stud. I delve beneath my mattress and take out my gunbelt. It contains two pistols, set up for a cross draw, and they hang low on my hips, clear of the smock's hem. I use a .357 Magnum Colt Python and a Desert Eagle automatic, in the same calibre. I appreciate the stopping power of the .357, invaluable when some crazy high on whatever's new this month is intent on making you make his day, and having both guns chambered for it means I can swap ammo if one gun jams. The wheel gun is my insurance policy – revolvers are practically foolproof. All the koppers are armed with them. But it only takes six shots and sometimes you need the extra capacity of the Eagle which takes thirteen. The best of both worlds.

I'm protected now against the hostile environment of the city

(my city)

and I'm going to be late if I don't get a move on. I leave the flat in a permanent state of chaos, the Multiscreen babbling to itself in the corner to fool any would-be intruder that I'm home, I've had a bad day, I'm cleaning my guns at the kitchen table and it wouldn't be a good idea to piss about with me. Not tonight.

The door slides shut behind me on hydraulic rams. Later, when I return, an eyesafe laser will scan my retina for identification before I can get back in.

What? Paranoid? Are you kidding? You obviously don't live in this city, any city.

(my city)

My mountain bike is chained to the stairwell below with enough metal to sink Houdini. It's another of my prized possessions, a lightweight proto-alloy model from Muddy Paw, with an automatic Shimano transmission powered by a rechargeable NiCad pack. Integral lights and nylon-reinforced tyres. Jet black. Very sleek.

The usual Saturday night crowd are on the street. Pimps, hookers, pushers, gangsters, mobsters, plain-clothes koppers (sticking out like bulldog's bollocks, nervous seventeen year olds far too clean shaven for their Technicolor ravewear), street vendors and posers. But it's a dangerous district downtown if you're not a native. An item of clothing, and inflection of speech, an accidental look can bring sudden violence. Still they come from uptown and the suburbs to see what all the fuss is about. Goddamn tourists. Maybe it would have been better if they *had* declared martial law. At least then we would know who to shoot at.

I keep my head down and keep pedalling through the rainslick streets. It's stopped raining and there's little traffic apart from the (very) occasional police cruiser, windows up and travelling at high speed. They think of downtown as a safari park and we're the monkeys and tigers. Don't stop at a junction, kopper, or we'll rip your windscreen wipers off. If you're lucky.

The nightlife spills from the pavements and dominates the abandoned streets. I veer and chicane through drunken revellers and sullen-faced street dwellers. I see familiar faces from my own time as a scavenger and street-survivor. Some of them were friends, but not any more. To be a survivor, you have to rise to the top of the heap, float on the scum pile until you get a chance to jump off. I did some nasty things to get off the street and there are no doubt debts still to be paid. I'm far from ready to honour some of them. If some of my 'friends' knew that I had an apartment and a job, they would not think twice before removing my eyeball with a finger and using it to fool the ID laser, then steal everything I've worked so hard for. I've not been away from the street for long enough to make new friends who might protect me from such an eventuality.

But I do have a brother. His name is Marty, and here he is on a street corner, striking a deal. I pull up short on the kerb twenty metres away and watch him. He's only fourteen but he's already got hoods twice his age working for him. I wonder why he's down here on the street, putting himself in danger. His footsoldiers should be doing this for him.

He looks nervous even from this distance, shifting from foot to foot and taking swift, shallow pulls on a skinny reefer. His clients, one white and two black youths in Halcyon Turf sportswear, are examining the packages he has handed to them. There are loud exchanges and contorted faces and my gut knots as I realise something is about to happen.

The packages are hurled to the ground at Marty's feet and split open, spilling white powder into the gutter and puddles. Marty reaches inside the green padded flight jacket he always wears. I reach for my guns too in an instinctively protective movement but realise that Marty is too far away for me to back him up without risk of hitting him.

The youths backpeddle, hands scrabbling for concealed weapons, but Marty already has the Uzi up in the aim and is cocking it with his left hand. The night air is split with a thunderclap and my retinas burn with muzzle flash. Marty hoses the Uzi left-right and the three youths go down as if the world has collapsed on to their shoulders.

Marty stops shooting and the street is filled with false silence from buzzing ears. Marty, oh so cool, looks over his shoulder at the street people emerging sheepishly from behind dumpsters and storefronts, deposits the Uzi back into his shoulder holster, and runs from the scene.

I follow. I'm much faster on the Muddy Paw than even Marty's long-legged stride, but he starts to duck and dive down alleys and back entrances. I stop at the mouth of one and unclip my mask, hoping he'll recognise me. Marty is a shadowplay puppet at the other end.

"Marty!" I shout. He stops and I see him turn, the Uzi in his hand again and rising into the aim. My blood chills in my veins.

"Marty! It's me! Luisa!"

The muzzle drops sharply and I breath again. He makes his way down the alley toward me. The Uzi is still in his hand, hanging at his side.

"Luisa," he says, giving me one of his brief cursory hugs that pass for his version of brotherly love. "I nearly popped you. What are you doing here?"

"I'm on my way to work," I say. "I saw what happened. What's the matter, can't your hired guns be trusted to cut deals on the street anymore?"

He grimaces and for a moment looks very much like the little boy he really is. My little brother.

"A miscalculation, Luisa." He makes a shrug that implies cynicism way beyond his years. He's a hood leader again. "The Halcyon Turf insisted on dealing face to face. Now I know why. It was a hit. I think they were hired by the Snugbury Close Family. Or maybe the koppers. We'll see."

Sirens interrupt us, the piercing rise and fall of the cop cruisers mixed and dubbed with the wail of an ambulance. Marty stiffens and noses the air like a retrieving hound.

"I got to go, Luisa. Take care. Stay out of trouble. You know how to find me if you need me." He pecks my cheek and for a moment the Uzi is a dead weight against my thigh, like an unexpected erection. Then he's gone.

I pedal back through the litter-strewn alleys to the burning neon of the main street. It is a carnival of light and sound, police cruisers and ambulances slamming to a halt at aggressive angles, body-armoured police assembling in riot phalanx. The people turn their music up several notches, as they always do when the koppers are out in force. The effect is overwhelming. The sounds of loop-rhythms, pulsing basslines and tortured electric guitars combine to hinder the koppers' concentration. In desperation they call for the big boys and soon a bright blue battle tank is nosing down the street, amber emergency lights strobing and big gun tracking across the storefronts.

Downtown is in uproar, a usual Saturday night. Animosity develops through fistfights into knifefights, knifefights into gun battles, and gun battles into full scale turf war, all fuelled by long-standing hatreds and alcohol and drug consumption.

My city is a war zone.

(my city)

My place of work is at the end of the main street, a ground floor unit fronted by a huge plate glass window that gets protected by an armoured screen out of business hours. There's an alley to one side and it leads around the back to the tradesmen's entrance. And the kitchen.

"Where's you been?" Joe Takei roars as I chain my bike up in the litter strewn yard. He's standing in the kitchen doorway and he's got a filthy apron tied over his business suit. He's the fattest Japanese man that I know. He's elbowed to one side by Davy coming out of the kitchen, shrugging into a Gore-Tex smock like my own.

"Good luck kid." Davy winks at me. "He's in a foul mood tonight."

Davy's my shift partner on Tuesdays and Thursdays but tonight he's pulled an early shift. He unlocks his own bike and rides off down the alley, giving Takei two fingers once he's a suitable distance away.

"You five minutes late," Takei blusters, pulling off the apron. "This your job, not mine. I dock your pay."

"I'm coming Joe," I say, snatching the apron from him.

He's all wind and importance and I don't take his threats too seriously. He pinches my arse too often for comfort and I'm hoping I can keep this job without having to fuck him. He *can't* dock my pay – I'm working a whole hour a day every day for five days every week and it's just enough to keep the flat and keep me fed. I can't *afford* to have my pay docked. Maybe Takei will get what he wants in the end.

Joe Takei's is a sushi-bar. The sign above the door reads

EST. 1998. 25 YEARS THE FINEST SUSHI IN MANCHESTER

I prepare fish for the meals and also for the display in the window, which features live fish. I have to hold fish down on the marble slab and scoop the flesh from each flank in turn, from gill to tail, with a razor-sharp filleting knife. The fish continues to flip and flop for some time. I place them in the window with the raw vegetables and flower arrangements. Every few hours they have to be replaced with fresh ones.

I steal a glance through the swing doors as I start work. There's a party of twenty or so suited businessmen and their bimbo wives from Cheshire, laughing loudly and spilling wine on the tables. They've probably been helicoptered in tonight to get a taste of the authentic Manchester. Later, after their meal and a tour downtown in armoured limos with police escorts, they'll fly back to their cosy secure estates in the countryside with their razor wire and rottweilers, and the men will be too pissed to fuck and the women won't care. They'll fall asleep thinking, hoping, that none of the zoo animals they've seen tonight will feel like repaying the compliment, and visit them.

I push my filleting knife under a fish's gill. It struggles. They say fish have no nervous system. Sometimes I feel we have none too.

Takei moves smugly among the suburbanites, who ignore him. He increases the polarity on the glass window to the shield them from a group of beggars who have taken up station outside. I know in a minute he's going to get me to move the beggars on.

Perhaps Takei's customers would like to take a tour of the city

(my city)

a city with no nervous system, a city immune to shock, a city where everyone and everything is your enemy.

My city.

(my city)

(my city is a war zone)

Medical Ethics and Stone Cold Killer

ILLUSTRATION BY DAVID GOUGH

Medical Ethics

The gunshot wound to Felix's arm was bad but Clute had seen worse. There was a half-finished tray of Thai take-out cooling and congealing on the table behind him, and Clute was fully intending to finish it once he had stitched up the exposed muscle in Felix's upper arm. It was hot in the surgery - shit, it was *always* hot *everywhere* these days - and Clute had to stop to wipe sweat out of his eyes with his shirt sleeve.

"Five point four five millimetre," Felix said. He grinned at Clute as he worked in the surgery's bad light. Thin, greasy hair, metal teeth, filed to points, breath like bad fish guts. "A nasty bullet. Never taken one of them before. Shit, never saw it coming. From an AKM copy. Don't see many of them in Purgatory. Narrows the field down a bit."

"Who could you have possibly upset, Felix?"

"You're a funny man, Doc. There'll be dancin' in the streets the day someone gets lucky and takes old Felix out. Until then, Purgatory sleeps with one eye open. I'm their worst fucking nightmare."

Clute sealed the wound with a neat row of butterfly stitches. He had fixed up the hitman so many times he was beginning to look like a patchwork quilt, more catgut and nylon than flesh. One ear was missing - it had taken Clute three long hours to make good the repair that night, roused from his usual fitful nightmares by Mario or Vince or one of the Director's other footsoldiers - he couldn't remember which - sent on a pain-of-death mission to return with Purgatory's sole doctor to save the life - again and again and again - of his favourite, immortal, infallible, unfeeling gunman Felix the Cat. It had happened so many times that Felix had begun to look upon Clute as a friend. Clute was aware of this. It made his skin crawl.

Clute cleaned the newly-sealed wound with a sterile swab and grunted to Felix that he was finished. Felix examined the doctor's handiwork with curiosity before clucking his satisfaction and rolling down the sleeve of the black-and-white urban camouflage fatigue shirt he habitually wore, holed and stained with the blood of previous encounters. He wore it, unwashed since god-knows-when, like the medals of a war veteran. It smelt only marginally better than his breath.

Felix's pistol lay on the table next to him. It was a Steyr-Mannlich 9.5mm automatic, resin-bodied, metal-free construction, ceramic firing pin igniting carbon-fibre cartridges. Undetectable to surveillance devices at airports and police stations, not that there were very many of either in Purgatory. The gun was a gift from the Director, a novelty remnant of some arms deal. The Director was Felix's sole paymaster - Felix was his favourite hitman. They both paid lip service to the idea that Felix was a freelancer, theoretically for hire to anyone with enough cash or desirable goods to meet Felix's price, but the Director was the only man in Purgatory with such resources. So Felix was a name on the Director's payroll just as much as Mario and Vince were. They just never said so. The relationship was mutually agreeable and highly professional in its conduct.

Felix noticed Clute looking at the gun.

"She's a beauty, is she not?" Felix picked up the gun and sensually ran his mottled fingers over it. He had never touched a woman like that. He was a master craftsman and this was a tool of his trade.

Clute had turned his back to the hitman, stripping of his bloody rubber gloves and washing his hands in the surgery's stone sink. He wished Felix would fuck off. He didn't like making small talk with a man he regarded as a devil.

"An unusual gun for an anonymous hitman, Felix. Guns like that are one-of-a-kind in Purgatory. Like the AKM that nearly took your arm off. Stamps your seal on every job like fingerprints. Or is that the idea?"

Felix jumped down from the surgery table, mildly offended.

"Oh no, Doc. The nine point five millimetre isn't for work. Only amateurs and posers use distinctive guns. No, it's strictly for pleasure. Special jobs."

Felix laughed. Clute was reminded of a blocked toilet being repeatedly flushed.

Felix left. Later, one of the Director's men would come with some money or a TV set that worked or a refurbished jeep carburettor or something else that he needed, either to this ramshackle surgery set up in an old dentist's office or to Clute's own place a block from here, overlooking the river. If he lived in the surgery he would be working twenty four hours a day. Clute would accept the blood money offering. Here in Purgatory, it was his only way of staying alive.

The jungle smells of burning flesh. Darkness has fallen like damp black fog but the pyre can be seen through the maze of trunks, red pokers spearing eyes.

The patrol moves forward cautiously. Safeties off, locked and loaded, nervous fingers hovering oh-so close to delicate triggers. Half of them are boys who will piss themselves with fright at the sight ahead, the other half are psychopaths who will revel in it. There is, on average, six months of age and three months of in-country time difference between the boys and the madmen. The patrol leader is one of the latter and he'll enjoy seeing the boys squirm. Nobody here is over twenty.

The heat is intense in the clearing. Eyes accustomed to darkness screw up at the light of the fire. Heat singes soft downy moustaches and eyebrows. Hands shield faces.

"Oh fuck," says one of the kids. "Oh fuck. Oh fuck.

Oh fuck."

If you look carefully you can see the pyre is a mound of human bodies. They squirm in the inferno, limbs twitching, torsos leaping upright. It looks like they're still alive but its the heat making muscles and tendons contract. The kids don't know this. One or two start vomiting. A couple faint. The patrol leader grins.

The kids don't see the line on the other side of the pyre. A group of soldiers, dressed in the same uniform and saluting the same flag as themselves herd a line of dark-skinned peasants toward the fire at bayonet-point. Close to the fire, they are forced to their knees and despatched with a pistol shot to the back of the head by a man with officer's bars on his shoulders. Two soldiers throw the bodies on to the fire.

Burning flesh. No other smell in the world quite like it. Kind of makes the mouth water..... are we all cannibals at heart then, wild beasts, bloody red meat eaters lurking within?

The keening and crying and Catholic prayers of those about to die rises above the roar of burning and the crackling and the regular head-jerking drumbeat of the executioner's gunshot. Men, women, children, all reduced to fuel for the fire. And all crying, crying, crying.......

" - crying out loud, Joe! It's four a-m. I've just finished patching up Felix. I don't feel like - "

"She's still alive, Clute."

Pause. Deep breath.

"You've got to help her, Clute. There's no one else. I can't leave her here. This is wild dog territory. She'll be lunch in half an hour."

"Is it that bad, Joe?"

"Worse. I know you got a strong stomach, Clute. I don't even know if you can save her. Maybe the only thing left is to put her out of her misery."

"I'm on my way, Joe."
"You're a fucking angel, Clute. You don't belong in Purgatory."

She was six, maybe seven years old. Naked and lying face down with Joe's coat underneath her, a piece of plastic sheeting on top. A thin warm drizzle was drifting down. No respite from the heat in Purgatory, not even at night.

Joe, fifty, grizzled, heavy-set, had manoeuvred her into the recovery position when he found her here, whimpering like a pup, before he called Clute on his Motorola.

She was still breathing, but only just. Clute knelt on the damp concrete by her head, feeling gently for the faint pulse at her thin wrist. He thought she had blond curls but it was kind of hard to tell as the back of head was missing, and what was left was a congealed mass of bone splinter and blood.

"She shouldn't be alive." This from Clute.

Joe was standing a little way from the mouth of the alley, smoking, back to Clute and the girl. He was an ex-cop and had seen plenty, but his cheeks were still streaked with tears like warpaint. He had kids of his own, across the river, in the other world, safe from all this shit. He thought about them a lot but their mother didn't like them thinking about him. He was looking at Clute now, seeing himself fifteen years ago. More hair - darker too - thinner body, better muscle tone. Clute looked like a scrubbed college kid who did not belong in Hell.

"Will she live?"

Clute tugged the plastic sheet over her head and stood up.

"She's dead."

"Shit." Joe threw the cigarette stub to the ground and ground it out violently with his heel. "Shit. Shit. She's the fourth in as many months. That's all Purgatory needs. A fucking child killer. Was she - ?"

"Yes." Clute took out a pack of Strikes and offered one to Joe. He took it hungrily. They lit up from Clute's zippo, heads leaning together to shelter the flame from the rain. "There's glass and blood around her anus and vagina. Broken bottle. Same as the last three. Then a gunshot to the back of the head and dumped in an alley. I'd say all this took place within the hour, from the condition of the wounds. Only this time - "

" - he didn't do as thorough a job, did he?" Joe snorted with barely restrained anger. He felt as if a personal curse had descended upon him, to have found this poor girl in the last pitiful moments of her life, to share them with her. He should have been honoured. He felt debased.

Clute turned back to the girl, crouched down at her side. His eyes cast around the pile of trash where she had been dumped - burst boxes, rotting vegetables, dog shit. No place for a child to die. Christ, what *was* a place for a child to die? A crib? The womb? A mother's arms? *You're a sentimental fool, Clute.*

There were odd scrapes on the wall. The light from the sodium on the main street was not good so Clute took a maglite from his pocket and shined it on the wall. Joe came over.

"What is it?"

Clute rubbed his hand along the brickwork, into the cement between the bricks. He examined his fingertips under the torch - *bloody.*

"Hold this." Joe held the torch while Clute peeled back the plastic sheeting and gently lifted the girl's pale hands. Her fingernails were torn, the delicate skin of the ends of her fingers shredded.

Joe knew what that meant.

"She wasn't shot somewhere else," Joe deduced. "She was still kickin' and screamin' when he brought her down here. He shot her right here."

The two men got down on their hands and knees in the puddles and the blood and the shit and began a fingertip search of the area. Clute held the torch in his mouth. After a fruitless fifteen minutes Joe stood up and mimed the shooting of the girl from different angles and projected where an ejected cartridge case may have landed, if the killer had been using an automatic. If it had been a revolver, they would have to dig the slug from her brain.

Joe found the casing in an overturned tin can. Clute held the torch so they could examine it.

"Looks pretty standard to me," Joe said. "Nine or ten millimetre, handgun calibre. I'd say this was the one. I - hey! What are you doing?"

Clute had taken the cartridge from Joe and was biting down on it. He took it out of his mouth and held it up to Joe again. It was unmarked.

"Brass will crush. This is carbon fibre. No ordinary cartridge."

He inverted it and held it close to his eye to read the inscription.

S - M. 9.5mm.

"You were nearly right, Joe. It's nine point five. But it's not from a standard handgun."

Joe raised his eyebrows quizzically. Clute knew he wanted the man that was killing these kids very much. Joe was a driven man, the closest thing that Purgatory had to a cop, just as Clute was their closest thing to a doctor. Clute took a swift mental decision to exclude Joe from this. He was way past his best and emotionally unstable. He would go in with guns blazing and this man, this child killer, this cold hard professional, would not think twice about adding old Joe to his tally.

Felix, thought Clute, *you son of a bitch. I saved your life so you could do this. You walked away from my fucking surgery and went and did this. Well, you've gone and made*

*me an accessory to the crime. So this is your 'pleasure'? I
should have let you bleed to death, you bastard.*

"Clute?"

"I need a drink, Joe."

"I hear what you're saying. I got friends will pick up
the body, make sure she gets a proper ...... send off, I guess.
Tell you the truth I don't know what that they do with 'em.
Least she won't be dog food. I guess we owe her that much
dignity. Whoever she was."

Clute turned away while Joe did his thing on the
Motorola. Somewhere in Purgatory the Devil slept with
blood on his lips and cock, while a mother cried at the ragged
hole torn in her heart.

Felix wasn't the sort of guy you could find in a hurry. As a
rule, Felix found *you*. And that was the last thing you knew.

Morning came, and with it the inescapable heat of day.
Purgatory sweated under a subtropical climate. If it was a
dark, rainswept dungeon by night, then a sweltering glass
house by day. The killing rate trebled on a day like this.
Mothers killed squalling babies, husbands killed nagging
wives, brothers killed jealous sisters, all driven mad by the
heat of the day. On a day like this, a child killer could roam
with impunity, just one more demon in hell. Over the river,
the City looked cool and clean and welcoming, distorted like
an unattainable mirage through the heat haze draped over the
rank waters.

A killing day, then, Clute decided, walking the two
blocks from his apartment to the Director's along the concrete
waterfront. Ten cent whores and streetmeat accosted him
from open windows in the riverside slam joints, until they
recognised his face and the calls for trade turned to ones of
greeting. He had treated most of them in his time here, for
gunshot wounds, beatings, hideous torture damage from
brutal johns and, most commonly, abortions. Many were HIV

positive - all of them for all he knew. He didn't have the kit to test for it with any degree of accuracy, but the symptoms had a way of becoming obvious. The whole of Purgatory, himself included, could be under the death sentence and he wouldn't know until it was too late.

Clute's shirt was stuck to his back with sweat, stained almost black. He probably smelled bad but the stink from the river overpowered everything else. Citizens of Purgatory liked to say they were immune from the smell but Clute knew better. No one was immune, just desensitised through familiarity.

A killing day. But for Clute alone that wouldn't make Felix's crimes any less heinous. Random acts of senseless violence in brutal a warzone could still shock. And Purgatory *was* a warzone. Clute, its healer, its doctor, knew that better than most. Amid the carnage, amid the cruelty - Clute had seen ten lifetimes worth in the jungle and the City - there was still room for that one further step. A rape or a torture that went beyond the accepted boundaries of such crimes. *Or the sex murder of a child.*

The sun glared down through the smog-shrouded brick canyons of Purgatory. Clute stopped by the old dock warehouse and watched a corpse swinging from a wooden gibbet mounted above a loading bay. The corpse was starting to rot. Seagulls had pecked out its eyes. A sign hanging around the corpse's neck read FOOD THIEF. Like a cattle rustler in the Wild West, a man who stole food in Purgatory could expect no mercy. In this urban arena of survival, to steal a man's bread was unforgivable. The corpse would hang there until it disintegrated, as a warning. Clute had seen this many times before.

The Director's offices were part of the old dock complex. His personal quarters were at the heart of a maze of abandoned outer offices and corridors, all wired with explosives and tripwires and surveillance devices. The

Director was nothing if not cautious.

Clute knew the way through. He was something of a privileged man in Purgatory, with access to people and places denied to many others, simply because of his skills. There weren't many on this godforsaken strip of an island that did not owe their own life or that of a family member or friend to Clute. The Director was one of these people. Clute thought of him as no more of a friend than he would have done Felix - *god forbid!* The Director was the ruthless overlord of Purgatory's organised crime. Drug dealing, arms supplies, prostitution, anything and everything to make money. Except food. The Director was a farm boy from Eastern Europe. He had suffered from malnutrition in his teenage years during the endless wars and changes of government that marked the politics of that region during the latter years of the last century. In his skewed personal philosophy he considered the interference with a man's food supply far worse than any other imaginable crime.

Clute had patched the Director up after a bungled assassination attempt. Shrapnel in the face and neck, gunshot to the palm of his hand. That gave Clute access to a moment of the Director's time, now and again. When he needed something. He needed something now.

There were cameras in these dark, damp, kind of cool corridors, with blinking IR sensors and passive metal detectors that tracked Clute eerily as he watched for the tiny splashes of luminous paint that indicated the safe route through. A wrong turn into an empty room would mean instant death. The Director knew he was here and recognised him, that he knew. Otherwise he would be dead already.

The corridor opened up into an airy, high-ceilinged shed. The roof was tinted glass, replacing the original corrugated steel, and shielded the interior from the worst the sun had to offer, giving the place a cool, dark ambience. The concrete floor was scrupulously clean, as if a squad of bootcamp marines were kept on hand to scrub it with toothbrushes. This was a place where someone lived and worked. The Director.

Clute halted inside a set of rubber swing doors that separated the corridor from the Director's inner sanctum. It reminded him of a hospital ER room. A camera mounted above his head swivelled to point at him.

In the centre of the chamber was an incongruous oasis of suburban calm. A chintz sofa, a burbling black-cased flatscreen TV, a standing lamp, a table, all standing on an immaculate circular Persian rug. The sofa was positioned with its back to the door. A man's bald head could be seen over the top of the sofa back.

"Clute." Flat, even tone. Not a request, not a greeting. Merely a statement.

Clute approached slowly. A man slipped from the shadows beside him and smoothly matched step, causing Clute to flinch. It was Mario, the Director's right hand. He was holding a Skorpion machine pistol with as much casualness as one could with such a wicked looking weapon. He grinned at Clute. Clute had seen him cut a man in half with that little toy gun. Once you had seen a man do a thing like that for no good reason, it was difficult to smile at him.

Somewhere, up in the rafters among the smoked glass or on an old overseer's balcony, would be Mario's counterpart, Vince. Vince was a Hispanic killer who hero-worshipped Felix. He wanted so much to be respected and feared like Felix but he was too much of a hothead, better suited to throwing himself in front of the Director and absorbing a rain of bullets than coolly taking out long-range targets. He would be Mario's back up. You could bet the sights of his gun were tracking Clute, from wherever he was concealed. Two psychopaths, two itchy trigger fingers, two automatic weapons, two chances to get blown away by a sneeze or an itch. The Director's paranoia was catching.

"Clute. Social call or medical check up?"

The Director was still watching the TV. Clute was right behind him, almost leaning on the back of the sofa. Mario had retreated to a safe distance, out of reach of Clute in case he tried to grab the Skorpion. Mario would ensure it would sting him if he did. They hadn't bothered to pat him down. The metal detectors told them he wasn't carrying. But Mario liked to think he was so fast, it didn't matter if Clute had a gun.

Clute could see over the top of the Director's bullet head to the TV. The set was old, the black plastic casing cracked. Lines rolled across the picture. They were watching themselves, from the camera positioned above the swing doors. The Director moved his head slightly, emitted a grunt, and the picture changed to a manga cartoon, a Lovecraftian beast rampaging through a city. The colours were all wrong. Blood was green. The monster was pink. It was most surreal.

"Let me see you."

Clute glanced at Mario, who gave a curt nod and traversed with Clute as he walked around the front of the sofa, as if they were at opposite ends of a taut rope, the muzzle of the Skorpion never leaving its aim. Mario was a diligent bodyguard.

Clute looked down at the Director. It always amazed him how the man was still alive. He sat near-naked in the centre of the sofa, clad only in a loincloth, great handfuls of flab flopping out from his torsos and thighs, discarded wrappers from candy bars littering his massive lap. He had no body hair whatsoever. Last time Clute had had a chance to examine him he had weighed in at twenty three stone. The skinny kid who had once almost starved to death was now an enormous, malevolent, fifty-year old chocolate-smeared Buddha with the density of an imploding star.

Scar tissue from the shrapnel bombs that tore his armoured jeep to shreds and killed two men ran in hard ridges across the right side of his face and neck, a warrior's tattoos. The Director extended a hand that bore the stigmata of a bullet entry wound and the brown smears of his last candy bar, and indicated that Clute should sit. There was no seat. The Director took up three spaces on the sofa. Clute dropped to his haunches.

"Your face is troubled," the Director said. His face betrayed no emotion, his voice less. Clute had never heard him shout, swear or raise his voice, never saw him rage or lose his temper. Yet this man was life or death in Purgatory, universally feared and respected. He had an army of willing footsoldiers at his command, and he controlled the supply of everything - except food - that the street people held dear.

"You lose a friend?"

"Not exactly."

"Then you have killed someone."

"No."

"No time for word games, Doctor. If you haven't come to examine me, confess to me or kill me, then you have come to ask a favour. No one comes to me for anything else. Speak."

Clute took a deep breath.

"Felix."

"Felix is alive and well, thanks to you. Do you wish to speak to him?"

"Felix is the child killer."

The Director raised one shaved eyebrow. He wiped chocolate from his mouth with the back of one huge paw. It was the most expressive movement Clute had ever seen him make.

"Go on."

"That's it. I found this at the scene of his last murder, last night. *After* I saved his life."

Clute unfurled one fist. On his palm lay the carbon fibre bullet casing. The Director stared at it.

"How do you know it is his?"

Clute's voice was steady, ever aware of the bullets trained on him, waiting to leap, but his words still dripped venom.

"You know damn well this came from his gun. You gave him the fucking thing. Now you know what he uses it for, what are you going to do about it?"

The Director looked directly into Clute's eyes. Steel blue met gunmetal grey. Clute was first to look away. He felt as if Mario would kill him for just *looking* at the Director like that.

"Nothing."

Clute was aware he was hyperventilating. Anger boiled up inside him. *Calm down, man, calm down. Or you're liable to do something stupid. Shit, this is how Joe would behave. This isn't going to solve anything, just get you killed.*

The Director cleared his throat. A faint flush had come to his cheeks.

"I respect you, Doctor. You're good to me, good to this shit pit of a city. I don't know why you do it, what makes you stay here. I do know you used to be a soldier. Which is why you'll understand this - soldiers who experience too much death and mutilation sometimes end up ..... becoming part machine. You know, you've seen it. Maybe you feel a little of it in yourself, sometimes. How easy it is just to switch the machine on and off.

"Felix is *my* soldier. Felix is my Hand of Judgement, ready to smite with instant vengeance any who raise hand or voice against me. Felix is very good at what he does. People who are very good at what they do for me please me greatly."

The Director steepled his fingers and leaned forward in the sofa. Flab rippled in a tidal wave across his bare flesh.

"If this is how Felix winds down or winds up for his kills, then so be it. The death of a few children is *nothing* compared with service he provides for me."

The blood was singing in Clute's ears. He wanted so much to smash the Director's fat face in with the heel of his hand, drive bone fragments up into his brain. Veins stood out in his neck. Mario noticed and shifted from foot to foot, nervous.

"There is one difference between me and Felix," Clute said, through gritted teeth, the taste of blood in his mouth. "We may have both been soldiers. But I have *never* killed anyone."

That wasn't strictly true. When Clute left the army he drifted listlessly through civilian life for the best part of a year. The draft had interrupted medical school and took him south to the jungles for three years, where his incomplete medical training meant he wasn't qualified enough to perform operations in the field hospital but was expected to do his stuff out in the bush, keeping boys alive long enough to make the casevac. He'd held more guts inside bellies slashed free by wirebombs than he'd care to remember. The sound of grown men screaming for their mothers while staring down wild-eyed at laps full of intestine loop and organs would follow him to his grave. It was the soundtrack of his nightmares.

Clute survived Hell for three years without pulling a trigger in anger. He didn't know how many of the boys he pulled from the jungle and passed still living to the choppers survived back to the real world, but there were plenty who'd died in his arms. But he had always done his best.

It was ironic that the blood that would stain his hands forever was spilt in civilian conflict. After completing med school on a veteran's scheme, he began to work as an emergency intern at a large city hospital. Saturday night shifts were always the worse - gang rumbles, cop shoot-outs, drive-by's. Sometimes he thought he was back in the jungle. One night a gang followed their victim into the hospital and finished what they had started in an alley, executing a boy on the emergency table in front of doctors and nurses.

Saturday nights. The flashbacks got worse. A police helicopter thundering overhead, a searchlight stabbing through a window, the arrival of an air ambulance, would all have him diving for cover, screaming. His colleagues were understanding - many were vets themselves. He managed to keep it together until the night of the anti-war demonstrations, when the hospital was flooded with tear gas and shotgun victims, cops with stab wounds, people with chewed-up limbs where they had been run over by police armoured vehicles, and a helicopter crew brought through in pieces when a demonstrator had brought them down with a well-aimed flare.

Clute had been on his feet for almost fifty hours straight. Woody, the grizzled old orderly, took him to one side. They were both wearing plastic aprons slick with blood. They looked like butchers. Woody pressed something into his palm and bundled him into an unoccupied office, locking the door behind him.

Clute smoked the joint and was asleep in five minutes flat. He didn't know if he'd slept for an hour or a day but the next thing he knew he was being shaken awake by another orderly and dragged back on to the emergency team. He could barely see straight, let alone operate. There was a cop on the table, a young cop with a gunshot wound to the stomach. He was screaming, screaming just like those kids in the cargo bay of the chopper, diamond-plate deck swimming with blood and shit, screaming for mother.

An air ambulance clattered overhead. This was no flashback, *he was there!* To the astonishment of the ER team, he picked up the injured cop and carried him from the ward, out through the packed waiting room and into the car park. The air ambulance wheeled overhead, its searchlight picking him out as it came into land.

"It's okay, son," he whispered to the cop, who was going into shock. "It's okay, I'm taking you home."

The emergency team and a burly nurse wrestled him to the ground and took the cop back inside. Clute fought like a wild man, breaking the nurse's jaw. Someone got a syringe of carbomazipam and banged it into his thigh, and put him out.

The cop died. If it had just been some cop, some nobody, Mrs Anyone's son, Clute might have claimed overwork, overtired and been reprimanded. He might have got away with it. But the cop was the youngest son of the chief of police. His other two had been killed in the war. He was very protective of his boy, and became an avenging angel once he discovered the manner in which he died. Clute's progress through the judicial system, the arrest, the cells, and the court was monitored every step of the way. His urine was analysed within hours of his arrest and found to contain proscribed drugs. The police chief visited him in his cell and spat in his face. Clute was set to rot in jail for a long, long time.

In the end, he was acquitted, but his career was in tatters. Character witnesses from the Veteran's Group, his old unit, his colleagues at the hospital and his superiors testified to his defence. It saved him from a custodial sentence, but he would never practice medicine anywhere, ever again. Except one place.

Here, in Purgatory, a man was judged not by his actions yesterday but those of today. It seemed as if Clute's hands had been stained with the blood of others since he was nineteen years old. But only one bloodstain remained to curse him, like Lady Macbeth's spot, and which brought him screaming out of his nightmares night after night after night.

He crossed the mined bridge, over the polluted river, to the damned island of Purgatory, and never went back.

"You know who he is," Joe accused, pointing a stubby finger at Clute. Clute drained the last of the Jack D and beckoned the barman for refill. "You know who he is and you won't tell me. Who or what are you protecting?"

The raw bourbon cleansed Clute's head and throat. Singularity of purpose was necessary.

"Are you going to get me the gun or not, Joe?"

Joe sighed. "You're a doctor, not a vigilante. You should leave this sort o' thing to guys like me." Joe swept back his duster coat. There were seven pistols and small pouches of reloading clips in his Elvis-buckled belt. He pulled the coat closed before anyone else in the bar got to see.

"Tell me, Clute. Let me deal with it."

"You don't understand, Joe. I just want the gun for self-protection. Been some odd sorts hanging around my place lately."

"Self-protection my ass!" Joe slammed the shot glass down on the wooden bar so hard he had the barman reaching for the pump action he kept beneath the till.

"Fuck you, Clute. I know you know who this son of a bitch is and you're going to try and take him down yourself. You're fucking crazy, you know that? I ain't a friend of yours no longer. You insult me."

Joe got up to leave. Clute put out his hand and grabbed the older man's elbow. They locked eyes. For a moment, Clute thought Joe was going to hit him or worse, pull one of those seven guns and shoot him. Then the old cop's eyes softened.

"Seven point six two millimetre Beretta. Laser sight. Image intensifier. Bipod. For home protection, right?"

"That's right. Home protection."

Joe snorted.

"Let go of my arm, Clute. I got some shopping to do."

Felix was a hard man to find. Clute waited for a day and a half in the cool loft of a warehouse overlooking the river and the goods yard of the Director's place. He had a sleeping bag and some cold cuts but the thermos of coffee had run dry that morning and he hadn't brought the stove. Felix was jungle-trained, just like Clute. But Felix had been trained to kill people, not save their lives. He would smell an amateur like Clute heating up coffee a mile away, and either steer clear or outflank him. Clute's only ace was to remain undetected and hope that Felix decided to visit the Director sometime soon. He was known to have done so in the past, but like all good survivors sensibly kept no rigid timetable. It was a slim chance, but the only one Clute had.

The second day dragged in to the second night. The boredom was mind-numbing. Clute's thoughts began to wander, senseless paranoia setting in. Surely people would be looking for him by now? Would Joe cover his trail? Suppose Felix found out that Clute was missing? Would the Director tell him that Clute had discovered his secret? Would Felix then deduce that Clute had gone underground to kill him? Was Felix, even now as Clute's mind tore itself apart with a series of circular, unanswerable queries, hunting Clute down?

Clute jumped awake with a start. He didn't know how long he had dozed for, it could have just been one of those momentary lapses that shit you up when night driving. If Felix had found him, he could have had his throat cut peacefully in his sleep. *Sweet dreams, Doctor......*

There was noise and movement below. Clute rolled onto the sleeping bag and peered down the rifle's image intensifier. He was several feet back from the glassless window, invisible from the outside.

In the grainy green of the II sight, Clute watched a jeep pull into the loading yard below. He flicked the sight to times ten. A figure clambered from the driving seat, back to Clute. *Felix?* Hard to say. The jeep was unfamiliar - could have been a gift from the Director to his favourite child killer. The image in the II sight was a green blur, meshing and distorting. A positive identification was going to be hard.

Another figure joined the first, this one walking from

the dock warehouse. Right size, right height, right rolling swagger for Vince. He seemed excited, animated, touching and pushing the other man, in fun not malice. Definitely Vince. And if Vince was excited, that meant -

Felix. He turned and looked directly into Clute's sight. Clute could make out every feature on his face, that hideous grin, those filed metal teeth. He was glad he had not switched the laser sight on - Felix would have taken it straight in the eyes and instantly gone for cover, temporarily blinded. He had to wait until Felix turned away and Vince was in front of him, so neither would see the tell-tale red dot until it was too late. As Felix turned Clute took a deep breath, switched on the laser and resettled his position behind the rifle.

Deep breaths. Steady breathing. Inhale. Exhale. Inhale. Exhale. Pause. Squeeze, don't jerk. Nothing to it.

Felix, you son of a bitch, you'll never know what hit you. You'll be lying on your back with your brains hanging out, and you'll never kill another child again, and no one like me will ever have to feel guilty for depriving another of life simply by saving yours. Shit, Felix, if only I'd let you bleed to death last time 'round, one more child would be alive and none of this would be happening.

Inhale. Exhale. Inhale. Exhale.

Felix was standing stock still, as if calmly awaiting his fate. The laser dot on the back of his greasy skull looked like a green searchlight through the sight, diffused by the II. Clute's finger tightened on the trigger.

You son of a bitch! Why me? Why do I have to have your blood on my hands now as well as his?

Inhale. Exhale. Inhale. Exhale.

Motherfucker! Why do you make me do this? I'm not a killer! Does your evil corrupt everyone you meet, Devil?

Inhale. Inhale. Inhale.

Felix, you bastard......

The 7.62mm Beretta ended up at the bottom of the river. He had paid Joe top dollar, but it seemed wise to dispose of it.

Clute walked the streets for an hour afterwards, until returning home and sleeping his calmest, deepest sleep for years.

The shrill tone of the Motorola jerked him back to reality. He tumbled from the bedclothes and hunted for the phone in the pocket of his pants, draped over a chair.

"Clute."

"Come to the surgery. You're needed."

"Vince?"

"Yeah. Felix is down. Real bad. Come quick, Doc."

Sun was rising over the river. Tried to burn away the smog but the smog always won. Just trapped the heat.

Clute skimmed stones for a while on the waterfront, then bought a rusty can of Coke from a stand on the square. He rapped with the seller and a couple of tired-looking whores heading home after a busy night, then headed across the city. Purgatory was waking up around him. Slowly, reluctantly, without much enthusiasm. Purgatory was a night city.

The surgery was just a block, maybe fifteen minutes walk away from the waterfront. He had run it in five before now. This morning, it took him forty.

"Felix is dead!" Vince screamed, grabbing Clute by the lapels of his coat as he stepped into the surgery. Tears streaked Vince's ferrety face. "Where have you been, you fucker? Where have you been?"

Clute didn't answer. Vince relaxed his grip and backed off, reaching for his pistol. His shirt and jacket were stained with blood, Felix's blood, from carrying the dying hitman up here. In his eyes, Clute had let his idol die, and he was going to make him pay.

Felix lay on the table. His throat was slashed from ear to ear, a flap of flesh hanging grotesquely down on to his sternum. It was a second, hideous grin. There were stab wounds all over his body.

Vince had a pistol in his hand. He was shaking all over.

"That's enough." The unmistakable inflectionless tones of the Director.

Clute turned. The Director filled the doorway behind him, literally. He wore a multicoloured kaftan and sandals. Mario loitered on the stairs, the stinging Skorpion in his hand.

"Leave us, Vince."

Vince blubbered something that a raise of the Director's eyebrow silenced. He holstered his gun and pushed past Clute. The Director let him go to join Mario on the stairs and shut the door behind him.

"You have anything to do with this?"

"No."

"You lie to me, Doctor, I swear you'll be on the next bus behind Felix."

"I didn't kill him. Looks to me like the AKM punks got lucky second time around. Decided to get in close this time."

"But you're not sorry."

"No. He deserved to die."

"And you let him?"

"I.... yes. Yes, I let the mad fucker die."

"Hmmm." The Director waddled across the surgery. Felix's blood lay in pools on the floor, where it had dripped from the table. He lifted Felix's head by a handful of hair, stared into his still-open eyes, and let the head fall back to the table with a dull, wet smack.

"There will be others. He was good. But there will be others."

The Director went to the door, pausing with his hand on the knob.

"Don't get the taste for this, Clute. The power over life and death is reserved for the few. You wouldn't like it, I assure you. It's a great burden."

Clute nodded.

"We're even now. Remember this in all our future business."

The Director left. Clute could hear Vince's whining protestations as they descended five flights of stairs. Vince wanted to cut off Felix's trigger finger as a memento.

Clute flipped open the Motorola. He needed Joe and his disposal people. He wanted this piece of shit removing from his surgery.

It was going to be another hot day in Purgatory.

Clute stepped out into the street. He needed a drink. he reckoned Joe might join him for one. He took in a lungful of the morning air. The smog burnt his throat, but the air tasted just a little sweeter than it had yesterday.

Just a little.

Stone Cold Killer

It was in the third week of the summer of the Long Rains that Hilary's patience finally snapped and he buried his care warden's beloved gold-nibbed fountain pen in the bastard's left eye, straight through the faggot's burgundy-tinted contact lense. He wouldn't be unzipping his flies in anyone's room after lights out anymore. As the sirens wailed and the security gates clanged shut, Hilary went over the wall with his US Army issue ALICE pack slung over his shoulder and a brand-new pair of welfare supplied Nikes on his feet. They would never catch him. Not tonight at least. He paused to catch his breath in an alley downtown. Even over the rotted stench of a corpse in a dumpster, he could smell Purgatory, to the east, over the wired and mined bridges and the river. The river.... if you could call it that. A river was supposed to be made up of flowing water, not sluggish stagnant sludge. A police Humvee slipped by like a prowling shark, motion detectors and lasers strobing the alley. Hilary clung to the corpse in the dumpster and shut his eyes, playing dead. It wasn't hard. When the cops were gone, he clambered out and vomited copiously on to the ground, into a deep puddle of oily water. it was, of course, still raining. Soaked to the skin but eager to be out of the city, Hilary navigated the alleys and back streets, heading east, never looking back.

Never, *ever* looking back.

Virgin Mary agonised over the decision for weeks. She didn't want to do it. She knew the risks she would run, maybe fuck things up forever, if she hadn't done that already. She didn't even know if Clute would do it for her, or how much it would cost her. Clute wasn't the sort of guy you could buy with a blowjob. Not for an abortion, anyway.

Finally, she called him up on his mobile, from the only

working booth in a square mile, right outside his surgery. Rain thundered on the booth's starred glass sides.

"Clute? It's Mary."

"The Virgin Mary?"

"The very same. Can I come up?"

"As long as you're not squeamish. I'm sewing up someone's belly."

"I've seen worse, I expect. I'll be right up."

The dim light in Clute's surgery made the scene appear even more medieval and grisly than it was. A fat Hispanic man lay partially anaesthetised on Clute's table, a rolls of blubber exposed amid a squall of garish clothing, silk shirt and embroidered waistcoat, an emergency case too urgent to undress. A blood spattered sheet was all that concealed the man's hideous belly wound from his sweating face. Clute worked intently on sewing up the mass of fat, skin and muscle, a caver's light on his head illuminating the stitchwork. The patient craned his neck to take a look.

"Don't bother, Valmer," said Clute. "You won't like it. Wait 'till I've finished and I'll show you what a beautiful war-scar you'll have to impress the ladies."

Valmer thumped his head back on the cold steel table. His fingers found the grooves in the sides where the blood drained away into pipes and plastic buckets. Clute had liberated it from an abandoned butcher's shop.

"Six inches lower, Valmer never be no use to no ladies never no more. I swear they were no more than seven years old, Doc. Came at me outta nowhere. Didn't ask me for money, didn't steal anything from my stall, just cut me open. What they call it? Wilding, or something? Just wounding and killing for kicks."

Clute unspooled a length of nylon wire and rethreaded the suture needle. "You know, you should really think about losing some weight, Valmer. This is going to cost you plenty in catgut alone."

Valmer laughed and instantly regretted it. A shudder ran through him and his face turned pale and cold.

"Shit, *shit*, that hurt. Don't make me laugh, Doc. I need to lose weight? I sell dead cats and dogs and bits of newspaper and pass them off as hotdogs and burgers. One thing I never do is go hungry."

The door creaked and the Virgin Mary walked in, dripping. Clute had his back to her, his face buried in Valmer's rolling belly.

"Take a seat, Mary. I'm nearly finished with Val."

Mary say quietly in a wooden high-backed chair to the right of the door. Valmer hung his head off the side of the table to get a look at her. He couldn't remember if he'd fucked her or not, but he recognised her as one of the hookers who hung around the Temple bars, looking for trade. She was speciality. Twenty five years old. Looked fourteen. Boyish figure, no tits, short blonde crop with black roots. Wore army boots, crop top, denim shorts. She sat in the chair and blew bubble gum, like she was showing off in a peep show window. Bubble-bang, bubble-bang. Pink stuff all over her lips and chin. Valmer sucked air through his clenched teeth.

"Stop that, Mary," said Clute sharply. "You're putting me off. And Valmer's got other things to worry about." Clute pressed his elbow into Valmer's groin, leaning on his growing hard-on.

"Sorry Doc," Valmer said guiltily. "Always had a thing for the young ones. You know how it is."

Clute finished his stitching with neat, precise knots. He bandaged Valmer's belly tightly. "Stay away from the ladies, Valmer, *especially* the young ones. Come back and see me in three days."

Valmer climbed gingerly from the table, placing his feet firmly on the floor before taking the weight off his ass. His shredded, blood-drenched shirt flapped pathetically around his torso. He grimaced and took a few steps to the door.

"What are you taking in payment these days, Doc?" He shot a glance at the Virgin Mary, sat like a well-behaved child awaiting a promised treat. "Or need I ask?"

Clute frowned at him. "You know that's not my scene. I hear you're reprogramming mobiles. I need one that lasts longer than a week." He picked up the battered Motorola from the table, banged it against the side of his head.

Valmer nodded. "Sure thing. I got a new contact over the river who reckons he can keep dead numbers open indefinitely. Give me a few days, I'll see what I can get you."

Valmer hobbled away down the stairs. Clute listened to him go as he sluiced down the butcher's table with a rubber showerhead fixed to his sink taps. It took Valmer a full five minutes to descend the two short flights of stairs and leave the building.

"You got something I can drink?" asked Mary.

"If you mean Pepsi or a cup of coffee, sure," said Clute, stripping off his blood-slick plastic apron. "If you want beer or bourbon, then no. What's it to be?"

"Pepsi."

Clute took a rusting can from a vibrating old fridge. He rinsed a cloudy glass and handed it to her. It looked as if it had held someone's false teeth. She cracked the can, vintage cola foaming and spilling over her hand, and poured it into the glass.

"You can get Pepsi from Valmer's stall," said Clute, "and you have what he wants as payment, so your credit's good. What's the problem, Mary?"

"Just how good a doctor are you, Clute?" She sipped demurely at her Pepsi, left a pink lipstick trace on the rim of the glass.

"If it's plastic surgery or a heart transplant you're after, you're probably out of luck. Most other things I can cope with. What did you have in mind?"

"A termination."

"A hit? I'm a doctor, not a sniper. Try Mario or Vince."

"No, silly. A termination. An abortion."

"An abortion? Shit, I haven't heard it called that in years."

"Never mind what you call it. Can you do one?"

"Sure. I mean, I could - "

"Could? Would? What's the problem?"

"I've never actually done one before."

"Is that a problem? You're a doctor. You've got books. How difficult can it be?"

"Not very difficult at all. But there is a problem."

She pouted up at him. "Which is?"

"I'm a Catholic, Mary. I can't do it."

Mary rolled her eyes. 1 "I thought we'd left all that shit behind in the Twentieth Century. They don't even appoint popes any more, Clute, not since the woman one. Here we are, living in Purgatory-on-Earth, and all you can do is bug me with your archaic religious beliefs."

"I didn't say it was what I believed in. I said it's what I am. Some things run real deep, Mary. I'm sorry." He turned away from her, continued with his clean-up.

Mary closed her eyes and took several long deep breaths.

"No, I'm sorry, Clute. I'm sorry to have to blackmail you, but if you don't do it for me, I'm going to have to it myself with a length of welding rod. And you'll have to clean up the mess afterwards."

Clute slammed down the steel kidney dish he was rinsing so hard into the stone sink that Mary flinched from the other side of the room at the clatter.

"What am I, Purgatory's fucking guardian angel?" he raged, face reddening. Mary blinked and swallowed, she had never seen Clute like this.

"What gives you the right to march in here and demand I sew you up after you choose to mutilate yourself? What is it to me? Have I been cursed forever to keep everyone alive just so we can all suffer a little bit more?"

Mary sensed that his anger was abating. "That's the story I heard. So maybe you'd better accept it, and quit bitching."

Clute was hyperventilating. He threw the steel dish down into the sink and kicked open the doors to the iron balcony that overhung the street. Rain lashed in, hot and stinking. Clute stood in the arch, allowed the rain to soak him to the skin. He tried to light a cigarette but the pack he had taken from his pocket were sodden. He threw them into the street in disgust.

"You'll catch a cold," Mary said.

Without turning, his back to her : "Hardly."

"Then you'll catch something worse. Come back in, Clute."

Clute watched the deserted street for a little while, ignoring her. Then he stepped back into the room and closed the glass doors behind him. The influx of rain had cleared the air of the metallic tang of Valmer's blood, but had replaced it with the smell of something far worse. The smell of the sins of Purgatory being washed away.

"It's been raining for thirty five straight days and nights," Clute observed, hunting out a dry pack of cigarettes in his jacket hanging up on the door. He pulled a Marlboro free and lit up. "Another five and I'm starting work on the ark."

Mary was puzzled. "The what?"

"Doesn't matter." He exhaled a long stream of smoke from between his front teeth. "You know, with this much rain, you'd think it would wash all the shit into the river, never to return."

"Scum will always rise to the top," Mary replied. "Getting idealistic in your old age, Clute?"

"Idealistic is an awful big word for a fourteen year old bar hooker."

She looked genuinely hurt. "I've never pretended to anyone that I was fourteen."

He hung his head. "I'm sorry. That was a cheap shot."

"You're damn right it was. Now, are you going to stop whinging about what you've been put on this Earth to do, for better or worse, or am I going to have to go and find me something long and sharp?"

Her logic and determination were chilling. Clute didn't relish the task he might have on his hands if she were to stagger back here in a few hours, torn and ripped by her own doing. He imagined her half-drowning herself in bourbon first.

"I got to make a living," she explained, her eyes liquid. "I don't like this, anymore than you do, Clute. Maybe a whole lot less."

"Lay on the table," he said. She did as she was told. She lay her head back on to the steel that had not yet cooled from Valmer's greasy, sweaty bulk. Clute vanished for a few minutes and returned wheeling an old supermarket trolley with a tray welded to the top. On the tray were things that would not have looked out of place in a mechanic's toolbox. She swallowed hard and a single tear squeezed from her eye. The Virgin Mary didn't cry easily.

She could hear the rain drumming like machine-gun fire on the tenement roof as she reached down and unbuttoned her cut-offs. Clute slid them down over her thighs. She wasn't wearing any panties. She trusted Clute more than she had ever trusted anyone before.

"Better get started on that ark, Clute," she said, before the touch of sharp cold steel took her breath away. "It ain't never gonna stop raining. Not ever."

* * *

Hilary lay panting in the lee of the abutments of the great stone bridge. Rain crashed down in heavy sheets from its edge. It had taken him over two hours to make his way across, consulting a sketch map of the mined and boobytrapped areas that he had bought from a guard at the detention centre. Amazingly, it had turned out to be accurate. There had been a lucky moment right at the Purgatory end of the bridge when he was about to set his foot on the island. A stray dog had followed him through the minefield, watching him intently with intelligent eyes as he sidestepped barricades and clambered over burnt out police vehicles, remnants of some forgotten last stand. It decided to dash past him as it caught the foetid scent of the streets, running into a tripwire that detonated a nail bomb jammed into a drain grate. The dog was shredded and Hilary received a nasty shrapnel wound to his cheek. He ran for the cover of the abutments, knowing that the noise and the smoke would bring curious eyes, eyes he would prefer to hide from for now. He didn't know that the flowing wound on his cheek would also bring those who were excited or enraged by the scent of blood. In Purgatory, there were all kinds of hunters.

Hilary took a beer from his ALICE pack. The bottle was still frosty-cold from the store fridge he had stolen it from, in the last gas station back in the real world. He knocked the top off with the heel of his hand and took a long draft. It tasted good. Beers used to cost him blowjobs back in the detention centre. Then their taste was spoiled, wasted, washing the salty-sweet tang from his mouth. This one tasted so much better. It tasted of freedom.

Hilary drained the beer, then tossed the bottle into the water. It floated on the rain-spattered green slick, caught by the current, headed slowly back toward the city. Through the curtain of rain he could see the blur of civilisation. Some people might call it that. Hilary thought it was Hell. A hell of buttfucking bent care wardens and random violence. Far better, he thought, to live in Purgatory than live in Hell, seeing as he wasn't going to make it to Heaven. Not a stone cold killer like Hilary. The human cesspit called Purgatory was his best - *his only* - hope.

Billy the Skid was Purgatory born and raised, as feral as the fatrats that clogged the sewers and the packs of wild dogs that cruised the streets like raptors. Billy and his razorskaters patrolled the abandoned sidewalks and flyovers in the Temple district, preying on the old and the weak and the vulnerable, teasing victims with high speed passes on their skateboots, slashing and hacking with balisongs until their targets collapsed bleeding into the street. Then Billy's boys would strip them naked like vultures, taking everything of conceivable value; bootlaces, earrings, pocket junk, leaving behind torn carcasses. Billy the Skid and his razorskaters liked to think of themselves as professionals.

Billy was seated on the parapet of the Temple flyover, idly picking concrete out of the lip with his bronze-handled balisong, when he saw the intruder entering his territory. A city-boy, he could see that even from here, ten metres away. Sneakers too clean, gait too cautious, as if the ground was about to blow up in his face. Bill the Skid snickered, and let out a yabbering cry, calling his razorskaters to action from wherever they were scavenging, sleeping, fucking. *Come on, come on, come on, rich pickings here, shiny city boy to tease and spoil and cut.*

They heard his call and tumbled from plastic dumpsters, from sunless attics and squats and from the suspended barrios of the debris-encrusted fire escapes hanging like tumours on the flanks of crumbling apartment blocks. Bleary eyed, hungover, hungry, angry. Heeding Billy the Skid's feral call not because they were scared but because he was their leader, the fiercest coldest killer amongst them. *Always something going on when Billy's around*, went the call. Skatewheels touched tarmac and wet concrete, squealing and spinning, looking for the prey, searching out Billy the Skid, heeding his call. *Blood in the air*. Hunting like airborne sharks.

Hilary heard the screech of skatewheels before he saw them coming. He had been heading toward the pink neon of the Temple district, pale bloodstains in the night rain. Maybe he would find what he was looking for there. If not, maybe someone could point him in the right direction. He had money, but he had no idea that a piece of paper with a dead man's head on it had no value here.

They came at him from all angles, balisongs and nunchuks flashing, cutting the straps of his pack and battering at his legs, forcing him to his knees. He cried out and tried to keep hold of his pack but it was torn away as he fell. He looked up - there were seven or more of them, so hard to tell, spinning around him in a whirling dance of death. Knives flashed in, cutting his outstretched palms, nunchuks thumping the back of his head. Then, just as suddenly as it had begun, it stopped. The screeching stopped. The razorskaters - he knew know what they were - stopped. He looked up into the tattooed warmask of the biggest, their leader, obviously. If Hilary was to fight back, it would be this one he would have to battle.

"I am Billy the Skid," said the ferocious creature. "Who invades our territory? What is your business here?"

He talks like a Dungeons & Dragons character, thought Hilary. *Okay, play the game....*

"I come in peace," said Hilary, spitting blood. "I seek the one called Felix."

Billy the Skid threw back his head and roared and his boys did the same.

"He seeks Felix the Cat!" Billy yelled. "Felix the Cat! You'll be seeing Felix sooner than you think, city boy."

Hilary wiped his mouth with the back of his hand. "Why's that?"

Billy suddenly became sombre. He bent forward, almost nose to nose with Hilary. Breath of metallic tang. Long tongue flickered out and licked Hilary's torn cheek. Hilary flinched.

"Because Felix is dead, city boy."

Hilary snarled. "That's not true! You're lying. Felix is the greatest hitman in Purgatory! He can't be dead!"

"Felix is dead, city boy. And you know what? We killed him."

"You're a fucking liar."

Billy the Skid *was* a fucking liar. Every gang and posse and two-bit punk in the city had laid claim to Felix's murder, until Vince and Mario had started to gun down those who 'admitted' their part in the killing of their hero. The loss of novelty had obviously failed to filter down as far as Billy the Skid's level just yet.

"We killed him, my skate boys and me. Cut him from ear to ear we did." He made a slashing motion with his balisong across his own throat. "Cut him so bad, even the Doc couldn't fix him up. I heard he bled so much that the red juice was running down the Doc's stairs for a week afterwards, like a fucking waterfall. Felix the Cat used up all his nine lives that night, oh yeah."

Hilary's nostrils flared. The shiv was in his hand even before the hawk eyes of Billy the Skid saw it, and Hilary brought it around in a roundhouse fist that would blindside Billy. But one of his skateboys saw it coming and barked a warning, at the same time stepping forward and burying a balisong up to its hilt in Hilary's lower back. Hilary screamed and went rigid and the blade of the shiv, a sharpened screwdriver from a trucker's toolbox, skidded along Billy's cheek, tearing it open, and on into his left eye socket where it impacted into the soft jelly of his eyeball. Hilary went down, face forward into a greasy puddle, the balisong still buried in his back. A cold wave washed over him, and he vomited. He heard Billy screaming and the squeal of the skates, shouts of older voices from the direction of the Temple bars. Billy cursing and crying, his skateboys dragging him away. The cold wave broke. Hilary felt peaceful. He breathed out into the puddle of water and grease and vomit, and was surprised when he didn't feel like breathing in again. Hey, death wasn't so bad, was it?

He had been in Purgatory for twenty nine minutes and thirty seconds.

"Another piece of gutter waste for you, Clute."

Joe thudded the lifeless body down on to the slab. Clute looked up from his desk.

"This the dead one you phoned me about?"

"As the proverbial. Better here than clogging up the streets, hey? Just certify him, Clute, and I'll take him away before he starts to smell."

Clute stood up, pushing his chair back, and rubbed the bridge of his nose. He was weary, Virgin Mary's abortion had been messy and traumatic and had taken much longer than he had expected. She was sleeping it off in his bunk in the room next door. He hoped she wouldn't come out and see the dead boy, but then again, what if she did? Anyone who walked Purgatory's streets at night must get used to stepping over corpses.

"You're fighting a losing battle, Joe. Who gives a shit about death certificates any more?"

Joe leaned against the cool wall and lit a cigarette. "*I'm* fighting a losing battle? At least mine are dead, Kemo Sabe. I'm not the one trying to save the whole fucking world. Anyway, I got funding."

Clute raised an eyebrow. *"Funding?* Someone's sending money? Into Purgatory? You have got to be fucking joking."

"Not money, but useful shit. Cameras, film, body bags, a laptop, Anonymous benefactor. Someone out there - " He jabbed a grimy finger to the west . " - wants some stats about what's going on in here. And that can only be good news."

Clute snorted. "You think so? Last time anyone took an interest in what went on around here was when they renewed all the mines and explosives on the bridges. Cheaper to have blown them all up."

"Yeah, but they didn't, did they? They keep us penned in but they keep their options open. Don't give up hope completely, Clute, it doesn't suit you. Now, take a look at our victim here. Not a Purgatory kid."

Clute ran a professional eye over the body. Hi-top Nikes. ALICE pack straps wrapped around one shoulder, the pack torn and its frame buckled. Cuts to the face and hands. Pale through massive bloodloss. The kid might have been attractive once, blond hair and fine bone structure in the face. Joe laid the bronze-handled balisong on his chest.

"I took this out of his back."

Clute stepped forward and placed two fingers on the boy's neck. His breath caught in his throat.

"Not a Purgatory kid," said Clute, ripping the boy's shirt open. "And not dead either. Your mouth-to-mouth any better than your diagnosis, Joe?"

The cigarette dropped from Joe's mouth. He floundered as Clute leapt into action. "Alive? Shit, I.... I'm sorry..."

"Don't be. You've probably saved his life. Go in the fridge for me. Behind the coke and beer there's two blood packs. Bring them to me."

While Joe fetched the blood Clute cleared the boy's

airway and clamped his mouth over the boy's lips, inflating his chest. The weak heartbeat appeared to stop for a long moment, then restarted with a hiccup, slightly stronger. It quickened in pace as Clute filled the boy's lungs. Joe busied around, setting the blood bags up on a stand strung with plastic piping. He had done this before.

Clute took his mouth away just before the boy spluttered and vomited. Clute turned the boy's head to the side to clear it from his throat. The boy's eyes fluttered open momentarily, and looked at Clute.

"It's okay," said Clute. "You're going to be alright. I'm a doctor." Clute thought of all the people he had said that to over the years, many of whom died with the words ringing in their ears, as he set up the drip, and began to put blood into the boy's body. With Joe's help he found the near-lethal wound in his back and started to repair the damage.

"Inch above the kidneys," said Clute. "Lucky son of a bitch."

Joe looked down at the pale ragged form on the slab. He didn't look particularly lucky. But then, wasn't anyone who was still alive in Purgatory lucky? No, not really. There were worse things out on those streets than death. Joe had seen some of them first hand.

As he worked, Clute flashed a weak grin at Joe. "Sorry, friend. Looks like this one won't reach you mysterious benefactor's statistics. I think he's going to make it."

The Virgin Mary was woken by the two men going about their bloody business. She recognised the deep tones of Joe, the friendly old cop. She waited in the hot, dark room until the noise had ceased, and could hear two sets of footsteps retreating down the tenement steps. She swung her legs off the bed and stood up. Blood was still running down her thighs. She staggered, caught herself. A sound like a puppy whimpering was coming from Clute's surgery. Mary liked puppies. She had been given one by a john who could not pay. She had looked after it, but then someone had stolen and eaten it.

There was a light on in the surgery, a table lamp over a desk scattered with papers that cast a sickly glow over the sickly room. Mary peeked around the door and saw the skinny boy lying on Clute's slab. Pale, blood-stained, he looked like a young vampire washed in by the rain, a gutter-scavenger. She thought he looked beautiful, scarred by war. She padded barefoot across the wet tiled floor , and laid a warm hand on his cool cheek. His eyes fluttered open.

"Who are you?" he asked, his voice barely a whisper.

"They call me the Virgin Mary," she said, stroking his cheek. He closed his eyes and a fat tear squeezed from beneath his right lid, rolling down through the dried blood on his face.

"Then I did die. But at least I made it to Heaven."

Mary suppressed a laugh. "Not Heaven. Purgatory. What are you doing here?"

"Dying."

"You're not dying. Clute's a good doctor. I've seen him patch up people cut up much better than you. I mean worse. Why have you come here, city-boy?"

"*City-boy. City-boy.* That's what they called me."

"Skaters." Mary had picked up the balisong from the metal kidney dish where Clute had dropped it. "Bad boys. Bad, bad boys."

"Not as bad as me," he whispered. "Where I come from, I'm the baddest of the bad. That's why I'm here."

Mary let herself laugh this time. "So, you're so bad, little brother. You want to be the baddest badass in Purgatory. Well, join the queue for the morgue. You're already halfway there."

"Wanted to be Felix, just like Felix." Dreamily.

"Baddest hitman. The best."

Clute had been listening at the door. He held in his hands a brand new Motorola and a clutch of batteries. Joe was not with him.

"Feeling better?" This to Mary. She nodded and shrugged simultaneously.

"You should get some more rest."

"I suppose I should. But I got to work."

Clute placed the mobile phone and the batteries down on a battered table.

"Nobody's going to be hiring you for a while yet, Mary," he said softly. "Get some rest. Stop bothering our friend here."

"She's no bother." His voice barely rose to the audible. Clute approached the table and placed his palm against the boy's forehead. His temperature was returning to normal. Clute examined the apparatus of the drip. Joe had done a good job.

"So you want to be a hitman, hey?" Clute said. "Felix's apprentice."

"They said Felix is dead. Is that true?" His eyes looked like those of a kid about to be told Santa Claus doesn't exist. Clute took a deep breath and shattered the myth.

"Yes, Felix is dead. He died on the same table you're lying on now. I'm one of the few people in the city who doesn't claim to have killed him. But I could have done. Then again, maybe I did. But you wouldn't have liked him."

"I didn't want to like him. I wanted him to teach me how to kill."

"Felix wasn't the type to teach young boys. He thought young boys and girls were for other things. Like suffering and dying. In his spare time, Felix was a child killer."

Hilary closed his eyes and his lip quivered. Clute felt like shit. It was a familiar feeling.

Mary saw a shadow in the doorway over Clute's

shoulder. Her mouth moved to warn him, something told her it wasn't Joe returning, but before she could utter a word a tattooed elbow rose and fell and struck Clute on the side of the head, knocking him over Hilary's body.

"We've come for the city-boy," said Billy the Skid, grinning. "Got no argument with the doctor-man. Just gonna take our prize 'n' go."

Billy looked grotesque. Two of his skateboys flanked him, holding balisongs out, waving them about. Billy's face was a swollen mess, his left eye socket a slitty, puffy mass. He hyperventilated through gritted teeth.

Clute had fallen across Hilary. He turned, gripping the table, his own body covering Hilary's. The intimation was unmistakable. *Over my dead body.*

"Got you all stone cold," Billy said. "You ain't holding any cards, doctor-man. If I have to go through you to get him, I will. Don't want to, but I will."

Clute straightened up, still keeping himself between Hilary and the skaters.

"Nasty looking eye wound you got there, Billy. Want me to take a look at it?"

Billy squinted with his good eye, confused. He couldn't understand why the doc was offering to help him when he was threatening to stick him. It had to be a trick.

"One good eye'll do me fine, doc," he grinned, wincing at the pain. "Now give us the city-boy."

"Won't skate too good with one eye, Billy," Clute continued. "Your 3-D vision will be useless. One of your boys will knock you off your skates, become the new chief, just you wait and see."

Billy eyed his boys. They looked pretty rock solid and loyal to him. *He was Billy the Skid!*

"Enough jive talk, doc. Get out of the way."

Hilary propped himself up on his elbows, a movement which took massive effort. Mary, watching from the side and ignored by all, wanted to go to his aid. Blood flecked foam at the corners of his lips.

"I'll take the punk on," he whispered.

Clute turned, not hearing Hilary's words. As he did so, he heard a bang and flinched automatically, recognising the sharp report of a handgun at close quarters. Wetness sprayed his face, and for a second he thought he had been shot. When he looked back, he saw Billy the Skid draped over Hilary's legs, gore running down the sides of the old butcher's table, and the two skateboys cowering to either side, holding their balisongs out like optimistic magic wands, hoping to ward off evil, hands quivering. And in the doorway, draped in a wet overcoat, stood Joe, a big magnum handgun in his fist. His eyes were steel. He indicated the two skaters with a sweep of the big gun's barrel.

"You two, fuck off. I see either of you again, you get the same treatment as your boss here. Got that?"

The skateboys remained frozen in terror. One had pissed himself.

"That means *go*," Joe reiterated. The one with the weak bladder moved first, dropping his knife and dashing past Joe, out the door and down the stairs, the other following right behind him. Joe put away his gun, picked up the knives, and hurled them down the stairwell after their owners.

"Sorry I had to do that," Joe said. He pulled Billy's body off Hilary's legs. Billy's chest was an open red rib cage. Hilary was drenched in blood, his eyes wide with horror.

"Don't be," said Clute, regaining his composure. His ears rang from the deafening gunshot in the small room. "Thanks, I think."

Joe dropped the body heavily to the floor and stepped over it, looking down.

"Didn't want to do it." It was as if he was talking to the boy he just killed. "Been a long time since I had to do that.

Don't let anyone tell you it's easy, you never get used to it. Never, ever."

"You hear that?" Clute to Hilary. Hilary nodded, slowly.

"Still want to be an assassin?"

Hilary looked at his blood-stained clothes, at the dead body on the floor and the sad ex-cop stood over it. Real tears ran down Joe's face and landed on Billy. Hilary shook his head, real slow.

The rains stopped seven days later. Clute put off plans to build his ark, and instead turned his attention to fixing the roof.

The Virgin Mary dropped by later that day, accompanied by Hilary, who looked pale and weak. Clute redressed the bandages around his torso and gave him a few of the precious antibiotics. They chatted about the loft that Valmer had given them to stay in. Mary had not been back to the Temple bars since her abortion. She had been looking after Hilary ever since, although no one had asked her to. Clute saw from the looks and words they exchanged that they had become lovers. He hoped she was being gentle with him. He watched them from the iron balcony as they walked away from his surgery.

The streets steamed in the murky heat, returning the waters to Heaven. The familiar rank smells began to rise again from the gutters.

It would take more than forty days and nights of rain to cleanse Purgatory of its sins, thought Clute.

The Brightside and Monger War

ILLUSTRATION BY NIGEL DOBBYN

Two hundred and fifty years after the Worldships left Earth, and the Brightsiders and the Mongers had partitioned and begun lifetimes of bitter warfare, Ankh and Banshee fell in love.

They met in the least romantic of circumstances. Ankh was teaching a class of podders Morality Tales when his schoolpod was attacked by Banshee's Monger special operations team, a fledgling outfit on their first and last mission. Of course, they were caught and held in the schoolpod's passive gumweb. The virgin warriors bit down hard on their tongues and took the imbedded poison. Banshee's implant was faulty. She hung there among her dead comrades, black clad from head to toe like big flies, crying softly, not because she had failed but because she was still alive. Ankh approached her, frightened smoke-smeared podders clinging to his legs, and gently removed her fearsome warmask. Coils of flame-red hair spilled out over the genetusks that curved up in wicked arcs from her lower jaw, and she regarded the pale young Brightsider with nothing short of hatred through emerald eyes and a curtain of sweat-damp locks. She scowled and spat the dead poison sac into his face. It left a streak of vile purple goo through the short blonde hair on his left temple. He thought that she was the most beautiful thing he had ever seen.

After Banshee was passed into the custody of the Polite Police and spirited away into the forgotten bowels of Brightside, Ankh couldn't get her out of his mind. He thought about her as he taught his class and looked at the strands of pink gumweb still hanging from the clean white tiles of the schoolpod ceiling. He decided to get himself appointed as Banshee's ReEducation Angel.

Their first sessions together were nightmarish. Banshee fought in the suspended crucifix of the web, trying to move her hands enough to tear out Ankh's pale white throat, but they had clipped her geneclaws and of course she was well secured. He tried to stay out of spitting range in the confines of the custody pod while attempting to soothe her with rehabilitory platitudes from the ReEducation Angel Manual, Volume One.

"Anger and hatred are negative forces, and entirely illogical. The gumweb is unbreakable, why do you still resist it?"

"You know we mean you no harm. Monger prisoners-of-war are re-educated and released, not punished. All you have to do is learn, and you can go home. Don't you want that?"

Banshee's anger was a red cloud concealing all reason from her. All her training, all the Monger battle indoctrination - they were not prepared for capture and imprisonment, they were prepared to die valiantly in the service of Mongerkind. She had heard about this insidious form of interrogation, where gentle, considerate Brightsiders cajoled information with empty promises of rehabilitation and repatriation. On the face of it, all you had to do was smile - admittedly not easy with genetusks - and agree, and maybe they would be true to their word. But her information said otherwise. No Monger warrior had ever been sent back alive. It was all lies.

Ankh became increasingly despondent at ever penetrating the armour of Banshee's conditioning. His colleagues at the schoolpod ridiculed him and he was carpeted by the Mastertutor for arriving late for work because of his commitment to the ReEducation Angel project.

"Civic duty is commendable," said Mastertutor Ono, standing in his plush office with his back to Ankh, overlooking the arcologies of Brightside's eastern zone below. Arcoworkers scurried like insects along the ribbed nylon tracks between the bloated fruit-bearing trees. "And responsibilities to your employment is quite another. You are setting a bad example to the podders, Ankh. I had big hopes for you, my boy. I know you have dreams of becoming a Mastertutor yourself. But if there is no change in your attitude, Ankh, I don't see how I can keep the conscription board away much longer."

The mention of military service sent an icy shiver down Ankh's spine. It was his worst nightmare. Imagine having to *strike* another person, even an enemy. Imagine *killing* someone. The thought was too terrible to even contemplate. He resolved to set his alarm earlier and to give Banshee one week to respond to his please. After that.... he would have to make a choice. His attraction to her, a sworn enemy, was as illogical as her stubborn refusal to be rehabilitated. Surely she knew that all she needed to do was acquiesce, and she could go free?

Two days into Ankh's self-defined final week, during a particularly tedious bout of questioning, Banshee's mask finally slipped, in the most unusual of circumstances.

"The Brightsiders are peace-loving people," Ankh had repeated for the several-millionth time. "We wish only to reach a settlement with the Mongers, so that no more of our people have to die."

She had snarled and spat a bloody clot of phlegm into his face when he got to close. Something snapped and he hurled the hard plastic-coated manual he had been reading from straight at her, screaming *"Why won't you let me help you? I love you and you'll rot in here or get killed trying to escape and I love you!"*

The book had bounced off her face and split her nose. She was silent and startled and hung there in the web, immobile, staring at him. She probed gingerly at her injury with a long pointed tongue.

"How can you love me?" she growled softly. They were the first words she had spoken to him. "I am your enemy. I came here to kill you."

He regained his composure and retrieved his book from the tiled floor of the detention pod. He wasn't sure what to say next. His manual dealt only with the gentle destruction of a prisoner's resolve with logical, peaceful, inarguable sentiments. It said nothing about breaking their noses.

"I've loved you since I first saw you," Ankh heard himself say. He approached her, well within spitting distance, the manual held loosely at his side. "We are not enemies. Only the credo of the Monger makes us enemies. There is no need for us to be at war." He placed his hand on her blood-smeared cheek and she snapped at him at first, but when he did not withdraw, she let him keep it there. She thought it felt......*nice*. Yes, *nice*.

"The credo of the Monger is all I know," said Banshee. "War with the enemy Brightside - total control of the Worldship - a return to Earth to destroy those who dared to banish us into space. I was born in Hive Thirty-Eight, Vat Seventy-Three, Valhalla Legion. I have no mother or father. Monger is my family. I graduated from Valhalla seven days before my mission to Brightside. This is all I know. I know nothing of your.....*love*, Brightsider. You are my enemy."

"If we are enemies, at least let us know our enemy's name," said Ankh, pacing the floor of the detention pod and invisibly returning to an orthodox procedure from his manual. "My name is Ankh. It means -"

" - Peace. I know. We are taught your naming conventions in our Intelligence Studies. And I am Banshee. It means - "

"- an ancient wailing creature of mythology, a harbinger of death," said Ankh, smiling. "We have our own Intelligence Studies, too. You see, are we so different?"

A flicker of a smile crossed Banshee's face. Ankh saw it and his heart fluttered. His perseverance was being vindicated but above all his affection was being returned, even in this tiny manner. He didn't think she was faking. He didn't know that she would not have known how. Monger warriors were brutal and cruel but they were not liars. They had a code of honour that even a Brightsider would understand.

Ankh's ReEducation Angel supervisors were pleased with the progress he was making with Banshee - a particularly difficult case in their opinion - and reported the matter to Ankh's Mastertutor, Ono, informing him how impressed they were at the conduct of his schoolpod in allowing their brightest tutors to participate in the Angel project. The report landed on Ono's desk the same morning as the conscription request from the Self-Defence Forces. Ono read the report, and carefully omitted Ankh's name from the request return, condemning instead Sportstutor Pollen and the Applied Agriculture teacher Bethlehem to their year defending Brightside. Ankh was blissfully unaware of how close he had come to being handed a gun.

"Tell me more about a Brightsider's love."
    They had graduated, with the permission of the Angel supervisors, into a lower security level where Banshee could be seated in a restraint chair yet be allowed full upper body movement. It was far more civilised than the crucified stress-position of the gumweb.
    Ankh had abandoned the ReEducation Angel manual. His sessions with Banshee were freeform and unscripted. His supervisors encouraged this, pleased with his flair for, as they called it with wicked humour, 'soft torture'. Ankh thought of it as no such thing. He was simply trying to win the love of a woman, and persuade her to renounce the war culture that was poisoning her.
    "The love of a Brightsider is a wonderful thing. We love the air we breath, the flowers we grow, the animals we

tend, and the men and women whose lives we protect by defending ourselves against Mongerkind. There is no greater love than the love of a Brightsider." He paused and looked deep into her fiery eyes. The fire softened slightly. "You should be honoured to be the recipient of such love. It is a precious thing."

Banshee's eyes flared. Ankh settled back into his seat with a sigh, knowing he had said a wrong word and angered her. Had he preached too much? Had their relationship gone beyond a point where he needed to constantly harangue her?

"You speak as if I know nothing of love," she said, her voice harsh but tinged with sadness, as if he had wounded her with his insinuation. "Mongers know how to love. Our love is the love of our race, and our desire for revenge and retribution. It is this that you do not understand, Brightsider - "

"Ankh," he interrupted. "Please, call me Ankh."

"Ankh," she acquiesced, with a tilt of her head. A week earlier she had still been trying to bite off his face. Now she had a range of almost cute gestures. Progress, indeed.

"It is love that drives us to victory," she continued. "You assume that we hate you but we do not. Hatred, as you said, is a negative force. Were we to hate Brightside it would deflect us from our ultimate goal - the control of the Worldship, the return home. Brightside merely stands in the way. This is what you do not understand. A Monger is capable of love, Ankh. The love of the Legion to which a warrior belongs, the love of battle, the love of victory -"

"-the love of an enemy?"

Her mouth opened and closed slightly, stunned by his question. For a fleeting second she was just a vulnerable girl, not a fearsome warrior, and he recklessly leaned across the table and kissed her full on the mouth, taking care not to cut himself on her genetusks. She gasped and spluttered as he sat back down, shocked at his own impetuosity.

"What was that?" she asked.

"We call it a kiss," Ankh replied. "Did you like it?"

She licked her lips, her face curious. "What does it do?"

Ankh rolled his eyes. "It doesn't *do* anything. It's a gesture of affection."

She nodded sagely. "Monger Legionnaires have a similar gesture of affection. It is the highest form of respect to leap on warrior's back and wrestle him to the ground, then mark the back of his neck with your tusks."

Ankh swallowed hard. Not for the first time he was glad she was tied up. She let out a barking laugh.

"Ha. That was an untruth. Did you believe me?"

He spluttered a nervous laugh. She had cracked a joke!

"No, the highest endearment of a Monger warrior is to cut the head off a dying comrade, using his own bladed weapon, and then to use that weapon to slaughter twenty enemies in his honour."

There was no humour in her voice this time. Ankh stared at the fearsome visage he had just recklessly kissed, and realised he still had a long way to go to tame this savage beast.

"What do you mean she's gone?"

The guard stared back at him, silent to the redundant question. He had lost an arm in the breakout and a medic was attending to his wound, clamping a graft housing over the bloody stump. He was in no mood to entertain a hysterical young tutor.

All around them were the smoke-blackened signs of battle. Ankh listened as the guard repeated his story. They had come in force to take their people back, a slamship penetrating the hull, foam sealing the outer break, nosecone peeling open and spitting Monger troopers out like semen.

"A veteran squad, no virgin soldiers these. Sonic

stunners, sticklebombs, masers. We stood no chance. They killed all the Kind Police and rescued the Monger prisoners."

Ankh dropped to his knees in despair, head in his hands.

"The girl. Banshee. The one I had been visiting, remember? They took her too? Did she go gladly?"

The guard's brow creased as he pondered the question. "The girl. No, the girl fought them. She did not want to go. A Monger electrostunned her and carried her off."

Ankh's heart leapt and sank in a split second. He had discovered that his love was reciprocated and then he had lost the giver of that love in the same breath. He sank back to his haunches, and cried.

Banshee had been away for Monger for a little over a month. She awoke as the stolen maintenance brute crossed through one of the many portals from the Nogozone into her nation, and she took a great lungful of heavy, dirty Monger air.

She lifted herself up on her elbows, sore and groggy from electroshock, and surveyed her surroundings. She was laid out in the open rear of a tracked Brightside arcology drone along with five or six Monger corpses - it was hard to tell from the tangle of limbs - and half a dozen extremely alive warriors in black special operations clothing. Some of the corpses were dressed the same, some wore the white overalls of the Brightside detention units. There seemed to be no other living prisoners. The warriors grimaced and growled at her. Their uniforms were marked with sigil of a Legion unknown to her. She sensed their displeasure at the loss of their comrades in return for her escape, and shrank back into the corner of the drone, drawing her knees up to her chin. She felt threatened and vulnerable. They were unfamiliar feelings, and ones that she didn't like at all.

Monger rolled by as they headed through its streets. Banshee looked upon it with new eyes, comparing its dark innards to the clean lines of Brightside. Monger was a world turned inside out, the conduits and passageways of its commerce and lifebloods visible and pumping, its engines of industry filling the air with a ceaseless hum. Rusty gantries hung from the Worldship's inner hull, with colonies of precarious dwellings clinging to them like tumours around an organ. Architecture like a madman's vision of hell, where the recycling of scrap was taken to its ultimate limit, a war economy where everything was satisfied for the greater good. A gutted, hollowed out world, that Banshee called home.

Banshee had been brought across close to her own hive, the local divisional commander would be her Valhalla Legion chief. He would no doubt want to see her immediately.

The drone rolled on through streets dripping with electrical conduits, sagging glassfibre communications webbing and steaming pipes. Mongers shuffled by, going about their daily business, hidden beneath cloaks and hoods. Mongers who were not warriors - even those who administrated and supported the war - were second class citizens. All Monger's ruling elite were warriors.

The sullen rescue squad dumped Banshee unceremoniously on the steps of the divisional headquarters, along with three corpses in the white custodial uniforms. As the drone sped away, she overheard the warriors planning days of feasting and drinking to celebrate their successful mission, and to mourn their dead comrades.

Banshee stared up at the huge grey steel doors of the headquarters, disorientated and confused. The doors swung open and headquarters staff came out and retrieved the corpses. Dazed, she followed them inside and reported her arrival to the clerks.

And then, her nightmare began.

"How much information did you disclose?"
"Nothing. I followed procedure."

Fire in her veins, electroshock applied through the diamond plate floor to naked feet. Banshee squealed and danced.

"Why are you doing this to me? I am a loyal warrior. I did nothing but fail to complete my mission!"

"Then how are you still alive? That is not standard procedure. All Monger special forces operatives are fitted with poison sacs."

"Mine was faulty."

The disembodied voice fell silent, as if discussing something that they did not wish Banshee to hear. Banshee recognised the voice of the main interrogator as that of Killdevil, her Legion chief.

"That is impossible. You chose not to die."

"That's not true! I tried to take it. It was faulty."

Another blast of blue fire, throwing her off her feet. She was naked in the featureless grey chamber. She landed heavily, grazing the backs of her thighs.

"You lie, warrior."

"I'm not! I cannot lie. I don't know how! You taught me how to kill, how to die. But you never taught me how to lie!"

"Centuries ago, the Monger were banished from Earth for crimes they did not commit, and because they refused to lay down their arms in the face of aggressors who would destroy them."

"This is true. This is spoken."

"The banishment condemns Mongerkind to share the Worldship with the Brightsiders, agents and co-conspirators of this wrongful punishment."

"Death to Brightsiders. Destruction to all their ways."

"The Monger creed calls warriors of all Legions to join glorious battle, destroy Brightside and return to Earth to wreak vengeance on those who cast us out, that we may once

again breath the air of the world of our birth."
"This is true," said Banshee, her voice hollow. "This
is spoken."

The interrogation - or "debriefing" as they referred to it - lasted for days. It reduced her to a sobbing heap. She had left Monger a proud, idealistic warrior - now she was a physical and mental ruin. What had she done to deserve this?

They released her, apparently happy with her version of events, but with a discharge notice. To Banshee, it was as if they had killed her. She was a warrior, born and bred into a warrior society. A discharge notice - ironically, it stated 'mentally unfit' as the reason - was equal to a death sentence.

She was shunned by her hive brothers and sisters and excluded from her Valhalla Legion, the worst possible insult. Clanless, she was given a menial job in a military stores unit staffed by mental and physical defectives. She lasted an hour before overpowering the disabled veteran appointed to oversee their work, and became a fugitive, on the run in Monger.

There was only one place for her to go and only one person who could help her.

"Tutor Ankh!"
"Uh?"

He had been daydreaming again. The class of podders had got out of control while he stared into his register, far away, and now Agritutor Oasis had come into the pod and discovered him. She was bound to report it to Mastertutor Ono - the recent conscription of two of their members into the Self Defence Forces had set all the remaining tutors at each other's throats in an effort to escape the draft. Now, no misdemeanour would go unreported between colleagues if it meant that their own chances of staying out of the war could be bettered.

"I'm sorry, Tutor Oasis, I've not been getting a lot of sleep lately."

"So I see. Catching up in school time then?"

"No, I mean - "

"There is a message for you, on the terminal in my office."

He was surprised. Who would contact him on Oasis' terminal? "A message? Who from?"

Oasis was tight-lipped and brusque. "It is untagged. That in itself is very rude, but if you could ask your ...... *friend* .... to use your personal terminal in future, I would appreciate it."

Ankh chanced leaving the podders unattended as the office was just along the corridor. He slid in behind Oasis' excruciatingly tidy desk and thumbed recall on the terminal.

MESSAGE FOR TUTOR ANKH. RECEIPT ACKNOWLEDGEMENT.

- ACKNOWLEDGED -

YOU MUST HELP ME. I AM A FUGITIVE. MONGER HAS SCORNED ME. I HAVE NO ONE TO TURN TO. YOU SHOWED ME HONOUR AND LOVE.

His hands gripped the corners of the desk. It was Banshee!

"Have you finished?" Oasis at the door of her office, a steaming mug in her hands.

"Leave me!" Ankh barked. Oasis' eyes widened in shock at his outburst. She spluttered and scuttled away, no doubt heading straight for the Mastertutor's office.

Ankh had surprised himself with the ferocity of his rebuff, but he had to read the message in private. What were the penalties for communicating with Monger citizens over unmonitored channels? He shuddered to think.

I HAVE TAKEN REFUGE IN THE NOGOZONE. I NEED YOUR HELP, ANKH. I NEED YOUR HELP.....

* * *

The Nogozone stretched the entire length of the Worldship, a lawless warren of tunnels, shafts and conduits, along which flowed the lifeblood of both Monger and Brightside - water, air, power and waste. Many battles had taken place here in the early stages of the war, until both sides had suffered greatly through loss of critical life supports. Thus the Nogozone had earned its name, and it was a rare military operation from either side that breached its sanctity, other than as an escape route. It had become a home for deserters and miscreants and undesirables, particularly from Monger, but it was a refuge for a fair share of disillusioned Brightsiders too. Not all Brightsiders were obedient citizens.

It took Ankh many hours to find Banshee. Her message had contained rudimentary co-ordinates of her position based on the communication grid she had clipped into to contact him, which narrowed down her location to a cubic half-kilometre. The Nogozone was three-dimensional, and finding her even in that small box would take time.

There were many unguarded routes into the Nogozone from the Brightside quarter. Paranoid Monger used up vital resources trying to secure its own border, but Brightside considered this unnecessary, which explained why it was a favourite escape route for Monger commando units such as the one that had extracted Banshee. Ankh, armed with a helmet-mounted beamlamp and a screwdriver, slipped into the zone through an air-ducting and vanished into the forbidden darkness.

Ever the methodical tutor, Ankh mentally quartered the cube he had located her in and began a painstaking search. Many times he was surprised by families of hunched people - Mongers or Brightsiders, he could not tell - nursing blind, zone-born children in squalid alcoves among humming machinery. He saw packs of opportunist rodent creatures cruising the tunnels, looking for easy pickings, which he sent scattering before him with the harsh beam of his lamp. He heard a pack descend on someone or something helpless and the screams echoed along the dark passageways, nightmare voices.

When he finally found Banshee, many hours later, she was huddled on the shelf of a louvered heating unit, sucking warmth, filthy from head to toe and bleeding from many cuts sustained through her arduous passage through this dark realm. Her eyes flared feral as his beamlamp illuminated her face and she leapt at him, clipped claws scrabbling for his face. But she was weak and he fended her off easily until recognition dawned over her face.

"Food!" she hissed, "You have brought me food?"

He was deflated. "No. I....I didn't think."

"I'm starving!" she gasped, drawing herself up into a tight ball above the humming heater. "I asked you in the message to bring me food. Are you a fool?"

"I didn't think," he repeated glumly, climbing up on to the shelf next to her. It didn't strike him that this was the first time he had been this close to her while she was unrestrained. She didn't seem so scary anymore - just a dirty, hungry, frightened girl.

"I was in so much of a hurry to find you," he explained. "But now I have, you can come back with me, and I'll feed you-"

"No!" she exclaimed. "I cannot go to Brightside. I am a prisoner of war. Brightsiders died when the commandos rescued me. I would be executed for sure."

Ankh snorted. "We don't execute prisoners! We re-educate them. All the same, you're probably right to be worried. The Polite Police would take you in to custody. I couldn't hide you forever."

She looked up at him, eyes wide and bright in the darkness, completely vulnerable. One of her genetusks was chipped. "Will you come back with food, then, Ankh? I am so hungry."

He nodded and slipped from the shelf of the heater. "Now I know where to find you, I can be back here in a couple of hours. Here, take these." He gave her his padded jacket and a spare pocket beamlamp. "If those funny things come near just shine the beamlamp in their eyes, They can't stand it, they'll run away."

"I know," she said. "I've seen them before, a few days ago, when I first came here. One of them was the last thing I had to eat."

He swallowed hard and tried to fight the rise of bile in his throat. She was good at reminding him what she was.

"I'll be back soon."

"Be swift."

He felt compelled to voice his feelings. "I love you, Banshee."

"I know you do," she said, "and that is why you are going to help me. Go now. I hunger."

Ankh returned to the Nogozone later that day with a parcel of food for Banshee, which she devoured immediately, some blankets and spare cells for the beamlamp. He begged her to return with him to Brightside, even if it did mean imprisonment again. He was frightened for her in this dark place, with its monsters and hidden dangers, but she was adamant that she was staying. She was, after all, a Monger warrior. Maybe the denizens of the Nogozone had more to fear from her than she did from them.

He visited her many times over the following days. Sometimes he had to wait hours for her past their agreed time of meeting, as she explored this dark new world she had chosen as her home. She would arrive back at her hide breathless and dirty and sometimes bloody. He thought she was hunting the fat rats or preying on the other inhabitants of the Nogozone, even though he unquestioningly brought her everything she could possibly need. She never offered an explanation for her behaviour, he never asked for one. His love for her was completely unconditional.

"Do you still love me, Ankh?" she asked, quite unexpectedly, one day after he had waited two hours for her to return from one of her wanderings. He was crouched in her nest of grubby blankets, sullen and sulking at her absence.

"Of course I do!" he snapped, and it sounded unconvincing even to his own ears. He softened his tone. "Of course I do. That is why I come to you, day after day, and bring you food, and wait here for you when you know I have come-"

"If you really loved me," she said, squatting on her haunches in the dim light in front of him, "you would come to here to live with me."

He was shocked. It was the first time she had suggested it.

"Leave Brightside? I could never leave. How would I survive here? You only survive because I bring you food and clean water."

She smiled a wicked smile and leaned closer to him. Her breath was hot on his face, hot and foul. "I appreciate what you bring me, but I don't need it to survive. I could provide for us both here, Ankh." And he knew exactly what she meant. His stomach flipped.

"I - I don't know," he said, drawing his knees up to his chin. A strange thrumming was building up through the metal floor, an uncomfortable vibration passing through the thin soles of his boots. Banshee appeared not to notice.

"We must be together," she urged, gripping his legs. "We cannot go to Monger - we would both be killed. We cannot live together in Brightside - I would be imprisoned, you would be punished for aiding an enemy."

"Re-educated," Ankh corrected. "In Brightside, no one

is punished." The thrumming was audible now, no longer simply a vibration, and was accompanied by a harsh metallic clattering like the bashing of cymbals. Faint blue light, like electrical arcing, shimmered in the darkness.

"We are both outcasts," Banshee continued, oblivious to the rising crescendo. "Our love makes us fugitives from our people. Only the Nogozone offers us sanctuary. You must come here to live, Ankh. I love you."

His heart leapt. She had said it! She had actually said it! He leaned forward to kiss her, and as he did so the beam of his helmet lamp swung down the narrow passageway outside her hide, and swept over the death black flanks of the source of the noise, a ton of tracked dirty steel heading their way. He was suddenly aware that the noise had risen to a deafening crescendo, he had barely heard the last few words Banshee had spoken. Still on her haunches, her body was half in the passageway, in the thing's path. Ankh reached forward and grabbed her filthy smock, and hauled her in.

The black steel monster cruised by with a thunderous roar, a medusa's nest of prehensile limbs tipped with blades and flails and scouring heads of steel cords, all ricocheting off the passageway's metal walls in clouds of sparks and dislodged debris. Banshee lay on top of Ankh, panting, as they listened to the sound of the thing die away. The rank smell of burnt ozone, hot oil and sheared metal hung in the air.

"Cleaning drone," she said, in answer to the bewildered look on his face. "Fully automated. Some of them are as old as the Worldship. They pass this way all the time. Sometimes they wake me up."

He wondered if she realised how close she had come to being cut in half. Nothing seemed to scare her. He remembered she had just told him that she loved him. He kissed her full on her mouth but the moment had been tainted by his brush with death. Again he was reminded that they were very different creatures. Could he give up his people for her and live in this forsaken place?

* * *

"Many, many years ago, the Human Race lived on a place called Planet Earth. Planet Earth was very green and very beautiful, and the Human Race lived there happily with many kinds of animals and plants.

"But then the Human Race invented machines, and these machines produced nasty gas and horrible waste that polluted the green and killed the plants and the animals, and Planet Earth was no longer such a nice place to live.

"When things became so bad that even the air was not good to breath, the Human Race decided to build huge spaceships to send as many of its people out to the stars, to live in clean environments and find new planets on which to start again. There were many of these spaceships, known as Worldships, and they were sent out to all corners of the galaxy.

"On one particular Worldship, a quarrel broke out between two different peoples. An aggressive and warlike people had banded together and decided that they had been banished from Earth because it was they who had been bad, rather than the air. They wanted to return to Earth and get their own back on the people who had sent them away. Using weapons and violence, they seized control of the Worldship's power source, and tried to turn the ship around.

"The rest of the people on this particular Worldship were peaceful and wanted to carry on and find a new planet, believing that they had been saved from the dying Earth. They did not want the bad people, who began to call themselves warmongers or Mongers, to take them back to Earth against their will. When the Mongers gained control of the ship's power, the peaceful people, who called themselves

the Brightsiders, decided that they must be stopped, and took control of the Worldship's navigation computers, preventing the Mongers from finding their way home. The Mongers cut the power, and the Worldship stopped moving, neither going back to Earth nor going forward. This is called a stalemate.

"All this happened many years ago, before your father's father's father's were born. Since then the quarrel has become a war, fought mainly on the outer skin of the Worldship, and many have died from either side. Many youngsters..... many..... many.... oh, fuck it!"

Ankh slammed the plastic manual into the desk top and ran from the pod, leaving thirty bewildered podders staring at an empty chair. Mastertutor Ono found them twenty minutes later, lured from his office by the sound of their playful rioting, and found a relief tutor to calm them down. He returned to his office where another form had arrived on his desk from the Self Defence Forces. Ankh's behaviour had grown increasingly irrational over the past few days. This time, Mastertutor Ono felt that he had left him with no choice.

Banshee had not seen Ankh for many days. She tapped into the comms grid and left hourly messages for him, but none were answered. He had failed to turn up at all of their arranged meetings for the past few days, and she had even begun to wait for him at the proper time, but still he failed to show. Had she upset him? She remembered their last meeting where she had told him she had loved him and he saved her from the renegade cleaning drone. Perhaps her insistence that he join her permanently in the Nogozone had frightened him. Perhaps she had asked too much. Perhaps he was taking some time to think through a decision, or to get his affairs in order before joining her. Perhaps.

She had not seen him for ten days and became convinced he had been killed, or worse. There was only one thing left for her to do - she would have to enter Brightside and find him. It was a drastic decision for her to take - her Monger disfigurements marked her indelibly as the enemy, and her time in the Nogozone and turned her into a filthy, decrepit specimen. She mugged a zone dweller for an oversized hooded cloak and used the last of the fresh water that Ankh had brought her ten days previously to clean herself up as best she could. She found a section of mirrored steel plate and regarded herself in it. She looked like a nightmare apparition, even by Monger standards. If her hivemates could see her now ... she had forgotten that they had forsaken her, already. Maybe they were all dead by now. Life expectancy of Monger commandos was extremely low.

Mustering her courage, she clambered through one of the access points that Ankh had shown her before, and entered a remote and quiet passage in Brightside.

Banshee was free in Brightside for several hours before the Polite Police's DNA scanners were alerted to her presence and she was arrested by a frighteningly efficient snatch team in a busy public thoroughfare. She put up no resistance. She had spent the previous hours wandering aimlessly through Brightside in a daze, unable to comprehend a way of finding Ankh, and blinded by the wonder of the place, which she had never really seen. It was so clean, she thought. White surfaces, no visible pipes or wiring, so many corridors and boulevards where people could sit and talk in peace and quiet - so quiet! - huge expanses of green, *and the arcologies....*! She was pressed up against the clean glass of a viewing balcony, frosting it with her breath as she looked down over the green sprawl when the Polite Police found her and fired pink gumweb over her, pinning her to the cool glass.

She was taken to the same detention pod where Ankh had first come to visit her. She asked to see him but no one would speak to her. She remained in the silent pod for hours until a voice raised her from fitful sleep. The voice was flat, artificially generated from a routine in a database program, absolving her jailers of the terrible act it was about to commit on their behalf.

"Prisoner Ex - thirty eight. Monger citizen designation 'Banshee'. You are charged with the murder of seven Brightside citizens during your escape from custody. How do you plead?"

She didn't know what to say, so she said nothing.

"How do you plead?" the voice insisted.

"I want to see Ankh," she said.

There was a pause. A subroutine ran and returned some data.

"Re-Education Angel 'Ankh' no longer reports to this detention pod. Individual is now a member of the Self Defence Forces assigned to the battlefront in Alpha Sector."

Banshee's heart fluttered. "No! He is a tutor, a gentle soul. I love him! He could never be a warrior! Never!"

"Individual is now a member of the Self Defence Forces assigned to the battlefront in Alpha Sector," the voice repeated gracelessly. "How do you plead?"

She said nothing. She started to cry.

"In the absence of a plea by the accused, available data will be processed in order to generate a verdict and appropriate sentence. This may take a few moments. Please be patient."

Banshee's eyes widened as the cold voice fell silent. Sentence? Ankh had told her no one was punished in Brightside, only re-educated. What did the voice mean?

"The verdict has been reached. You have been found guilty. The sentence is disintegration."

"*Disintegration*?" She clasped her hand to her mouth, just before a maser ray flickered from a hidden slot in the wall and wiped her cleanly from existence, as was the Brightsider way.

As a method of spooking the defenders, the Monger armoured division *Iron Thunder* broadcast their battle mass over the same channel used by the Brightsider footsoldiers for their helmet comms. The howling of the combat prayers and the blessing of the weaponry by the chaplain deafened the young Brightsiders huddled in their smooth steel trenches with the infinite blackness of space pressing down on them. Several ripped off their helmets and ate vacuum, dying even before the Mongers had even fired a shot.

Ankh held the gun in his hands like a dead weight, still unable to believe that he had been sent here. Even as he had gone through the stages of his call-up - the last interview with Mastertutor Ono where he had failed to satisfactorily explain his behaviour, the goodbyes to his secretly-relieved colleagues and his bewildered podders, the training camp, the swift and almost cursory training and finally the deployment - he had been convinced that it had all been some terrible mistake and that someone was about to call out his name and tell him just that and take him away from it all. It had never happened. Now he was here, with hundreds of others just like himself, no doubt hoping the same thing, about to defend Brightside against what intelligence sources held to be Monger's biggest offensive in many years.

A thrumming passed through his feet, much deeper and faster than the warning he had felt from the drone in the Nogozone with Banshee. *Banshee.....* he had had no chance to contact her once he had been conscripted, everything had happened so fast, and he knew he had been under surveillance by the Polite Police in case he had tried to dodge his call-up. He wondered what had become of her. Strange, really, how he had lost her for the second time just after he had discovered that she really did love him. Would she be proud of him, he wondered, as a warrior? No. That was her way, not his. She loved him for what he was. He hoped that wherever she was, she was surviving. He suspected that she was. She was good at that.

A gasp rippled along the battle line. Cresting the horizon, where the hull of the Worldship dropped away into infinity, a Monger armoured division approached, vast destroyer leviathans riding on steel cables running across the surface. The song of the hypertensed cables whispered to the defenders through the soles of their boots. It sang of death. Beneath the flared ceramic armour skirts of the destroyers, cableskater troopers moved like swarms of insects, chrome suits reflecting starlight back into the void, fearfully beautiful.

The shrill whistle sounded across the helmet comms channel. The Brightsiders formed up on the ladders and ramps of the steel trenches, clutching weapons, waiting for the second whistle which would send them into battle. A black cloud had sprung from the lead leviathan - sticklebombs bearing down on them, evil little things that stuck to a spacesuit and blew hundreds of tiny holes in it and its wearer. One of the nastier, but by no means the only, methods that Monger had developed for young Brightsiders to die.

Second whistle.

Ankh took a deep, sweet breath.

Over the top.........

A Night on the Town

ILLUSTRATION BY RIK RAWLING

"El capitalismo convirta a Caracas en un inferno"
- graffiti on Caracas bus station

Miguel is trying so hard to impress her, he really is. He has greased his hair and brushed his teeth - twice, with the new American toothpaste that nanotechnically scours your mouth - and lightly rouged his cheeks. He is wearing his older brother's favourite outfit (Carlos would kill him if came back from his school outward bound holiday on Margarita Island and found him wearing it) - nylon and leather parachutist's boots, baggy cotton pants and skinny-rib black T-shirt showing off his concave stomach and multicoloured Inca sunburst tattoo encircling his navel. He looks gorgeous, like a rich seventeen year old alone with a beautiful young woman in his family apartment in Nuevo Caracas should look. And *still* she is not impressed.

She sits in the moisture-slicked bay window, looking out over the firefly city as the sun is eaten by a storm sky, toying with a narcotic All-Day Sucker, her long brown legs dangling naked from the dramatic split in her halter-necked blood red ball gown. She does not even flinch as the slam thunder rocks the city. Maria is eighteen years old and a raven-haired Latin beauty. A year older than Miguel - it may as well be a hundred. She has made an art form of cynicism and world-weariness. The narcotic lollipop that Miguel bought her from a street vendor on their way here should be making her buzz. Instead, it appears to intensify her boredom.

Miguel is desperate. Maria is a goddess, her body curved and voluptuous. He very much wants to return to school on Monday and boast of his sexual adventures - which he will of course, even if he does not bed this impressively unimpressible siren. But the conditions are so right! His botanist parents away on a field trip in the rainforest - no school until Monday morning - a Saturday night city stretching and limbering thirty stories beneath them - his creditocard full and active (*Praise Jesus!*) and his father's brand-new red Ford Machos "Matador" Special Edition waiting in the basement garage. They can go anywhere and do anything. God, what will it take to make this woman horny?

He slumps in the formocouch and watches her. She slips from the window sill with a bored sigh and is momentarily highlighted by sheet lightning as the storm breaks over Nuevo Caracas, wild photons Dopplering her bare shoulders with jungle tiger patterns. She moves toward him with liquid grace, bare feet padding on thick carpet. She kneels at his feet and places her hands firmly on his splayed thighs. He stiffens.

"I need to eat," she breathes, running her tongue across her glossy lips. A faint whiff of lemon drifts from her breath, the scent of the narcotic.

"Take me to dinner," she insists, settling back on her haunches like a karate fighter awaiting a bout.

He swallows hard before answering her.

"What would you like to eat, Maria?"

Her dark eyes flare. The first sign of passion he has seen since he brought her here.

"Something special," she purrs. "Something unusual. Something exotic."

As she speaks her fingers trace the inside of his thighs. He feels the pressure of her sharp nails through the thin cotton pants.

"Take me somewhere different, Miguel." It is, he thinks, the first time she has spoken his name. She makes it sound like treacle being poured on velvet. *Miguel. Miguel. Miguel.*

So, he thinks, let's recap. Saturday night. Parents in the forest. Carlos on Margarita. Apartment free. City buzzing. Ford Machos "Matador" Special Edition in garage, keycard in pocket. Money no problem. Beautiful, high-as-a-kite Maria Del Fuego in a thigh-split red cocktail dress on her knees - *on her knees!* - in front of him. There is, of course, as mad as it seems, only one serious course of action.

There are myths and legends that permeate Nuevo Caracas like no other city on Earth. In this place where the rainforest hugs the cyberscraper as it smothers the congested, disease-ridden barrio, the *brujo* or witch-doctor of the forest tribes is as respected as the Catholic priests who ply their trade from streetside booths, whispering Latin mantras from under smog masks and rain capes. There is a story that Miguel has heard many times and which he is frantically trying to recall the details of now. The story concerns a brujo in the southern part of the barrio that rings the cybercity. The brujo owns a restaurant situated in the abandoned ruin of a 19th century mission church, a tiny collection of crates and candles stuck in wax-encrusted wine bottles, huddled beneath corrugated plastic sheeting. In this "restaurant" the brujo weaves culinary magic that brings the affluent down from their crystal towers to run the gauntlet of muggers and lepers and beggars, of car thieves and body-part bootleggers and army deserters fleeing the war with Ecuador. The brujo accepts no money or creditocards - only trade for things he will find useful, or can trade on. What will Miguel give to him? The dish tonight - for there is only ever one dish on the menu, no choices - will be the *mutopargo*, an enormous multi-headed, many-finned mutant fish caught upstream in the poisoned Orinoco, where the chemical sprays that help the rainforest survive drain into the water. The fish are resilient and difficult to capture. When they are caught they often remain alive through days out of water as they are brought to the city. Miguel has heard that some are even still living as they arrive at the diner's table, to be eaten raw like Japanese sushi, a dozen eyes watching mournfully and fins flapping as the knife cuts home. Why would anyone want to partake of such a grotesque and cruel experience? Because the flesh of the mutopargo is the most delicious known to man. *It is the food of the rainforest gods.*

He stands and puffs out his shallow chest. She gets up and does the same - her plumage is much more impressive. She draws on her red spike heels and is taller than him by a head. He sucks in a breath.

"We will go to see the *brujo,*" he tells her. Her eyes sparkle - she knows the story. He thrusts one hand into his pocket and closes his fist around the comforting keycard of the Ford Machos "Matador" Special Edition, and he knows now that he has her.

Nuevo Caracas, at night:

Black hardtop rolls by beneath the Ford Machos "Matador" Special Edition's fat tyres. The car corners like a tram and Miguel holds the tiny electronic steering wheel with one casual hand. His other caresses Maria's naked brown thigh, revealed by the split of the red dress. So smooth, so smooth. She does not complain, nor does she agree to his touch. Ambivalence comes naturally to her.

Nuevo Caracas, at night:

Half the population is nocturnal. As the sun sets and the thunder clouds sweeping in from the forest fast-darken the sky, these creatures scuttle from their daylight boltholes to play or work, whether that work be selling their bodies (or body parts) or preaching infernal Papist damnation to anyone who will listen. The air is thick and damp and heavy with acidic ozone. Not that it bothers Miguel and Maria - the Ford Machos "Matador" Special Edition is equipped with an aerospatial-grade air conditioning system that keeps humidity, temperature and pollution levels within the car to acceptable levels. It is, perhaps, a little chilly. Miguel's nipples are erect beneath his brother's T-shirt. As he turns the corner where the polizei are threatening streetdwellers with electric batons, he decides he will see if Maria is similarly affected.

Nuevo Caracas, at night:

The city is a living organism, mutant child of the rainforest, an amoeba split in two, the squalid barrio and the cyberscrapers, with the streets the neutral ground where beggars and bankers can be murdered or raped or hustled by armoured riot-ready polizei, without fear of prejudice. Nuevo Caracas is nothing if not democratic. Bolivar would be proud.

Nuevo Caracas, at night:

The landscape changes as Miguel begins his ascent into the domain of the barrio. The Ford Machos "Matador" Special Edition's massively overpowered engine grumbles sulkily in its restraint mode under the sensuous haunch of the bonnet. Miguel's foot is barely touching the accelerator. He reluctantly forsakes Maria's delicate thigh and grips the wheel with both hands, begins to pay more attention to the road. If a barrio gang emerge from a side street armed with a battering ram made from old crane parts, he will stamp his foot and the Ford Machos "Matador" Special Edition will - stylishly - carry them from nought to sixty in four seconds. The veloured bucket seats press their flesh reassuringly, ready to catch them if the Ford Machos "Matador" Special Edition rears like a stallion making a mad dash for freedom.

"How much further?" Maria whines, shifting in her seat.

Miguel is loath to take his eyes from the road. Street lighting disappeared a few miles back and the Ford Machos "Matador" Special Edition's powerful headlights spear the dark tunnel of the way ahead, picking out figures moving to either side. They pass a solitary polizei-mobile, parked on a junction with its doors and windows sealed, a single red light glowing weakly on its roof, like the last gas station for a hundred miles. They flash by at speed, into the dead heart of the barrio.

The barrio, at night:

In Nuevo Caracas, money changes hands and business is the order of day and night, the pursuit and accumulation of wealth, whether the vast riches of the interbankers or the savings of the whore hoping to escape the streets. Here in the barrio, there is only one business - the business of day to day survival.

The barrio, at night:

The city is alive but the barrio is dead, its heart ripped out by corruption and greed and man's inhumanity to man. Here life has been made cheap. A child can be sold for a meal. A man can be killed for a bottle of beer. When people have nothing, they have nothing to lose.

The barrio, at night:

Victim of the city, the barrio lies crushed between the cyberscraper and the mountains, compressed by need for that most valuable of commodities, real estate. A thousand people living in the space for a hundred with no power except for that which they might generate through ingenuity or desperation. A thousand people with dead hearts and dead minds and dead lives. A dead city to mirror its neighbour, so very much alive.

"How much further?"

Miguel swallows hard and prepares to admit that he has no idea. The Ford Machos "Matador" Special Edition has slowed to a crawl and is making its way along steep winding streets choked with debris and the detritus of life in the barrio. Suspicious eyes view him from behind heavy hessian drapes and the paint smeared windows of old trucks and buses that some of these people call home. He feels that if he stops moving, they will descend on the car like a plague of locusts and strip it of everything of value, including himself and Maria. In the barrio, everything has a value, including things that the city dwellers consider trash. That strange, sad thought terrifies Miguel.

The streets of the barrio are almost deserted, the thunder and lightning driving the people indoors to their shacks and shanties, to cling to their possessions in case the coming torrential rain tries to sweep them away. Miguel needs directions or they will circle this godforsaken place all night, and he knows Maria will not be impressed by *that*.

Instead, he thinks, she will be impressed by his nonchalance at stopping the car and asking one of the barrio residents for help. He has a small amount of currency in a billfold in his pocket, he knows that these people will want paying for information, and you cannot expect barrio dwellers to accept creditocards! He smiles at the thought as he parks the Ford Machos "Matador" Special Edition by a large black injection-molded dumpster where the blue glow of a television screen seeps from the edges of a filthy sheet slung over the propped lid. Maria turns to him, horror on her face.

"Don't worry," he says. "I just need to ask the way."

And he gets out of the car.

Miguel is a foolish, ill-informed, spoilt youth of the cyberscraper culture. He knows no more of the barrio than the wild stories of the brujo and his ilk. He does not know that there is no reasoning with the people of the barrio when you have something that they want, especially when you are dressed in your older brother's best clothes and have a beautiful woman by your side. Maria could have told him this, if she was not paralysed with fear. Her family are less affluent than Miguel's - they live in the borderlands where you can smell the barrio, not just imagine it as a dark horizon or a scattering of twinkling fires in the distance. Maria has arrived home to find barrio kids in her room, rifling through her underwear draw. She thought Miguel knew all this. She trusted him. Now, he has turned off the engine of the car, unlocked the door, and *got out*.

Miguel does not want Maria to know how frightened he is. He feels very vulnerable in his smart borrowed clothes as he approaches the dumpster. The side of the plastic box is painted in psychedelic swirls of luminous paint, cryptic symbols and figures. One resembles the Inca sunburst tattoo on his bare stomach. He fingers the tattoo self-consciously. He doesn't know what the tattoo symbolises, he just thought it looked cool. What if it offends a follower of one of the barrio's myriad religions?

He gingerly lifts the hessian that obscures the dumpster's lid. A child is inside, sitting crosslegged on a carpeted floor, leaning forward with its face pressed up to a television screen, nose almost touching it. Miguel cannot tell at first if it is a boy or a girl. The inside of the dumpster is strung with cheap Christmas tree lights, thin wires leading from them and the television up to the makeshift power lines sagging from the building next door. The supply is dangerous and unreliable and every few seconds the television picture recedes to a dot and then springs back again, each time apparently changing channel. The child does not seem bothered by this unintelligible assault on its senses.

".... *stay tuned stay tuned will you open the box or take the money buy the new CoCo-narcobar NOW it's full of flavour and can help prevent twenty types of cancer Ecuadorian paratroops landed today in northern sectors scandal hits new mining complex on the Orinoco delta stay tuned stay tuned stay tuned.....*"

Miguel stubs his foot against the dumpster and the child jumps up, an enormous hunting knife in its small hands. Miguel sees now that it is a boy, no more than ten years old, with raggedy clothes, copper hoop earrings and a dirty face. The boy does a double take at Miguel's clothes then waves the knife around in front of Miguel's nose. Miguel jumps back.

"What you want, clown man? You want my ass, huh?

Not for sale, clown man. Go somewhere else! Unless you want to speak to my brother." The boy waves the knife again. Miguel presumes that this is his 'brother'.

"I'm not going to hurt you. I just want directions." Miguel holds up the palms of his hands in a placatory gesture. The boy's rodent eyes glance from empty hand to empty hand, and he relaxes slightly.

"I just want to watch my television, clown man. Why should I help you?"

Miguel keeps one hand outstretched and digs in the pocket of his brother's parachute pants with the other, bringing out the thick billfold. The boy's eyes light up like his television screen.

"What do you want to find in the barrio, then, clown man? Not much in the barrio to interest city types. Girls we got. You want girls, clown man?"

Miguel shakes his head and peels off several notes from the billfold. The boy licks his lips hungrily.

"The brujo, little man. We're looking for the restaurant of the brujo."

Standing up to his waist in the dumpster, the boy is a head above Miguel, and looks over his shoulder to the Ford Machos "Matador" Special Edition parked behind him. He can see Maria in the passenger seat. He reaches forward for the money but Miguel pulls it away and the boy almost topples over the plastic rim.

"Directions first. I'm in a hurry."

The boy clambers from the dumpster, his 'brother' still in one hand. He wipes the other hand three times on his pant leg and offers it to Miguel, giving a slight bow as he does so. Miguel gingerly accepts the greeting.

"Bruno Del Santos El Rodriguez at your service," says the boy. "You want the restaurant of the brujo, and I am the man to show it you. But it is much too difficult to explain the way. I must come with you."

Miguel looks at the dirty boy and thinks of his beautiful car and the beautiful woman inside. He finds it difficult to imagine the two pictures in the same frame. But what are his choices? The boy has a big knife and information that he needs. He can only hope that Maria is not too appalled and that later he can clean any stains off the upholstery before his mother and father return.

"Okay," Miguel says. "But your brother stays here."

The Ford Machos "Matador" Special Edition roars around the barrio's narrow streets with greater confidence as Bruno leans forward from the narrow ledge of the car's back seat and points left and right, giving Miguel precise but invariably dangerously late directions. They are climbing into the storm sky, the ground above them thinning in its concentration of shacks and slums as they near the summit of the barrio.

Bruno is enjoying himself. He has never been in a car like this one and his seat gives him a perfect view down the girl's impressive cleavage. She slaps his face when he tries to touch her. She then spends the rest of the journey pressed against the trim panel of the passenger door, trying to get away from his hands and his pungent odour. He gives up and attempts to play with the myriad gadgets and screens on the car's dashboard, which earns him an equal rebuff from Miguel. He wishes he had his brother with him, then he would show these two some respect.

"There, there it is!" Bruno points at a skeletal ruin silhouetted above them against the lightning-torn sky. Miguel peers through the car's windscreen and uses the image to navigate his way through the last of the barrio streets, empty of life up here. Several dogs scatter from something large and dark they were gnawing on an alleyway. Miguel sees the steep, narrow road that will take them up to the mission church, and decides that he will drive the Ford Machos "Matador" Special Edition no further. He parks at the bottom of the hill and switches off the engine.

"Good job, city man, yes?" Bruno grins with yellow teeth and holds out his dirty palm. Miguel smiles at him and they all get out of the car. Miguel fiddles with the keycard until he arms the car's defence system. A blue light glows softly on the dashboard.

"Good job, you pay me now, yes?" Bruno is insistent, urging. Miguel smiles again and presses a single crisp note into the boy's hand. Bruno looks at the note with disgust and spits on the floor.

"You promised me more, city man. We had a deal. You pay up, or I fetch my brother."

Miguel leans forward and gives Bruno a fierce push, sending the boy sprawling into the dirt. The note flutters away and Bruno chases after it on all fours, grabbing it before it disappears into the trash piled in the gutters. He stands and screams an obscenity at Miguel and Maria. Miguel picks up a crushed can and throws it at the boy, who runs away, cursing them in vivid language. Maria laughs, and Miguel smiles. He was worried that the evening was not going as planned, but now she seems genuinely impressed with him. He really showed that barrio kid who was boss man, didn't he?

The old mission church stands out above them, an unfleshed corpse of a building, a relic of a colonial past. Miguel takes Maria's hand and together they walk up the narrow street. In the gaps between the ruins they can see the inky expanse of the valley they have left, the city caught between the rainforest and this hard, dangerous place. Nuevo Caracas is a crystal ship afloat in a black sea. It seems so far away at this moment.

As they near the old mission, they can see fairy lights and candles flicker in the shell of the church, teased by the storm wind. Sheet lightning periodically turns night to day.

Miguel begins to feel nervous. What if this *is* just a myth? They have risked their lives - *and his father's car!* - to come here. Maria is hungry and impatient, and he has chosen to take her to the ultimate restaurant, which may or not exist, to eat an exotic - and quite possibly poisonous - mutant fish! Miguel, you are *mucho lobo!*

Miguel guides Maria over the rubble-strewn courtyard. Big wooden gates lie forlorn to each side. Maria steps delicately and deliberately over the ground in her spike heels, allowing Miguel to steer her toward the softly illuminated plastic sheeting strung across the front of the mission. Maria stops and shrugs off Miguel's touch.

"There's nothing here!" she says petulantly. "This is no restaurant, it's just some barrio shack. Why have you brought me here, Miguel?"

"Come," says the brujo, stepping from the darkness, a slight figure in tapestry robes. "I've been expecting you."

Miguel and Maria freeze for a moment. The brujo is an old bearded man, not threatening in the least. Why should they be afraid of him? He smiles and beckons to them.

They follow the brujo without question. He sweeps aside the plastic sheeting and ushers them into his restaurant.

The interior is dark and smoky. Shadows chase shadows away from the glow of candles and lightning flashes. The restaurant is empty of customers. A dwarf waiter moves toward them with a glass pitcher of red wine.

The brujo shows them to their table - a packing crate covered by a cloth and marked with the logo of the Venezuelan Air Force, and two plastic picnic chairs. Maria graciously allows the brujo to pull the chair out for her before she gathers her dress around her and sits down. The brujo smiles toothlessly. The dwarf fills up their glasses with wine.

"You will, of course, be ordering our special," says the brujo, wringing his hands. It is a statement, not a question.

"Is it available?" asks Miguel coolly, raising an eyebrow.

"Of course!" says the brujo. "Otherwise, you would

not be here."

The brujo and the dwarf disappear. Maria sips at her wine and looks around the restaurant, trying to see if they are really alone. Dark shapes flit around the periphery of her vision, but she sees no one. It is so hot in here, moisture rolling down the rippling plastic sheeting. A light sheen of sweat covers Maria's neck and shoulders, glistening in the candlelight.

Miguel's attention is fixed on Maria. He plays with the stem of his wine glass and tries to think of cool things he can say to her. Before he has a chance to deliver a stunning fusillade of compliments, the brujo returns, accompanied by the dwarf carrying a huge covered silver platter.

"Your mutopargo," says the brujo, and unveils the platter with a flourish.

The fish is still alive, shuffling ineffectively on the platter, surrounded by fruit and vegetables and Venezuelan *cachapa*, maize pancakes, and *caraotas* beans. It is a two headed specimen, the most common mutation, and the two heads flip nervously in different directions, saucer eyes attempting to take in all threats. Multiple fins drum a beat on the metal dish. The dwarf places the platter carefully on the packing crates then retreats with the brujo, bowing graciously.

Miguel and Maria and the mutopargo stare at each other for a long time in silence. The dwarf returns and gives them both sharp knives and forks.

"It's so beautiful," says Maria. "It's such a shame to kill it."

"Some people say it is already dead," says Miguel, testing the edge of the knife with his thumb. "It will have been out of the water for many days. It is just electricity, making the fins and the head move."

Maria wants to believe him but the mutopargo looks at her mournfully, both heads swivelling toward her, as if appealing for feminine mercy.

"But it is supposed to be so good to eat," says Miguel, and makes a deep incision into the fish's flank. The fish shrieks and shudders. Miguel recoils and drops his knife. Maria licks her lips and picks up her own knife. She makes a bold, more positive incision deep into the fish's side, cutting a swathe of white flesh. The mutopargo stops moving. Miguel watches, awe-struck, as Maria slowly cuts the flesh on her plate and forks a piece into her mouth. She closes her eyes, chews and swallows.

"It is fantastic," she says. "It is the most fantastic thing I have ever tasted. Here, try some."

She cuts a swathe for him and he accepts it from her. He rolls his eyes as he tastes it for the first time.

"Excellent," he says. "More. *More.*"

He takes over and carves and feeds her, and in between takes pieces for himself. The brujo watches from the shadows, satisfied. He catches Miguel's eye and winks, then taps his palm pointedly. *What have you brought me in trade?*

Miguel freezes. How could he have been so forgetful? He reaches into his pocket and takes out two things - his creditocard and the keycard to his father's Ford Machos "Matador" Special Edition. The brujo accepts no cash. The Ford Machos "Matador" Special Edition...... His *father's* Ford Machos "Matador" Special Edition.....Is there no alternative? He looks across at the girl he has brought here. *Surely not.....?*

Maria Del Fuego looks even more beautiful with her eyes closed in the ecstasy of exquisite taste. When she does open her eyes to see why Miguel has not fed her another morsel, he sees a look in her eyes which was not there before, a look that says, *Good work, Miguel. You've won. I want you.*

He smiles and forks another mouthful of food into her mouth. In the end, the decision is not so hard, after all.

* * *

Carlos will kill him, of course, but it is a small price to pay for such a wonderful evening, and maybe when he tells Carlos of his fantastic adventure and how he made love to the beautiful Maria Del Fuego back at their apartment, he will forgive him. They are heading home through the barrio at speed, and he turns down the air conditioning as it is getting cold in the car. He is, after all, wearing just his best silk boxer shorts, with his creditocard tucked safely in the tiny condom pocket, just behind the condom. He smiles at the thought of the brujo dressed in Carlos' clothes, an old man in the guise of a superhip Nuevo Caracas kid. Maria giggles at his nakedness but her laugh has a saucy edge, tinged by red wine and sexual tension. Miguel fights the impending erection as best he can. That would be *so* uncool.

Word travels fast in this urban jungle. These people have no need of internet or phone. The Ford Machos "Matador" Special Edition was tracked as it entered the barrio and allowed to pass through an elaborate series of gates and predetermined routes invisible to the eye of city dwellers. As Miguel climbed to the restaurant of the brujo, these gates and routes were closed behind him, and makeshift roadblocks sprung into place. On their way back down, Miguel and Maria are blissfully unaware that they are driving straight into a precisely prepared trap.

As they descend, Miguel begins to realise that they are not travelling the same route they took on the way in. The car slows to a crawl through streets that become tighter and narrower until he can barely manoeuvre the muscular vehicle. Belatedly, he knows he has taken one wrong turn too many. An old Cadillac, rusted and choked with foliage, blocks the road ahead. He looks into his rearview TV screen, preparing to reverse, and sees a party of figures appear out of the gloom. They are holding things in their hands, long things, sharp things. A sudden lightning flash illuminates them menacingly. Miguel utters a curse and guns the engine in a threatening manner, wheel-spinning and edging backwards, startling Maria who lets out a cry. The figures break ranks and Miguel prepares to get the hell out of there, but a dark shadow blocks the way. The bastards have towed a couple of wrecks in behind him, blocking his exit. He swears and thumps the steering wheel in frustration.

Maria has been watching the dim glow of the rearview screen. She stuffs a fist into her mouth and whimpers.

"What are we going to do, Miguel? What do they want?"

The Ford Machos "Matador" Special Edition will strike easily through either barricade but Miguel is worried about the paintwork on his father's brand new car. Emboldened by his encounter with Bruno the barrio boy and his successful negotiation of barter terms with the brujo, he decides to try and reason with them. Maria clutches her face as he gets out of the car.

Their faces are terrifying in the half-light. Ninety percent of barrio dwellers are Indian or *mestizo*, half-breeds. Their faces are painted in colourful chaos patterns. He suddenly remembers he is practically naked.

There are seven or eight of them. Behind them is a tractor attached by chains to the wrecks that were dragged to block Miguel's escape.

Miguel tries his best confident smile.

"Could you gentlemen please move your cars, and tell me the fastest way back to the city?"

The mob maintains a stony silence then one nudges and whispers something to another, and they all fall around laughing and cackling. Miguel joins in, slightly relieved, but completely in the dark as to the joke.

"Bad night to be lost in the barrio, *caudillo*," says one of the men. "Storm coming. Barrio real bad place to be caught a storm. All sorts of scum float to the surface."

Miguel laughs a nervous laugh. The barrio dweller calls him *caudillo* - it means strong man, or big man. It is, of course, meant sarcastically. Miguel realises he has made a terrible mistake. He starts to back away. The mob move forward.

"Pretty lady in car."

"Pretty dress."

"Know how to treat a lady, *caudillo*?"

"That why you wear no clothes? You been playing *fiesta* with the lady, *caudillo*?"

"We show you how to play fiesta with pretty lady."

Miguel dashes for the sanctuary of the car. He decides to break out of here and to hell with the paintwork. These are not barrio kids, these men are evil banditas who will beat him and rape him and leave him for dead. He places a hand on the door of his car, and his world explodes in blue fire.

Maria has slipped over into the driver's seat and armed the defences. The car's bodywork is now electrified and near-fatal to the touch of an intruder. The force of the shock has sent Miguel reeling into a nearby wall where he slams with bone-crunching force. He shakes stars from his eyes in time to see the barrio gang attempt a similar feat, undeterred by his own fate. They are propelled away from the car with all the sudden force of colliding magnets. Maria revs the engine and wheel spins out of the confines of the alleyway, careening off the sides of the cars blocking the route and taking most of the paint off the Ford Machos 'Matador' Special Edition's right flank.

Miguel staggers after her, his bare feet slipping and stubbing his toes in the trash-strewn alley. The barrio gang moan and wail in the alley behind him, the effects of the shock much greater on them with their metal weapons and studded clothes. If he is lucky, he can get away from them while they are still stunned.

Maria turns the car at an angle at the end of the road, preparing to make her escape into the wider street beyond. Miguel assumes she is waiting for him. He is wrong. The driver's side window slides down a few inches.

"It's been a lovely evening, Miguel" she says, blowing him a kiss. And she is gone, in a roar of overpowered American engine.

Miguel sinks to his knees in the middle of the alley. He has no car and no girl. He is lost and has no way of getting home. Maybe if he just waits here long enough, the barrio gang will recover and come and put him out of his misery. After all, what other choices does he have? How far is he going to get in a pair of boxer shorts?

"Hey, clown man, city man. Where's your lady, hey?"

Miguel winces. Bruno clambers from a nearby trash pile, dripping rubbish, his grin a yellow slash splitting his dirty face. He has his brother with him. He swaggers towards Miguel with the confidence of someone three times his age. It's easy to know when you've got the upper hand, even when you're ten years old.

"Want to know the way home, city man?"

"I have nothing to give you," Miguel says dejectedly. He is no longer even frightened of Bruno's blade. "I have nothing left."

Bruno closes one eye and peers at Miguel.

"Those are very nice shorts," Bruno says.

Well, thinks Miguel, as he stands on the brow of the hill with his city glistening like a teasing, out of reach jewel below him, at least things cannot get much worse. No car, no girl, no clothes. He may be naked but at least he knows his way back to Nuevo Caracas. If Bruno was telling the truth. He didn't like the way the boy laughed as ran away waving Miguel's silk boxer shorts in the air like an enemy flag captured in battle.

The storm, when it breaks, is like a cool relief, rain washing his body and the streets, the sky venting its anger on Miguel's behalf, as if the rich of the city are wealthy enough to bribe nature, and the barrio must pay the price. Monday morning and some very awkward explanations are a lifetime away.

It has been, Miguel thinks, *a very interesting night on the town.*

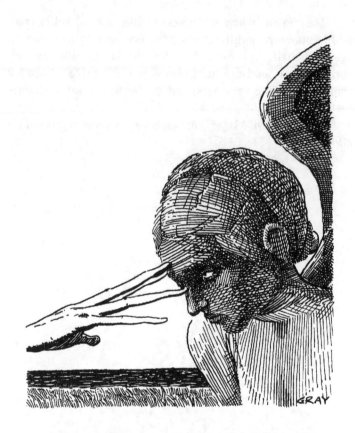

Thoughts on Life and Death
from the Tarkaha

ILLUSTRATION BY DEREK GRAY

"Tell me more about this *death*, Earthman."

They walked and talked in the cemetery on the cliff, the Earthman called Connor and the Tarkaha who had no name, and who had assumed the standard acceptable physical form recommended when associating with these fragile beings of blood and bone; large eyes, smooth hairless bodies, asexual genitals, pale grey skin tone. They resembled so much the Greys of contemporary UFO mythology that countless abduction and government conspiracy stories were vindicated until it was pointed out that the Tarkaha could assume any form they wished, and chose one which would be pleasing and acceptable to the human eye.

"Death is a great burden to a man," said Connor, who had once been a priest, a man of faith, but had seen so little in his life to make him believe that there was a higher benevolent power, and so much to suggest quite the opposite, that he had renounced his office. Somehow, the brand-new position of Alien Liaison Officer to the United Nations Extraterrestrial Affairs Committee seemed made for him, a born-again pragmatist.

"Knowing only oblivion is waiting at the end of sixty-seventy-eighty years if you're lucky," he continued, "or waiting around the corner, ready to strike you down in the shape of a runaway car, a murdering madman or a - heh - Act of God. It is the curse of mankind that we are the only creatures who are aware of our own mortality."

"Our studies inform us to the contrary," said the Tarkaha. "Elephants guide their dying to graveyards older than mankind itself, whales shepherd their sick to the safety of inshore bays."

"Ah, but our belief is that animals have no souls, that they cannot comprehend a life beyond the demise of the physical form."

"Death - Acts of God - souls," mused the Tarkaha,

rubbing its smooth chin with long delicate fingers, an expression of thoughtful contemplation it knew was visually pleasing and comforting to its human companion, even though the thought processes it was mimicking were being carried out by a virtual brain the size of a planet, that existed in a reality that humanity was only just beginning to understand. "Let us walk and talk more. We have much to learn."

They walked and talked some more.

"Death is a very difficult concept for the Tarkaha to grasp," said the alien, pausing by a weathered stone angel standing sentinel over an ancient mossy tomb. It ran its fingers over the angel's implacable, finely chiselled visage, worn smooth by sea air. "For the Tarkaha there is no death, no ultimate annihilation. The Tarkaha is energy - energy cannot be created or destroyed, you are familiar with the theory?"

Connor tilted his head and smiled. "Of course. It is the basis of the physical universe."

"Immortality is a heavier burden than knowledge of a finite lifespan," the Tarkaha continued. "The Tarkaha are, as far as we know, the only immortal race in the Universe, and as such we have an obligation to be its eternal guardians. Humans approach their obligation within the boundaries of their own mortality, and for the most part think no further than the end of their own lives, or perhaps that of their offspring."

"You are, of course, quite correct," said Connor. "We think as individuals, with an individual's petty concerns and grievances, and an individual's greed."

"The cult of the individual would have meant the destruction of the human race had the Tarkaha not presented humankind with the means of interstellar travel," said the Tarkaha.

"Yes. We would have been too busy killing each other,

we may have never explored another world, and eventually the sun would have boiled away. We *are* very grateful, you know."

The Tarkaha smiled. "Interstellar travel is the least of our gifts. If we had not repaired your ozone layer and rebalanced the chemical constitutions of your atmosphere and oceans, you would never have survived long enough to watch your sun boil and vanish."

Connor rubbed unconsciously at his bare arms. He was wearing a thin short-sleeved shirt and a tie, knot loosened at the neck. It still felt strange to be outside in direct sunlight dressed like this. A few years before, prior to the dramatic, sci-fi movie arrival of the Tarkaha, he would not have been able to stand on this exposed clifftop without a protection suit, a polarised sun visor and a heatshield canopy. They did indeed have much for which to thank the Tarkaha.

"Yet the Tarkaha are individual too," said the alien. "Individual and communal at the same time. While we can join together in a collective mind more powerful than anything you can comprehend, we can also exist as wholly individual entities, billions of physical light years from the Core Mind, in absolute solitude for aeons. We do this, sometimes, on missions to spread enlightenment and knowledge to progress wayward civilisations. We are, on occasion, called gods by cultures such as your own. Occasionally, we are misrepresented and our well-intentioned actions become counter-productive. We may be immortal, but we are not infallible." A strange smile crossed the Tarkaha's features. "The Tarkaha has visited Earth before, you know."

"I know," said Connor, smiling. It had been a bad few years for Christianity, Islam, Judaism and every other major religion (although Buddhism was bearing up remarkably well under the alien onslaught on humanity's main crutches). Even when the stark proof of the fictionalised Good Books was offered, many chose to stay shaken (if a little stirred) believers in the old ways. The mass suicides had been particularly spectacular, and fascinating to the death-obsessed Tarkaha.

"So, it is unusual to find that humankind is the closest philosophical relation to the Tarkaha in the known Universe," said the Tarkaha. "The evolution of your species to the higher plane, the shedding of the physical self, was well underway before we made contact, with your developments in silicon-based intelligence's and the investigations into the conversion of brain patterns into digital code. But you would never have survived to see those projects reach fruition."

Connor was becoming a little rankled. He was under strict instructions not to anger members of the alien delegation, but even the due deference with which he was treating his guest did not take the edge off a certain unpleasant fact. The Tarkaha were so damn *smug*.

"I'm not about to defend humanity in the face of such damning evidence for our ultimate destruction at our own hands," said Connor tactfully. The Tarkaha mirrored his wry expression with disconcerting accuracy. "But as you say we are the Tarkaha's closest philosophical relative, so we must have *something* to offer the Universe. Take our reproduction, for example. Man is born out of physical love." He thought about what he had just said. "Usually, at least."

The Tarkaha pondered this for a moment, looking out to sea. Dark shapes moved beneath the wind-frothed waters.

"Yet your apparent miracles are treated so blithely. Men are born with no apparent purpose, into squalor and poverty and societies bulging with bodies that cannot be fed. You feel it is your indisputable right to procreate with no interference from others, even those who may take ultimate responsibility, yet you have so little regard for the lives that you so carelessly create. Do you ever ask yourselves, what will be the purpose of the life we are about to create?"

"Rarely," said Connor. "Often, those lives are not even

allowed to reach fruition, and are instead terminated in the womb."

The Tarkaha shook his head sadly. "In our society, such abuses of life would be unimaginable. The conception of life, a *new* life, is a very serious decision. The origination of a new individual within the Tarkaha requires the consent and active participation of many other individuals. The process lessens us all, weakens our individual power - remember that we are energy and cannot be created or destroyed - and it is a decision that is not taken lightly. A new Tarkaha is born once every millennia, or so. It is not unusual for those involved to debate the matter with the Core Mind for centuries."

"You society seems so perfect," said Connor, watching the surface of the sea below them churn and a dark amphibious shape break the water. A dolphin - no, bigger than that - a pilot whale or something equally as huge. "Protected, venerated procreation to a higher purpose, then peaceful immortality, benevolent supremacy over the Universe. Have you ever known conflict? War?"

"War," the Tarkaha repeated, and the word sounded like it had discovered a bad taste in its mouth. "Yes, further back in time than any but the Core Mind can remember. When the Tarkaha were breathers and bleeders, man-forms like humankind. Beings who move in a frictionless, unfettered Trans-space environment have no appetite for conflict. Conflict is for physical creatures who resort to kinetic solutions to the problems that beset them. War is a flesh and blood thing. War is a *man* thing."

They watched in silence from their lofty vantage point as marine mammals frolicked beneath them. A school of dolphins, grey flanks shining in the evening sun, were mobbing what looked like a big pilot whale, sliding along its length and gently body slamming in oddly sexual movements. On closer inspection, the big creature looked like a whale, but was nothing of the sort. Its fins were too small, its skin too pale, its eyes too big.

"The Tarkaha take many forms," said the alien, nodding down at the creature, who ejected a plume of steam from its blowhole in greeting, "and commune with many forms on your planet. Many forms that you do not credit with comparable levels of intelligence."

Their discussion was interrupted by the drone of a squadron of fighter-bombers passing overhead. The human and the alien were momentarily shadowed by the delta-winged aircraft, made ponderous by the unusually large missiles secured to their bellies, like pregnant birds of prey. The squadron headed out to sea and over the horizon.

"War," commented the Tarkaha dryly, "that man thing."

A detonation cleared the sky. Pure light flooded from east to west, as if a star had fallen to Earth. A fiery cloud blossomed and mushroomed to the heavens. The Tarkaha froze, an odd expression fixed on its face, as information assaulted its senses. Connor examined his fingernails.

"Our official delegation," the Tarkaha said, incredulous. "You have.... *destroyed* them? You have *destroyed* Tarkaha? *How can this be?*"

"It wasn't easy," said Connor. "The best scientific and military minds on the planet - present company notwithstanding - have been working on the problem for years. How do you destroy that which cannot be destroyed? It was as much a philosophical question as a physical one. But we do have a talent for improvisation. It was a difficult decision, please believe that. But you can't just jaunt around the Universe pushing lesser lifeforms around. We do that man thing so well, you'll have to admit."

He watched the frozen creature as it abandoned all semblance of its puppet form. The illusion of physical presence peeled and wavered and a glowing sphere with a counter-rotating centre, like some form of elaborate executive desk toy, emerged from the shallow grey chest cavity, hovering and oscillating a few centimetres from Connor's face.

"The dolphins it is, then," the Tarkaha said, a little sadly, projecting its voice straight into Connor's brain, then took off as if startled. The glowing sphere circled the bay several times until it was joined by a second one, torn from the body of the whale-thing. They coalesced into a single shining star, and imploded.

Connor straightened his tie and walked back through the cemetery to his car, through the city of the human dead with its mossy tombs and guardians of stone.

The action would probably mean war, of course, but they were prepared for that. That man thing, as the Tarkaha had pointed out, that they did so well.

The Tarkaha, Connor thought, *were just so damn smug.*

Parlour Games

ILLUSTRATION BY DEREK GRAY

It was on his fifteenth birthday, during the long summer of their first year alone, that she first suggested the idea to him. After all, they could soon be the last boy and girl left alive in the world, if the television was to be believed.

"We can't," he protested, blushing fiercely, although she knew that he had already thought the wicked thought while watching her undress or swim or bathe. "I'm your brother."

James became distant then, staring out from his seat on the clifftop outcrop they called The Rock to the thin smudge of the mainland shimmering on the horizon. On a clear day like this, it never felt so close, yet so far away, all at the same time. He felt the familiar tears well up and he knuckled them away. He didn't like her to see him cry, even if she was a year older than him. She touched his elbow tenderly.

"It doesn't mean anything anymore," she said gently. "I mean, all the things we were told were right and wrong, good and bad. It all means nothing as long as we're stuck here, just you and me. We can do whatever we want. What's going to happen when everyone's dead?"

"How will we know?" he asked, turning to face her. "Stuck here, how will we know when everyone is dead?"

"When there's no more television," Suzanna said grimly.

Suzanna was right: he *had* been watching her bathe and swim, and he *had* felt something stir inside him, and he had enough schoolboy-hearsay knowledge in his head to know that what he was feeling was *wrong wrong wrong*. That night, after she had shocked him by asking him outright, he heard her running a bath in the big old bathroom upstairs, and he found himself tiptoeing to the keyhole. He knelt before the oak door and pressed his eye to the brass latch.

She was slim and pale and blonde - she didn't revel in

the sunlight like he did. Over the last year her hips had widened and her breasts had swelled. He remembered the morning she had rushed downstairs, tearful, with bloody sheets bundled in her arms. He watched her examine herself in a full length mirror. It was not the vain self-adulation of a movie star or a model, more a detached, technical inspection. She sucked in her belly and stuck out her chest, turned and posed. She clambered into the steaming bath, a gothic monstrosity of ceramic and festering green ironwork, and began to soap herself down.

James rose from the door, excited and ashamed, and bumped against the banister in his haste to leave. Suzanna heard the noise and listened, hearing his muted retreat down the stairs. She smiled secretly to herself.

The house was an enormous Victorian folly, commissioned by a 19th century writer driven mad by apocalypse fever on the eve of the new century. One hundred and twenty years later, it stood on the clifftop promontory, gazing out over the straits to the mainland like a lonely stone sentinel, exiled and outcast. It had over thirty rooms, a maze where children could run amok. Suzanna's and James' father had bought it in 2010, before their mother died, and before he took the trip to Mars. He was a rich man by then - air force pilot, politician, writer. To be chosen as the sole European to join the joint US/Russian expedition to Mars was a great honour, and one he accepted instantly and publicly. His wife died in an air crash three weeks later. He was expected to stand down from the trip. Instead, he packed James and Suzanna, still grieving, off to boarding school, and threw himself into his training. James had been too young to fully understand it all. Suzanna had been more aware of the betrayal and abandonment, and had never forgiven him for it. Sometimes she wondered if this whole mess had not been brought on by her own curses and wishes, like some evil voodoo.

The parlour boasted a state-of-the-art watchwall, a huge television display that was completely incongruous beside the Victorian splendour when it was not hidden behind sliding oak panelling. It had become James' and Suzanna's sole window on the world they had left behind, after James smashed their radio in a tantrum one afternoon. James would sit in front of the watchwall, mesmerised, for hours, even as the nature of the programming changed from game shows and home shopping to constant news and civil defence broadcasts and endless streams of useless 'expert' advice. It seemed at times as if the whole world had caught fire.

James was sitting watching it numbly. Suzanna, unable to at times to take it all in, got up and left. Guilt pangs stabbed her every time she saw someone die on the watchwall.

She wandered into her father's study. James increased the volume on the watchwall and the commentary, strangely neutered of menace now it was detached from its visuals, followed her in.

"......*city of Berlin placed under martial law last night as supplies of vaccine perished in a rail crash en route from the Plague Centre in Vienna. Rioters took to the streets and burnt several buildings around the Bundestag until paramilitary police brought the situation under control......*"

The unmistakable sound of furious people burning their own city through frustration, the whoomph of petrol bombs, crack of bullets and gunning engines of armoured vehicles. *They are fools*, thought Suzanna, as she took a photograph from a dusty shelf. The photograph was a fuzzy digital one, snatched from a TV image, of nine spacesuited men standing in a group on a red desert terrain. She could make out her father in the group, even though the men were almost anonymous in their gold-mirrored helmets. He was the tallest, and he was giving a thumbs-up sign to the camera.

They are fools, she thought, *because the vaccine is a*

placebo. It alleviates the symptoms, the madness and the choking and the vomiting. It does not cure the disease. They would now that, these good people of Berlin, if they watched enough television, like James and she did. Then maybe the world would enjoy the last days of their lives in peace, and not burn down their beautiful city (and Berlin *was* a beautiful city, mother and father had taken her and James there, the year before Mars and mother's death). *They think they must riot because they think they are being abandoned to die.*

The photograph was covered in a layer of dust. Grey dust, earth dust, not the red dust of Mars. That was in a little vial that normally stood next to the photograph on the shelf. It wasn't there - James must have taken it. Hadn't she read somewhere that household dust was ninety percent human skin? Was the red dust of Mars, then, all what was left of its former inhabitants, the canal builders and the alien princesses that had cleverly hidden themselves from the eyes of her father and his colleagues as they walked its surface? He had thought it a clever joke to leave her an old Edgar Rice Burroughs paperback under her pillow the night he left for Mars, with a post-it note stuck to the cover that read -

I will bring you back a gift from Barsoom, my Princess!

-love, Daddy

She had found the note insulting, as if she didn't know what was really happening. She knew exactly where, what, and how far away Mars was, how it was dry and had a poisonous atmosphere that no human (except for John Carter, of course) could breathe. Astronomy and Related Sciences was her favourite subject at school. If he had taken more interest in her, he would have known that. She found the flippant note when she woke and cried that morning as his rocket blasted off from Baikonur, on the other side of the world. Not because he had gone, but because he still thought she was a child.

".... still no idea where this plague has come from. It resembles nothing I have ever seen before. It does not respond to any of our most sophisticated treatments and defies categorisation......" Ah, another rent-an-expert, preaching doom. She had yet to hear an optimistic word on the subject. Better for the scientists to claim failure and ignorance, then unleash their miracle cure, rather than give people false hopes to be dashed. She was sure they would get it under control. They always did, didn't they? But she had thought the same thought a year ago. A lot of people had died since then.

The study had been left almost untouched since he had gone, properly gone. James had been in here once or twice - last time he appeared to have taken the vial of Martian dust. But it seemed to deepen his depression if he spent too much time in here, surrounded by the mementoes of his father's life. The photographs, the bits of Mars and detritus of former careers. A cased medal for valour in action over the former Yugoslavia, a UN citation as a member of a negotiating team in an African republic civil war, the books he had written on air combat and his work with the UN in far-flung conflicts. He had hardly been with them during their childhood, always away, always turning up on television, tanned and confident. Suzanna often thought that she had seen more of him on the TV during the first ten years of her life than she had in the flesh. It had been like having a movie star for a father. Now all they were left with was this room full of legacies to the things he had done and the places he had visited and the people he had met, when he should have been with them. Then he would have known that she knew where Mars was, and none of this would have happened. She opened up a desk drawer and took the familiar, worn envelope from it, and put it in her pocket.

"... someone is suffering from the symptoms in your family, contact a Civil Defence Patrol as soon as possible. Civil Defence patrol vehicles are painted yellow. Civil Defence workers wear yellow armbands. Remember, the sooner symptoms are reported, the more effective the application of the vaccine can be...."

James was still staring glumly at the screen when she went back into the parlour. She decided it was not the time to rekindle the conversation they had had yesterday - he had been withdrawn and dullish ever since. It had given her fitful dreams last night, dreams where she had ridden a stallion barebacked and naked over the rough heath of the island's hilly interior. It had been exciting and erotic. She had woken this morning damp and hot and guilty.

"I'm going down to the cellar," she said to him. He turned and for a second his eyes flared with something that could have been revulsion - this was something he could never bring himself to do. They had argued about it before, but she did it anyway. She thought he was about to protest, but he just nodded glumly, and returned his attention to the watchwall.

They should have really buried him, she knew that. But this was the most time they had been able to spend with him in their lives. He couldn't go anywhere now, not to fight someone else's war or to an alien planet. Because he was dead, and they kept him in the ice cellar.

They must still be drawing power from the mainland, Suzanna reasoned, as the island was unoccupied apart from their house and some abandoned crofter's cottages on the north side. All their electrical appliances still worked, giving them heat and light and supplying this huge walk-in refrigerator in the cellar. It was the sort of thing you would find in a large hotel or restaurant. Suzanna recalled when they first came here, all four of them. Their father had plans to raise cattle and make a living, self sustenance and all that. Their mother had complied with his plans, as she always did. He had intended to retire early and they could have all lived here, one big happy family. Then the call to Mars had come, and he could not resist. A bucolic future with his family faded into insignificance.

James had found his body and it had struck him dumb. He had run to her, she was out on The Rock sketching, she remembered it clearly. He pulled at her arm and her sketchbook had fluttered from her grip and over the edge. She was angry but James ignored her, making grunting noises in frustration (it was several days before he spoke again), pulling her to the house.

And there he was, in his study, propped up in his chair where he had planned to write his books and count his cattle, his eyes open and a line of vomit running from the corner of his mouth, empty bottles of pills scattered across the desk. Photographs cluttered the desk surface - the expedition shot of Mars, receiving his medal from a UN general, a portrait of their mother as a young woman. He had been sitting looking at them as he forced fistfuls of drugs into his mouth. In the corner of the room lay the modem from his computer and the household phone point, both deliberately smashed. All possibility of communication with the mainland was gone.

Suzanna and James had clung to each other in the doorway, terrified to enter, the irrational fear of a dead body. Eventually, Suzanna had sent James away and she had approached their father, felt for a pulse. His skin was so cold. On the desk lay an envelope with JAMES & SUZANNA written on it in brisk, business-like script. She folded it and pocketed it, and read it later when James was asleep, and cried until she thought she would cry forever.

James had helped her drag his body down here, and as far as she knew, that was the last time he had laid eyes on his father. Suzanna, on the other hand, visited him regularly. She knew that his body would decompose eventually, even in here, so she cherished this time with him.

The ice cellar had a steel door and a large throw lever lock. A small panel outside the door measured temperature and power level. She opened the door and a blast of cold air met her. Thrusting her hands deep into the pockets of her jeans, she went inside. One hand curled around the envelope in her pocket.

Dear Suzanna and James,

My dear children, what have you done to deserve such lives? The answer is nothing, you must not blame yourselves for any of the terrible events that have taken place as a result of my actions -

He lay on a long wooden table loosely covered by a sheet. She gently peeled it back from his face. It had taken on a bluish tinge and was becoming puffy. She knew there wasn't much time for them to be together.

I was never the kind of father you deserved. Always too wrapped up in my own world, never having time to be part of yours. I feel so guilty about the loss of your mother. If only I had never invited her to Baikonur, she would still be alive today, and you would still have her, and not be alone.

"You know we loved you," she whispered, "even if you never gave us the chance to show it."

This terrible, terrible disease. They know we brought it back and spread it to all corners of the Earth, why will they not admit it? It is their fault, and not mine, yet I am the carrier and I feel the blame. You seem to be immune, protected, just as I am - our genes are the same, of course.

But do you carry and spread, just as I do? I do not know, and that is why we have come here. You must never leave this island, children, and you must never allow others to come here.

"James has taken your dust," Suzanna said conversationally, stroking his cheek with the back of his hand. "I don't know what he wants with it. It could carry the disease, couldn't it? Perhaps that is how it came back. Perhaps you were not the carriers! I must get it back from James. If he releases it into the wind it could carry to the mainland and infect them, if they're not already."

I always thought taking one's own life was impossible. I was a pilot and a soldier, my survival instinct was often all I had to keep me alive. Some of us have very strong survival instincts. But too much has happened, I am to blame for too much death, too much misery. It eats away like cancer in my gut, each morning as I wake, each day as I try to work, each sleepless night. I have chosen the coward's way out, children.

Forgive me. I love you.

I have always loved you.

Forgive me.

Daddy.

"Goodbye," she said, and kissed him on his cold cold lips. "It was nice to talk to you again." She replaced the sheet carefully.

She paused in the doorway before sealing the steel door behind her. He was a faceless lump under the sheet.

"I love you, Daddy," she said.

Summer's heat faded into autumn on the island and the question that Suzanna had put to James on his birthday remained unresolved. There had been a brief encounter when he had fallen against the door while watching her bathe, and had tumbled into the room. She had stood up, naked and dripping suds, facing him brazenly with her hands on her hips. He had frozen, mesmerised by her body like a rabbit in a spotlight, then fled into the house. He did not speak to her for several days, and the incident was never mentioned.

The television stopped broadcasting some time before the first flurries of snow had begun to waft down from the north. James had become even more withdrawn and was often to be found in one of only two places - tending the vegetable patches that the bowling-green lawns had been sacrificed to accommodate, or in the parlour staring at the incessant visual static on the watchwall, as if willing the transmissions to return. Suzanna, by contrast, was glad to be rid of them. It was obvious to her, if not to James, that the world was dying. They and their tiny island had been spared. It was the eye of the storm that was engulfing mankind. Meanwhile, almost all communication between James and Suzanna had ceased. By the time the snow lay thick on the ground and they had turned to the canned supplies in the cellar to get them through their second winter here, she suspected he had even stopped watching her bathe.

And then the power failed. It happened quite suddenly one night. Suzanna was reading and her light blinked out. James had been watching the static of the watchwall and it too cut out. The house was plunged into darkness. Suzanna was abruptly reminded of the tenuous nature of their position. The world outside her bedroom window was white death. The electric heaters clicked and popped ominously as they cooled down.

James bumped and cursed his way through the house to her room. She waited for him and was surprised when he climbed on to the bed next to her, and put his arm around her. It was the first time there had been physical contact between them in months.

"I'm scared, Suzie," he said. "I was praying this wouldn't happen."

"It's going to be all right," she said with as much confidence as she could muster, but the big sister act was thin. The truth was, she had no idea if it was going to be all right or not.

They slept together that night for the first time since they were very small children, James spooned against her back for warmth as the house cooled around them. He was embarrassed the next morning when she awoke with the pressure of his erection against the small of her back. He vanished shame-faced into the cold house to dress and prepare some food.

The loss of power was not quite as catastrophic as they had first imagined. The house was equipped with a solid fuel central heating system that bypassed electric power and roared throatily into life once James had broken up enough firewood from old furniture and crates in the outbuildings, and stoked up two of the house's several fireplaces. Heating the entire house would be impossible - Suzanna found a plan of the heating layout and they went around together, turning off stopcocks and radiator valves to channel the heated water into specific radiators. They succeeded in heating their bedrooms, the study and the parlour, and abandoned the rest of the house, which had become as cold as the ice cellar. The only problem would be finding sufficient fuel to last them through the winter, which they knew could last until March or even April - it had the previous year. James gathered as much from the outbuildings as he could, removing doors and window frames, and began to examine the antique furniture that filled the house. Suzanna balked at this and ordered him out to forage amongst the crofter's cottages and the small woods that dotted the northern part of the thinly-forested island. The chimneys of the house streamed smoke for the first time in decades, sending an unwitting message to the world.

Suzanna and James are still alive, if anyone else is.

Suzanna did not visit her father very often during that winter. It was far too cold to roam through the house unless it was absolutely necessary, and she had delegated herself the task of keeping the fires permanently lit while James was responsible for the supply of the wood, which he gathered with the strength and energy of someone ten years older than his fifteen years. She went down to the ice cellar once to open the door, to prevent the air inside from stagnating now the refrigeration system was off. The temperature inside seemed to be no different - her father's body had not decomposed any further. She left him there, covered by the sheet. She would have to bury him, come the spring, if the power did not return.

James blamed the smoke - thin black lines of it had risen from two of the chimneys ever since they had lit the fires. Now there was a ship on the horizon, and what were they going to do about it?

They sat on The Rock, huddled in their jackets in the biting winter wind and watching the sea with a mixture of excitement and fear. Suzanna had on a big army-issue parka while James wore a flight jacket adorned with tour-of-duty patches, both taken from their father's study.

James had spotted the ship an hour earlier through a pair of binoculars and summoned Suzanna to the cliff. It had got much closer since then, but it was not moving very fast. It was a big white ship, the sort that is a peacetime cruise ship and a wartime hospital ship. This one had no visible markings and flew no flags. Its course appeared erratic, it was not on a direct heading to them, but it was definitely closing with the island.

"Maybe we should put out the fires," said James. "Maybe they haven't seen us."

"Of course they've seen us," snapped Suzanna. "They're coming ashore, there's nothing we can do."

They watched in silence for a while longer. They knew what this meant, but neither voiced it. Were they allowed to be happy, because people were coming at last, after their long isolation? Or were they carriers of the plague, and would infect anyone who came ashore?

"The ship is too big," James commented, watching through the binoculars. "They won't be able to come ashore, unless they swim."

"There are lifeboats on the side," Suzanna noticed, pointing. "They can use those." James nodded.

"You know what father told us," James said suddenly. Suzanna turned, startled. "That we should never let anyone on the island. To drive them away if we must."

Suzanna swallowed hard. The suicide note had never been mentioned before. She had left it for James to read shortly after the event and he had returned it to the study later, tearstained.

"How can we do that?" she asked.

"Father had a gun," James replied. "A rifle, in a locker under his desk. Ammunition too. I can fetch it -"

"No." She put her hand on his. "We can't do that. Why kill someone if they're doomed to die anyway? What's the point?"

"Death from the plague is terrible," he said, his eyes wide with television imagery. "We'd be doing them a favour."

"Do you think they'd give up because one person is

shooting at them?" Suzanna was almost raging at his stupidity. "They've probably got guns themselves. They'd probably kill *us*."

"Stop," he said, grabbing her hand. "Look."

The watched the ship. It had come close enough to them now for them to read a nameplate on is bow - *SS Thunderchild*. They could also hear sharp reports from the deck of the ship which they took to be gunfire. Stars twinkled along the decks in time with the noise.

"They're fighting amongst themselves," James observed. "Some must be sick, trying to-"

James sucked in air as the stern of the ship erupted in a dull, resonant explosion that rocked them on the shore a split second after a gout of flame had shot a hundred feet into the air. A second blast tore through the decks of the ship and they felt the heatwave reach out and touch them on The Rock. Suzanna vibrated with fear, James stared open-mouthed in awe.

"Someone's blown it up," he said. "She's sinking. So fast."

The ship sank stern first, water bubbling and foaming around it, dragging down the diminutive figures that leapt defiantly from its crazily-tilted decks. Suzanna and James watched in silence as the ship took all of three minutes to disappear completely from view, leaving behind nothing but an oily slick on the surface of the water and a strange stink in the air - hot diesel mixed with something worse, like burnt pork.

And a single, scorched lifeboat bobbing in the wake of the vanished ship, a figure in the lifeboat struggling with a single oar, striking out for the shore.

"I'll get the rifle," James said, and started to rise from The Rock. Suzanna dragged him back down and slapped him hard across the face. He was so shocked he made no attempt to retaliate. His face glowed, from the slap and from embarrassment.

"If we drive that man away, he will die in the sea, or he will put ashore on another part of the island, and still find us," Suzanna said. She had hold of both James' hands and was effectively pinning him down to the Rock. "He may already have the plague, or we may not be carriers. *Maybe maybe maybe.* We don't have the right to make the choice for him, James. Now help me get him ashore. If nothing else, we will find out what has been happening out there. Don't you want that? Isn't that better than your precious television?"

James struggled out from her grip and snorted. He thought she was making a bad decision. He told her so. But yes, he would help her.

The man was exhausted by the time he reached the shore, and had collapsed in the lifeboat. Suzanna and James negotiated the narrow icy track from the Rock down the cliff face to the shale beach below. James took off his shoes and socks and rolled up his trousers, and waded out to drag the boat ashore.

He was a big man, as tall as their father had been but heavier. He had long dirty-blond hair tied in a pony tail, and he had been burnt on his face and hands by the fire on the ship. It took them more than an hour to get the man up the track to the house. He drifted in and out of consciousness and was unable to stand so Suzanna and James had to support him all the way back to where they put him in Suzanna's bed. Suzanna kept a watch on him while James went to make some coffee.

Suzanna watched the man while he slept. He was in his mid-twenties and handsome despite his facial injuries. He was dressed in sloppy green fatigues, as if he was a guerrilla soldier of some kind, or an army deserter. While James was making the coffee, Suzanna went through the pockets of the jacket they had taken off him before putting him to bed. There she found a government ID card with his photograph on it. His name was Erik and he was a university student.

"You must leave," a thin voice croaked. Suzanna jumped and dropped the card and the wallet she had it taken it from. Erik struggled upright in the bed.

"What? What did you say?"

"You must leave me," Erik said, grimacing and blinking away tears of pain. "I have the plague. We were put on that ship, sent off to die. Some started fighting. Then there was an explosion - a bomb in the engines. We weren't meant to survive."

Suzanna pressed him gently back into the bed. His chest was hard and muscular beneath his shirt, burning with a fever she could feel through the shirt on the palm of her hand.

"Don't worry," she said. "We're immune. We'll help you. Try to rest. Trust us."

Erik was in no fit state to argue. He sank back into the mountain of pillows, groaning. He tore at his shirt with one hand, pulling it open.

"I'm burning up," he said. "I have to get these off."

Suzanna leant over the bed and helped him undress. He was fit and tanned beneath the scruffy fatigues. Hair spread across his chest and down the centreline of his flat belly, disappearing into the waist band of his trousers. She found her touch lingering on his body. She became aware of James in the doorway behind her, a tray in his hands.

"I've made coffee," he said redundantly, meeting her eyes evenly. He set the tray down on a side table. "I'll be getting wood, if you need me."

He left before she could think of something to say, some excuse for what he might have thought she was doing. She returned to undressing Erik, who was drifting in and out of consciousness. He was beginning to spasm occasionally, an early symptom of the plague, she remembered from the TV reports. She shut her eyes and pulled off his trousers.

* * *

Suzanna kept a lonely vigil by the young man's bedside. Night drew on and James had not returned. She was not too worried, on other occasions when he had been annoyed with her he had stayed out in one of the crofter's cottages all night, building a fire to keep warm. Where else could he have gone?

Erik regained consciousness for minutes at a time. He asked Suzanna to undo his pony tail and she spread his hair out in a damp halo on the pillow. Guiltily, knowing he was near death, she quizzed him about the mainland and the rest of the world. He painted a grisly picture of the most ferocious plague mankind had ever known. There was a working vaccine, he said, but people were dying far faster than it could be manufactured. If you and your brother are immune, he told her, smiling weakly, all you have to do is sit it out. Someone will come for you, eventually.

"Maybe it's for the best," he said resignedly. "There were too many of us, anyway, wasn't there?"

He slept again and when he woke later his fever was ferocious and he asked her to remove the bed covers. This he did, and he lay there naked and sweating in the guttering light from the candles she had placed around the room. His penis lay flaccidly on one thigh. She could not take her eyes off it. Erik's eyes fluttered open and noticed her watching him. A brief smile crossed his face, and he felt her touch upon him, cool in his fever heat.

The next morning she found James squatting beside a flickering fire in the nearest crofter's cottage, warming his hands over the flame.

"He's dead, isn't he?"

She nodded and crouched beside him.

"It's going to be all right, you know." And she really believed herself this time. She told him about the vaccine and the news Erik had brought. He absorbed the information glumly. She put her arm around him and he made an attempt to shrug it off. She held him closer.

"Come on," she said. "We have a job to do that will keep us warm."

The earth was partially frozen beneath the layer of snow. Suzanna broke it up as best she could with a pickaxe while James dug it out. By midday, two shallow graves lay close to The Rock.

They buried Erik first, fashioning a cross from two wooden staves and stapling his laminated ID card to it. Then they carried their father from the ice cellar and laid him finally to rest. Before they filled in his grave, James rummaged in his jacket and brought out the vial of red dust. He cracked the top and scattered it into the grave, over his father's shrouded body. They marked his grave with his old flying helmet, weighed down by a rock.

They survived to the spring on firewood and canned food, and before James' sixteenth birthday came around a military vessel had moored offshore and sent a spacesuited decontamination team ashore in a speedboat to examine them. They were interrogated, prodded and poked. Suzanna was terrified they would be taken away to be experimented upon, or worse. She breathed a sigh of relief when the team commander finally took off his helmet, and ruffled her hair.

As they waited for the launch to come and pick them up, Suzanna hugged James and reached into her pocket to touch something she had placed there. It was the tear-stained letter. It was the only thing she took from the island that day, and she never went back.

Some of us have a very strong survival instinct.

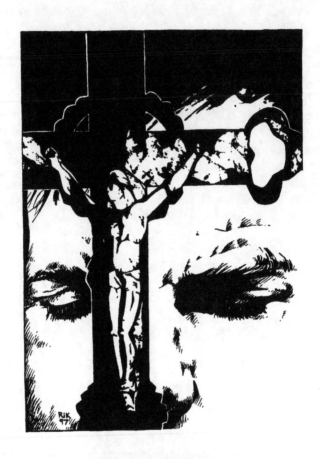

HyperGolgotha

ILLUSTRATION BY RIK RAWLING

Maybe it had been a mistake asking her to Jerusalem for the launch. Bryard wanted to break the news gently but he did still love her, in his own way, which of course would never be enough. Was it crueller to announce the end of a marriage in an exotic foreign city rather than rainy Manchester?

She had accepted in her usual bored manner, and gone straight out to buy a selection of clothes and travelling accessories, while he worked overtime debugging at Hyperreality Plc's complex in the Pennines, preparing the final touches and meeting various Israeli dignitaries who trooped through the consultations and presentations. They were invariably impressed, to say the least. Moments of public adulation for computer programmers were few and far between. Bryard was determined to enjoy the next few weeks. Having Judy out of his life was part of that.

His employers, along with the Israeli cabinet and the Jerusalem city leaders, had chosen an extremely high profile date to launch his creation upon the world - Good Friday, 2012 AD. Bryard had balked at this - the streets of the Via Dolorosa would be choked with crowds, where would they install the beamers to ensure maximum opacity? How could they secure cabling when so many pilgrims feet would trample it? What would become of him - and Hyperreality Plc - if it *failed*? The directors had taken him to dinner and reassured him that the tests carried out in the eerie full-size mock up buried deep beneath the Pennines (it always reminded him of stories of doppelganger towns built by Soviet Russia to train deep cover agents) had been more than adequate and they were confident that the Good Friday launch in the heart of Old Jerusalem would be an enormous success. As they smiled at him with dollar-signed eyes, he knew he was still carrying the weight of this project on his shoulders. If anything - *anything* - went wrong, Bryard would be crucified.

But still his decision to invite Judy nagged at him. They took
the suborbital from Ringway on Monday, which would give
them three days in Jerusalem before Good Friday, days filled
with systems installation for Bryard and his team, and
shopping and sightseeing for Judy. He promised her he
would be back in the hotel no later than nine p.m. each
evening so they could have a late dinner and maybe go
dancing, if he was not too tired. She had pouted and
demanded assurances that they would go dancing *every* night
no matter how tired he *pretended* to be, and he remembered
one of the reasons he was going to leave her. She was an
insensitive bitch, and she forgot all too easy how hard he had
to work to maintain the kind of lifestyle to which she had
become accustomed. Did she think she would be jetted off to
the Holy Land and indulged by a man who could guarantee
his working day finished when his wife wanted to go dancing?
Such a man, thought Bryard as he left her asleep in the air-
conditioned hotel room and went to join his team in the Old
City, did not exist. Women invented them to torture honest,
hard-working husbands.

There was so little for him to do here. He had a fine
team of enthusiastic young men (all, he observed, happily
unmarried) who stripped down to shorts and T-shirts and
installed the complex system of beamers, cameras, projectors,
reflectors and cables along the Via Dolorosa, sweating in the
stifling heat and swearing good-naturedly when things didn't
go to plan. Bryard supervised the construction of a
microwave link, then walked through the cool alleys of the
Arab quarter to visit the other end of the link, a Cray V
supercomputer situated in the King David Hotel. This wasn't
strictly his jurisdiction - Hyperreality had poached a dedicated
Cray expert from the parent company - but as overall project
manager he could be held responsible if anything went wrong.

He viewed the installation in the air conditioned room situated in an empty suite next to the huge walk-in freezer, and chatted on professional matters to Nbele, the Nigerian Cray man. There seemed to be no problems. Nbele appreciated the chance to meet and chat with Bryard. Among his peers, his reputation was preceding him.

He didn't think it was appropriate to tell her on the first night. It had been a wonderful evening, Jerusalem was such a romantic city with its fantastic, ancient architecture, its resonant place names, and the dusky model-girl soldiers who flirted on street corners with UN soldiers. Judy chattered over dinner about her day, and never once asked Bryard about his. They ate a wonderful chicken dish and the most delicious pitta bread Bryard had ever tasted, drank white wine and listened to a barmitzvah procession make its way through the street below the rooftop restaurant. As Judy wittered Bryard laughed or tutted at appropriate places. Sometimes he would do the wrong thing at the wrong moment and then he would have to admit that he wasn't listening, leaning across the table to touch her hand and explain that he was tired. But she would sulk and again he understood why he was leaving her. It would be so easy to tell her at a moment like this, when she was most unreasonable. But there was always tomorrow. He didn't want whatever histrionics she would perform to interfere with his work. Not before it was complete, at least.

On Thursday they scheduled a full test of the system. Jerusalem was thronged with pilgrims, and it required a sizeable detachment of the elite Golani Brigade and, it seemed, most of Jerusalem's policemen, to erect barriers and man barricades to seal off the Via Dolorosa. The policemen assumed they would be privileged with a glimpse of whatever this secret thing was, but Bryard had arranged for only his immediate team to witness the test. He had no intention of

SHENANIGANS

revealing the nature of the project to any outsiders, and to have it leaked to Israel's sensationalist press before Friday.

Such was Judy's lethargy that she declined an offer to join him for the test. She assumed he was putting on some sort of high-tech light show. He had never bothered to correct her, and let her go on a sightseeing trip to Bethlehem. He promised himself he would tell her tonight, to get it off his chest, so that he could enjoy his moment of triumph tomorrow to the full.

The test went better than he had ever imagined. One of his team, a talented young technician whom he knew to be deeply religious and who had lobbied relentlessly to work on the project, was so overcome with fervour that he fainted. Even Bryard felt a lump at his throat in seeing his creation in pixel-perfect motion on the Via Dolorosa, instead of the fascia board mock up under the Pennine hill. Later, the young man claimed he had been overcome by heatstroke after staying in the sun for too long. Bryard noted this and commented on the incident at length in his email to the directors that night, sending it from the terminal in the hotel before Judy returned from Bethlehem. He told them to expect a casualty ratio for the next day of around one in fifty, and to ensure that the medical services in Jerusalem were alerted. It seemed as if even the creator had underestimated the emotional power of his creation.

Judy returned much later than he expected, slightly drunk from too much red wine on the trip back from Bethlehem, and found Bryard sitting on the balcony in the warm evening air. Jerusalem, old and new, stretched out below them. Tomorrow, he would show it something it had not seen for two thousand years. But right now, there was something else that he had to do.

"It's over, Judy. I want a divorce."

She laughed at first, assuming he was joking or just annoyed at her for coming back late and drunk. But when he launched into a bitter, long pent-up tirade of reasons why he was leaving her, she sat dumbstruck on the corner of the bed, and absorbed the enormity of it. Without responding to him she tearfully collected up a few clothes and toiletries and dashed from the apartment, slamming the door. He waited for half an hour then phoned reception. They told him that they had given his wife an alternative room. He went to bed, satisfied that she was safe and that he had done what had to be done. Now, only tomorrow mattered.

He slept fitfully and rose early, breakfasted in his room. He should have felt buoyant, this was to be the greatest moment of his career, perhaps the greatest day in his life, but Judy had tainted it, even by her absence. He regretted breaking the news to her last night, he felt sorry for her even after the years of heartache she had caused him. Leaving the hotel, he left a message at reception with a pass that would give her access to his command post on the Via Dolorosa later that day, to join him for the launch if she wished. He hoped she would choose to do so.

Jerusalem was a pulsing, living organism. The hot, dry streets were packed with bodies as Bryard made his way to the temporary command centre situated high above the Via Dolorosa in a somewhat militaristic tower. A police patrol brought him in a dusty Toyota four-wheel drive, its impatient driver leaning on his horn and driving people out of the way. Bryard sat in the back, impassive, hands folded in his lap.

By contrast, the command centre was a sanctuary of calm. Bryard's young team, now smartly dressed, ran through cursory checklists and balanced clipboards on knees as they operated keyboards and specialised manipulation devices. Banks of screens glowed with soft light and the hum of machinery filled the air. This was Bryard's idea of heaven. He had never felt this way in his home or when out with Judy. Maybe that was part of the problem.

The dignitaries began arriving a little later. First, the two directors of Hyperreality Plc, Bennett and Henderson, weary from the suborbital flight, but in a near frenzy of excitement. Then the Israeli prime minister, Rukab, and several of his cabinet and Jerusalem city councillors, accompanied by secret service agents openly sporting weapons. A member of Bryard's team depolarised the long window on the wall unoccupied by screens and equipment, offering a breathtaking panoramic view of the Via Dolorosa. Far below them, the streets filled. Pilgrims, holidaymakers, market traders, citizens of Jerusalem, and many television crews, all vying for space in the narrow alleyways. Helicopters clattered overhead - mostly UN and Israeli patrols, and an enterprising television crew, who had to be warned off from hovering directly over the Via Dolorosa by a Cobra gunship.

"Mister Prime Minister," said Bryard, looking at his watch. "It is time. Would you care to do the honours?"

Rukab stepped forward and placed his finger lightly on a large red button.

"Let the world see," he said.

A louder humming filled the room as the microwave link with the Cray V cycled up, and began transmitting millions of lines of code to the beamers and opacitors in the streets below. The grid of hardware spread out across the city like an invisible nervous system, and a twenty metre Jesus Christ began his long, last walk up the dusty cobbles of the Via Dolorosa.

Silence descended upon the city, tangible even behind the walls of the command centre. Rukab spluttered as he had forgotten to breath. This was no mere hologram or pale light projection. A two thousand year old story was being acted out in front of them, as real as if they had been transported back in time.

Pilgrims and policemen watched in amazement as Jesus

of Nazareth towered above them, the heavy cross across His back, the crown of thorns drawing blood on His forehead. Roman centurions, equally as mighty, spurred Him on, stopping to kick and whip him as He stumbled once, twice, three times. Mary Magdalene stepped from the crowd and offered Him water, the Roman soldiers dragging her away. Other giants in the crowd jeered and threw sharp-edged stones, bearded men in long robes alongside smooth-chinned men in modern lightweight suits. The illusion was beyond perfect. It was *hyperreal*. People began to faint.

Bryard's chest filled with pride. He had worked on this project for ten years. Only his marriage to Judy had taken up a greater part of his life.

Mesmerised by his own creation, he did not notice at first the door to the command centre opening, and when he did he was surprised to see Judy, immaculately dressed in a pale green skirt and blouse, but her eyes darkly rimmed with smeared mascara. She had been crying. She didn't say a word. Instead, she reached forward and took an Israeli agent's gun from his holster as casually if she was taking a drink from his hand. She stepped back, the gun in her hands. The agent turned and froze. His colleague reached for his own weapon and paused when he saw Judy already had the drop on him.

"Have you come to kill me?" Bryard asked her weakly, almost whispering.

"No," she said. "Your mistress."

And she discharged the gun methodically into each of the computer controllers arranged neatly around the room. The directors and the cabinet members turned slowly, almost unwilling to tear themselves away from the scene below, even in the face of such danger. Bryard's team were already under their seats, sheltering.

Below, where the crucifixion of Jesus of Nazareth, King of the Jews, was taking place in the still, hot air above the hill known as Golgotha, the hyper illusion began to falter. The animation of Jesus froze with his eyes cast skyward, looking for help or forgiveness from God, or Bryard.

Rukab's bodyguards came to their senses and realised Judy had emptied the gun. They bundled her to the floor and disarmed her. Bryard stood over her, tears streaming down his face.

"Ten years," he said. "You have robbed me of ten years."

She looked him squarely in the face as the agents pulled her to her feet, hands bound behind her back.

"Then we are even," she said, and they took her away.

Later, Bryard sat alone in the command centre. The cabinet had gone, discussing in grave tones how this would effect their chances of re-election. The directors of Hyperreality Plc had vanished swiftly, muttering concerns over share options. Even Bryard's team had deserted him, heading for the bars to drown their sorrows. In the darkness above the city, electric ghosts of two thousand year old martyrs, whores and soldiers flickered across the sky, bringing salvation to no one.

Divide by Zero

ILLUSTRATION BY FRAZER IRVING

I remember the night they finally caught up with me.

Christ, do I remember the night they finally caught up with me.

Dickens had sent the instructions down the wire. The fone beeped twice while Bobby was hogging my portable deck in the living room, playing *Death Holocaust 2099* or some other illegal hyper-addictive shit, rubber eyecups masking-taped to his face, and I had to turf him off to get at my mail. He skulked away to the big monitor in our bedroom but mum had pinched it for the teevee session I had installed. She'd blown her set when she missed out on a big e-lottery win by one number - 24 instead of cosmic 23 - and she'd put her big fat furry-slippered foot through the screen. Bobby was pissed off but he knew better than to try and keep mum and teevees apart for more than a matter of minutes. Me, I would have rather have tried my chances cold-turkeying the Jizz addicts down at the mall.

Dickens liked to play his little secret agent games and give two beeps on the fone so we knew when to pick up instructions from our anonymous mailboxes. We were supposed to retrieve them, read them and delete the files within ten minutes or something, and never *ever* hardcopy. Thing was, much of the stuff was far too complicated to memorise - mail aliases, corporate web site addresses, credit card numbers, passwords, sign-ons. A single character wrong in the middle of any of that shit and you might as well not even have started, especially as the security procedures that any suspicious infringement called into play would have the Boys in Black knocking on your door within minutes. So I ignored Dickens' warnings about copies and evidence and auditable trails and dumped each night's instructions into a spare chunk of volatile RAM that erased itself when I switched the deck off. That way, I got to use accurate data in my work, cutting and pasting to minimise keystroke errors, and if the heat came down while I was on the job - well, illegal password ownership would have been the least of my worries. My deck, mum's teevee, the big monitor, Bobby's VR eyecups - everything in our house that was made out of black plastic or had an electrical plug was hotter than the centre of the sun.

Bobby took the hint and muttering something about not being wanted, bundled himself up in a thick quilted jacket with luminous kanji appliquéd on the back, and disappeared out into the gathering October gloom. I watched him cross the shattered concrete lot that fronted our housing unit, sidestepping deep puddles of greasy water, and vanish into the hinterland of twisted metal bracing and blackened shells of buildings, swallowed up by this shit pile we called our home. It was, like they say, a jungle out there, but me and my brother were trainee predators, feral beasts born and raised. We were survivors, if nothing else. Mum didn't even lift her head as Bobby left.

With Bobby out of the way and mum safely entrenched in front of the teevee, I jacked my deck into the socket I had rigged from the municipal LAN line that ran in a drain housing a few hundred metres from our house. I read somewhere once that there were more illegal nodes on most security-free municipal LANs than authorised ones. It was just too easy to break in with a length of fibrewire and an optical clamp, rather than pay the nominal fifty euro monthly fee. They were supposed to be free, introduced as the turn of the century under the *Information For All Initiative*, but like everything else had either been privatised or run down. I remember where I saw that nugget of info now - a security consultancy web page, where a little animated app showed a tracer program lighting up the network map like a neon spider, illegal nodes in red, good little fee-paying citizens in blue. Better red than in the red, I say. Safely connected - no marauding hunter-killer programs on the loose, my Sentinel tells me - I collected Dickens instructions.

Ten minutes later, I was deeply enmeshed in multiple layers of challenging security routines, firing off Dickens' passwords from my fingertips like a fighter pilot ejects chaff to decoy missiles, and sending the simpler security software agents off on meaningless tangents into password-interrogation subroutines that mimicked the legitimate attentions of the network analyst or sysop. The task that night, as had been the norm for a number of previous weeks, was to divert tiny amounts of currency away from the data flow of micropayments, fractions of euros for web page access, software updates, pay-for-view teevee, data subscriptions, mainframe processing time, or any one of the other million things you could buy and sell and sample digitally. Someone might pay 0.75 of a euro pfennig to view a pornographic picture (probably artificially generated, but who cared?) of this evening's short shelf-life teevee starlet, but would they notice 0.76 on the streams and streams of itemised billing that such commerce threw up? Most people requested not to receive such bills, many others had given up the mammoth task of checking them. Enter Dickens and his freelance team of young bucks - myself included. Dickens, apparently, was never one to miss the opportunity of exploiting a niche in the marketplace. Like a vulture, he spotted weaknesses from ten miles out.

I operated almost exclusively at the codeface, in text-based systems, and as such was deemed much in demand by Dickens because I was so much faster than the other guys - no diss meant, each to their own - who relied on eyecups and datagloves and graphical manipulation devices. In my opinion, interfaces devoured processor time and RAM that was far better spent cracking code. The Graficals, as I called 'em, attracted gamers and teevee addicts and VR jockeys who were used to interacting with data as great polygons of colour, texture and shape, towers and monoliths of things meant to

SHENANIGANS

represent data warehouses, stock control, corporate mainframes and the fairy-light matrix of the ubiquitous and poorly secured municipal LANs. Fine and dandy, but I got just as much of an adrenaline rush from my reversed black-on-white screen and my slashes and colons and asterisks. I got what I wanted faster too. And I never, *ever* got caught. Until that night.

I was close to my target for the evening when the Sentinel icon in the corner of the emulation window lit up like Bonfire Night. I exited the BankNet quickly and carefully, rolling up my audit trail just as Dickens would have liked, and examined the Sentinel's status panel. It revealed that a tracer had been tripped somewhere in the BankNet and was currently cruising the municipal LAN, looking for the culprit. Tracers could be killed or diverted easily enough but they left messy evidence in the net, evidence that could be tailed back to the assassin given a sufficiently talented or just downright tenacious DDS agent. Besides, I had not tripped the tracer - it had been one of Dickens' other little helpers that was abroad that night, jacked into the same LAN as me. Maybe Schonigen or Dykstra, both Graficals (snigger) from the Westside. So it would have been foolish of me to step in and zap the tracer on their behalf, and risk copping the flak for it. Far better for me to jack out and carry on my work through a fone modulator in a public booth, as per Dickens' instructions. So that's what I did.

I gathered up my deck into a black nylon despatch bag and sealed it tightly with Velcro webbing. My MTB was in the hall, covered in a pale grey concrete dust like everything else in here. I passed between mum and the teevee as I pulled on my bubble jacket and made my way out. She grunted as I blocked her view of the screen for what must have been half a second. I couldn't bear to look at her anymore. She must have been a hundred and twenty kilos. All she ever did was eat, shit and watch teevee. I guess she was 'mum' in the biological sense only. Bobby and me had been feeding and educating ourselves for more time than I care to remember. She just shared our house like some vast beached sea creature, consuming too much of every resource we had - power, food, air, water - and putting nothing back into the loop.

An MTB was the only way of getting around on the estate. Cars and motorbikes rattled to bits on the broken concrete hardpan within days. My MTB had pneumatic shockers front and rear. The guy I took it off fought hard and I had had to cut him. Maybe he had cut the person he took it from. Law of the jungle.

Our 'estate' was just that - an old industrial estate from the time when we actually made things, not just consumed them, retail units that had lain derelict for a decade since the Collapse until the Americans came and some bright spark decided to carve them up into housing units to cage up the growing bands of the Dispossessed who clogged the arteries of the country. Imagine living in a cement factory with asbestos walls and crushed glass carpeting and you'll get a pretty good idea of what it was like. Those of us born here had lung shadows like kids elsewhere had freckles. Even the incessant rain did little to keep the dust down, especially inside. Life expectancy wasn't too long so you fitted in what you could. I had done well to get to seventeen without major surgery (not that we could have afforded any). Bobby wasn't shaping up to be so lucky - he was only thirteen and had started to cough up ugly black clots of blood. I gave him two years, tops. Shame, he was a good kid. He was just starting to get interested in the underground movement AvaloNet, which conducted a campaign of violent resistance to any American interference in British affairs, an organisation that I viewed with some suspicion. But Bobby seemed to think they had something to say and was talking about joining their youth wing. I didn't want to see him planting bombs under US marines' cars or hacking intelligence systems on

AvaloNet's sayso, but I hoped he would live long enough to make that choice for himself.

A wide stretch of black tarmac led from the estate to a strip mall that was our town centre, shopping and meeting place, and the focal point of our 'community', if you could call us that. The off-licence had been raided at gunpoint so many times that the owner invested in a bullet proof glass pod like the Pope uses, and controlled entry and exit to his premises electronically. He had also bought a serious South African drum-magazined shotgun, which he kept under his till. He felt very safe, until some enterprising youngsters burned him out with jellied petrol bombs. Who said initiative was dead?

I cycled along the gravel and dirt to the side of the road as heavily laden thirty wheelers thundered past, heading east into the Pennines, their wash sending me wheeling into the scrubland as if I had been swatted by a giant hand. Rain clouds massed in the dark sky over Yorkshire. Good - a decent shower kept the dust down for a few days. We were never short of a little rain.

The strip mall loomed in the chill October dusk, all harsh sodium and Technicolor neon tubing. An old double-decker bus retrofitted with multiple axles was parked at an angle in front of *Joe Swo's Diner*, a tatty American theme fastfood restaurant, and a gaggle of tourists were drinking their Diet Cokes and soaking up the ambience of early twenty-first century post-Collapse urban Manchester. I wondered how much they had paid to be taken to a shit hole like this, probably the only stop off on the way to a rural theme village in the Pennines. Maybe they thought that we were a theme village too - a village themed on urban decay and social breakdown.

I parked my MTB close to a public fone booth and triple-locked it to a lamppost. Inside *Joe Swo's* I could see Bobby and two kids of about the same age, clustered around a dirt-streaked plastic table littered with Styrofoam food containers. One of the boys had a plastic bag with cables and wiring hanging out of it, and they were passing bits back and forth across the table. Two Jizz addicts shared an inhaler at a table nearby, their eyes closed, oblivious to all around them. I hoped Bobby would remember I needed more RAM for my deck but Christ only knew what he was trading for it.

The public fone booth was a smooth plastic cylinder that stank of urine. Why did people always piss in fone booths? It required a pfennig to enter but the short blade on my Silverman tool and a deft turn clockwise usually worked just as well. The door hissed open and I stepped inside.

Fone modulation was archaic and painfully slow but a whole lot safer than using the public data jack socket, which spat little apps into your drive and asked awkward questions of your system, questions that I didn't want to answer. I set up my deck on the plastic shelf and fitted the 69'er rubber couplers to the fone's earpiece and mouthpiece. I heard the dial tones then the hiss of connection, and the sweet burst of surf. *I was in.*

I guess they must have given me fifteen seconds or so to log on to the BankNet, just so they would have the satisfaction of catching me in the act. Later, I would realise that they knew my modus operandii down to the average number of keystrokes I made and my predicted behaviour under stress. Nothing if not thorough were the Department of Data Security.

My first indication that something was wrong came when I saw through the booth's scratched plastic windows the tourists scattering as if a wasp had flown into their midst. As they cleared the pavement I saw what had made them run - a navy blue armoured personnel carrier was driving up the pavement through them and toward me at high speed, its fat tyres crunching plastic bins and rubbish. Even then, my first thoughts were that I had been caught in the middle of some gang battle or that a robbed shopkeeper had called in an over-zealous tac-squad. I fought to get out of the booth, grabbing my deck and punching at the door panel, as the slab of blue armour filled the window. I still thought I was just going to be inadvertently involved in a nasty accident. I had no idea that they had actually come for *me*.

The APC butted the fone booth with its sharply-canted prow. The plastic crumpled in and the booth upended from its flimsy foundations and crashed into the road, taking me with it. Incredibly, I was uninjured. I brushed broken plastic out of my face and crawled out of the wreckage on my hands and knees, stuffing the deck and all its trailing paraphernalia into my jacket. Obviously, I didn't want to be quizzed by the koppers on what I had been up to.

I stared up into the yawning black muzzle of a Peacemaker submachinegun, singled out by the stabbing beam of a maglite strapped under its barrel. I knew enough about guns to know that the light meant that the kop on the other end had taken up initial pressure on the trigger. A twitch and I would be comprehensively ventilated.

"Stand up and place your hands behind your head. Interlace your fingers." The voice was electronically distorted, like a Star Wars stormtrooper. I did as I was told.

"I haven't done anything. You ran me over - "

"Are you Jason Packard, of Tumbledown Estate?"

A chill ran down my spine as I heard my own name. There didn't seem a great point in lying.

"Yes."

A number of the tac-koppers clustered around me now - all their Peacemakers spotlighting me, like the ghost-tracks of aimed but unfired bullets. The kops wore navy blue body armour, knee and elbow pads, shin guards, padded gloves and sinister grilled helmets marked with numbers stencilled in white. One ran a beeping detector over my body, and when it was discovered with a shrill whine, took my deck from my jacket.

"Jason Packard, you are under arrest on suspicion of electronic fraud, theft and possession of stolen goods. You are not obliged to say anything, however anything you do say may be taken down and used as evidence against you."

"Oh fuck," I said, which I thought was fairly innocuous. One of the armoured koppers behind me secured my arms with some sort of plastic binder that bit into my wrists when he pulled it. He shoved me in the small of my back toward the heavy doors on the rear of the APC. I was going down. I had heard so many stories about people disappearing in custody or killed 'resisting arrest'. I was about to find out first-hand if the horror stories were true.

Standing by the APC were the kop's commander, his rank-marked helmet tucked under his arm, and a man with crewcut hair, pebble glasses and a long tan duster coat - a typical DDS agent. He accepted a package from one of the kops - my deck in a plastic ziploc bag. He turned it over and over in his hands.

"Thanks for keeping this one alive, gentlemen," he said, his accent American. "Take him away. I'll take care of his toy."

They shoved me into the back of the APC, on to a webbing seat. I had to sit on my bound hands which hurt. The diamond plate floor was awash with thin gritty oil beneath my trainers. Before they closed the doors, I saw Bobby standing among a gawping crowd at the roadside. He looked at me and nodded. I nodded back. He turned and began to unlock my bike from the lamppost - he knew the codes. I hoped he would be smart enough not to go home - there would be nothing for him there. I think he was old enough to know that. The heavy door thudded shut, sealing me into a metal womb, surrounded by impassive masked automatons. I had never felt so alone, nor so utterly doomed, in my entire life.

It was, of course, just the beginning.

The journey took an hour, half an hour, twenty minutes, two hours. I couldn't tell as I was sitting on my watch. The stormtroopers to either side took off their helmets and shared a smoke, blowing it in my face. I asked them for one but they ignored me. All I could hear was the rumble of the diesel engine and the babble of radio communications from the driver's cab. Occasionally the vehicle would slow and one of the stormtroopers would pull a rubber flap off a little hull periscope and peer out, then grunt and pull it back into position. But we never stopped rolling until we reached our destination.

When we did, there was a flurry of activity and the back door of the APC was flung open, letting in a blast of warm, stale recycled air. Blinded by halogen arclights I was dragged out of the vehicle and into a dusty concrete hangar. For some reason I knew straight away that we were underground. I could almost feel the weight pressing in on the high corrugated ceiling. We were in some kind of underground installation, all loading bays and yellow-and-black striped ramps. Further observations were impossible as my head was pushed down and I was frogmarched along brightly lit corridors to a prison block and hurled into a small unlit cell with a bunk chained to a wall and a crusty bucket in the corner. The door slamming shut behind me sounded like the ringing of my funeral bell.

And then, my troubles really began.

"State your name, date of birth, place of residence."

"You know all that. You told me when you picked me up."

Mild electric shock through fingers and toes. I am naked and suspended upside down in some sort of nylon webbing harness, in a brightly lit tiled chamber. Cameras on the end of prehensile limbs like welding robots dart around my body, peering into my face. There is a cold, unfamiliar pressure between the cheeks of my arse, some kind of rectal probe, for who knows what reason.

"Previously validated facts are required for accurate truth calibration. Answer the question."

"Jason William Packard. Born July tenth, nineteen ninety seven. I live on the Tumbledown Estate, East Sector, Greater Urban Manchester-Liverpool Axis. But you know all this."

I try hard to be cocky but I'm really terrified and the blood is pounding in my temples.

"Are you familiar with the individual known as the Mirrorman?"

"No." Expecting more shocks.

"Mirrorman: data terrorist, information pirate. Other known aliases - the Scavenger, Zero, Dickens -" Pulse flickers in my neck at the mention of his name. The coldly modulated interrogation voice stops dead.

"The individual is known to you as Dickens."

Never grass, never speak, never tell - Dickens' words. No overt threats but I'd seen the arsenal his messengers carried.

"The individual is known to you as Dickens." Not a question, but a statement, a mantra, to be repeated over and over until I agree. This isn't an interrogation, it is a brainwashing exercise. What for? I was caught bang to rights. They don't even need signatures anymore to put you away for this sort of thing. As for being a minor - fourteen year old helicopter door gunners were responsible for the massacre of rioters in Tirana last year. Somehow I don't think being under eighteen will particularly affect my treatment. Two good shocks through the soles of my feet and I'm crying.

"Yes, Dickens, fuck, yes, I've worked for Dickens."

A ruby laser flickers from a glass bubble on the floor and projects images directly on to my eyes. I try screwing them up tight but I get a shock every time I do. I watch as a series of e-fit images, like an endless comic strip, scroll by.

"Indicate the individual known to you as Dickens."

"I've never seen him, never met him." This is true. I get another shock anyway, including one right up my arse. Not a rectal thermometer, then.

"For fuck's sake, are you sadists? You know when I'm telling the truth. You don't have to do this to me."

I grit my teeth and wait for more shocks. They don't come. The laser strobes and dies.

"Describe your first contact with the individual known to you as Dickens, and all subsequent contacts and business dealings."

I take a deep breath. Never grass, never speak, never tell. Fuck you, Dickens, you faceless bastard. You're not hanging by your balls in a stormtrooper's shower cubicle with a cattle prod up your arse. I spill my guts, before someone gets around to doing it for me.

The interrogation lasted for three days. I kept track of time as best I could as I was hustled from cell to interrogation room and back again. They fed me on vitamin pills, let me drink water, and let me shit in the bucket. They also let me sleep, but I didn't. *Couldn't.*

After the three days they left me alone for twenty four hours while my tired muscles, aching from hanging in an inverted stress position for seventy two hours, had a chance to recover. Then they threw in some old baggy combat clothing - American by the look of it - and a pair of nylon and leather boots. I dressed quickly, glad of the warmth, and waited. I tried to use the time to prepare myself mentally and ran through a list of possible outcomes to all this - execution, lobotomy, long imprisonment.

Nothing could have prepared me for what happened next.

* * *

The sergeant was maybe fifty years old and looked like Henry Rollins did right before he croaked, a block of chiselled rock. He seemed impervious to the biting Pennine wind, sticking out his chest and chin while the rest of us huddled pathetically. He wore nondescript combat clothing that could have been any western army, but the subdued badges on his smock pocket marked him as an American. He opened his mouth and confirmed it.

"Fucking sacks of shit," he said, the wind snatching the words from his mouth and hurling them down the valley. He had a vague Southern states drawl. "You disgust me. What have I done to deserve this?" He cast his eyes upwards as if seeking celestial answers.

There were five of us stood in front of him on the freezing, windswept tor high up on a Pennine fell. One girl, four boys, all faces downcast and avoiding eye contact. I didn't know any of the others but they all looked around the same age as me, all dressed in surplus military clothing, small bergen rucksacks at our feet. No one, least of all me, looked capable of surviving a night out here. But it was getting dark. And here we were.

An officer had come to see me in my cell the previous night. I couldn't tell if he was a kopper or a soldier - their badges and uniforms all looked so alike. His tone and manner were gentle and persuasive but no less threatening than the bullying guards or the harsh tones of the interrogation room. He explained that I could 'volunteer' for a short programme that would transfer me for a period of not more than six months to a military unit where my skills could be used in the government's interest - he didn't say which government -

rather than against it. At the end of six months I would be discharged, all crimes annulled. He didn't bother telling me what the alternatives were - he obviously presumed that I wouldn't be refusing.

I guessed that my comrades were similar offenders, but I had not had a chance to talk to them yet. The American sergeant led us on a route march across the top of the wet moor, accompanied by two sullen young soldiers with builds like marathon runners. One of the younger boys began to fall behind almost immediately, his boots looked as if they were two or three sizes too big. The sergeant and his men didn't pay too much attention to him, until we had entered some woodland to rest and the boy had disappeared in a wet fog that had descended. One of the soldiers went to look for him and came back twenty minutes later, alone. Nothing more was said.

And then there were four.

We camped that night in a thinly-wooded copse. The rain lashed us as the soldiers showed us how to make shelters from the plastic sheets in our bergens and the sergeant droned on about navigation, tracking, survival. I listened and learnt because his monotonous drawl gave me something to latch on to. One of the boys got into a fight with the sergeant for refusing to eat a stew made from a rabbit that the soldiers had snared and killed. When we woke just before dawn the next day, stiff and shivering in our aluminised survival bags, the boy was gone.

And then there were three.

The sergeant pushed us hard that day, over ankle-turning moor and fell, to strange ancient cairns on top of the hills, back and forth, over and over again, until our feet were bleeding and sore and our thighs ached and we were cold and wet and hungry. We stopped for a while in the dangerous-looking lee of a huge mossy boulder that looked like a fallen meteorite, while the two young soldiers dressed our bleeding feet with antiseptic sprays and plastic skin blister patches. There we were attacked by a pack of wild dogs, grown feral from strays let loose in the cities. One of the boys was literally carried away by a massive, wicked looking thing that appeared to be a cross between a Japanese Tosa and a Pekinese. The sergeant and soldiers seemed more interested in saving their own lives, and fired off a few desultory shots, which succeeded in driving the pack away.

And then there were two.

I began to get the impression we were nearing our eventual destination. The sergeant concentrated on his laminated map and GPS handheld and less on haranguing me and the girl or spouting countryside lore. We stumbled across a group of heavily-armed travellers erecting a big mesh satellite dish for some unknown reason. There was brief gun battle during which I hid behind a rock with my hands over my ears. The girl and both the young soldiers were killed.

And then there was one.

The sergeant took the loss of his men and all but one of his young charges in his sure-footed stride. He pushed me ahead of him, barking orders to change course as he examined the GPS and the map. I got the feeling that I had been the victim of an elaborate setup that had gone terribly wrong.

The sergeant halted on a smoothly domed hill. It was almost dark and through the drizzle I could see the sodium ghost of a city to the east, maybe the Leeds-Bradford sprawl, but it could have been a moonbase for all I knew. I stood in a desultory huddle while the sergeant scrabbled around on his hands and knees in the wet grass, like a sniffing dog. His stubby fingers found something and he grunted in triumph. With a firm yank, he pulled a turfed hatch clear of the ground and beckoned me over. I looked down into a deep shaft studded with steel rungs and dim bulbs protected by glass lenses. It looked bottomless. The sergeant ordered me down and followed, slamming the hatch shut behind him.

The interior of the hill was silent and antiseptic. I had heard about places like this, relics from the cold war where observers were supposed to seal themselves up to monitor nuclear attacks. I always thought that it sounded like the ideal job for a friendless, antisocial console jockey, until the electromagnetic pulse blew away all your nice toys.

The low-ceiling corridors smelt of dust, sweat and new plastic. The lighting was sickly and dim, just enough, like you find in the basements of old buildings. The sergeant led me along to a room divided up into cubicles by black steel mesh partitions where several soldiers hunched over notebook consoles. Other soldiers patrolled the room, watching the console jocks. Wiring and cabling intermingled like spaghetti on the floor. No one looked up. A man stepped from behind the door, duster coat swinging. The DDS agent from my arrest. He smiled thinly.

"This is your new home," the man said. "Remember this?" He indicated a spare seat and an open deck. *My* deck - I recognised the spray-graphics on the keyboard. That I had last seen polybagged in the hands of this man at the roadside by the mall. I felt a sudden lurch of homesickness.

"You are now in the employ of the government," he said. Again, he neglected to mention which one. He drew deeply on a cigarette and blew a smoke ring. The bunker didn't appear to be air conditioned. "You are part of a special team monitoring and fund-gathering on behalf of the security services."

Fund-gathering? Was that what I had been brought here for? To hack micropayments on behalf of the treasury?

"We call this bunker *The Cage*. Your every move here will be logged and monitored. If you try to escape you will be shot. If you try to contact the outside world you will be shot. If you attempt sabotage, you will be -"

"-shot?"

The man smiled coldly. "I think you understand."

"And after my six months?"

The man smiled again. "A sense of humour. Yes, you'll need that here." He walked from the room, paused in the doorway.

"Well done on surviving the selection course by the way. Few do. You should be very proud of yourself."

The routine in the Cage was little better than the interrogation centre except for the chance to use my deck. There were clocks so that our bodies could adjust to a certain degree. We worked in cycles of eight hour shifts, day or night was irrelevant, you just slept or ate the rest of the time. My comrades were a mixture of army 'volunteers' and a couple of other offenders. They didn't encourage fraternisation which was doubly frustrating considering one of them, another prisoner, was a pretty girl. I tried to watch her dressing and washing as discreetly as I could. She seemed brainwashed by the ordeal and unaware of what effect her feminine lines and smells were doing to the rest of us in the bunk room with her. I wonder how she coped, trying to sleep at night to the sounds of boys masturbating.

The sole point of reference for me was the deck work, but even that was tainted by the conditions I worked under, the long hours and the intrusive monitor Sentinels - now *watching* me, not watching *out* for me - that winked away in the corner of the screens, logging our every keystroke, and the human monitors, soldiers and koppers who walked around the Cage between the partitions, keeping a close eye on our work. But for all that, there were times when I imagined that I was at home with Bobby and mum, receiving my instructions from Dickens and preparing to work for the night. But my wings were securely clipped here. I felt like a windsurfer on a short leash.

Days passed. I began to think about the DDS agent's reply to my question. No one was ever going to walk out of here. As if to confirm this, the pretty girl began to cry in her sleep. Her work deteriorated. She vanished. Simple as that.

Knowing that you are doomed can concentrate the mind wonderfully. I began to amass a huge amount of knowledge about the complex network that the Americans, bless 'em, had installed over the length and breadth of Britain. The nature of the work gave us access to nodes and systems that even I would have had trouble cracking, if I had known they had existed. I knew then, if I had ever had any doubts, that I was not leaving here alive - I already knew too much. I noted weak points in the systems and mentally formulated possibilities for sabotage, then turned my attention to the Sentinel that was preventing me from doing anything about it. I noticed a loophole in the Sentinel's command lines and began to explore the innards of the monitor program itself, while running a cover routine that made it seem as if I was busy. The soldiers who looked over our shoulders didn't bother so much when their sergeants or DDS agents weren't around, just played cards or watched teevee in an adjoining chamber. I took the opportunity to explore the inept programming of the Sentinel. Of course, government-written software was always inept - if civil programmers were any good, why would they need us pirates? I prodded and poked at the Sentinel day after day, until I was sure that I could bypass it if necessary. Now I had the ability to contact the outside world through an email drop or website. The question was, who to alert? Dickens? If he was still alive and not in custody, he would want me dead. Bobby? He was just a kid. Mum? *Please.* A newspaper? I was a prisoner of the government in a remote illegal covert operation. A reporter would not get within twenty kilometres of the place.

The answer came sooner than I had expected when the apparent high-quality of my work led me to be assigned monitoring duties on the jingoistic website belonging to AvaloNet, the anti-American activist collective. I traced email support letters, online forum users, gave out fone numbers and M-LAN ids. I followed individuals through their day at every point where their lives intersected with some node of the on-line world - *0900 fone wake up call, 0930 used pay-per-view for early morning news, 0950 located in mall by CCTV network, 1015 withdrawal of two hundred euros from personal bank account.* No doubt a lot of stormtroopers made a lot of overtime and a lot of people either died or got locked away. I wasn't sorry - in my opinion, AvaloNet were gangsters and cared little about American expansionism. I'd had school mates blown up by their car bombs on Anglo-American Friendship Days. No, I wasn't sorry about blowing the gaffe on AvaloNet supporters and activists. But I had found a way in.

Monitoring AvaloNet's site I placed a very short and very concise message using as simple code that they used and I had cracked, but had successfully concealed this fact from the Sentinel. The message outlined the approximate co-ordinates of the bunker, the nature of our covert activities, and the times of the shift changes of the soldiers when the defence systems would be down. The message slipped out under the Sentinel's gaze. All I could do was sit back and wait.

I found myself a storeroom where old hardware awaiting repair or new stuff awaiting installation was stored. There were huge polystyrene cartons in there. Slipping away during a mealtime I made myself a bolt hole where I could hide from AvaloNet's attack, if and when it came. I neither wanted to be discovered or killed by them. AvaloNet were as merciless as the government and no doubt had their own imprisoned hackers somewhere, doing just as we were.

Their attack came less than thirty six hours after I had posted the message. I was lying half-awake as I had taken to doing during the soldiers' shift changes, and heard a commotion at the top of the shaft, then the flat crack of gunfire. While the others in my room propped themselves up on elbows and wondered what was happening, I was up and out and into my hideyhole, where I pulled old screens and steel racking around me, and hid my head in my hands.

I listened as the AvaloNet team assaulted the bunker. There was no attempt to leave anyone alive, as I had suspected, just the incessant hosing of automatic gunfire, and the crackle and pop of a needle laser, blue flashes and a burning smell leaking into my hiding place. The door to the storeroom banged open and a stray burst shredded the foam over my head, but no more bullets came. After a while, the gunfire died. Then came the screams and the odd isolated gunshot. Then silence.

I sat in the box and forced myself to count to one thousand, twice. Then I did the same again. Then I climbed out.

The AvaloNet team had killed everyone. Several soldiers lay in the corridor, which was swimming with blood. All my comrades had been machine-gunned in their bunks. I was the sole survivor. I saw an unfamiliar face among the dead in the Cage - an AvaloNet terrorist. She was a girl in her late teens. She might have been very pretty until a guard's bullet had hammered at the back of her skull and the resulting exit hole deformed and ruined her face.

The AvaloNet terrorists had emptied hundreds of rounds into the Cage and swept the needle laser over everything, melting plastic tracklines through all the hardware. LCD screens lay shattered, the multicoloured innards of decks smoking and sparking. I dug about in the rubbish and found my own deck. It was cracked and scorched but it seemed intact. I thumbed the power and it booted up. I found a working connection and logged in.

Freed from the constraints of the Sentinel and the gun to my head, I flexed my wings, and did what I do best.

Dawn is breaking. I clamber over the lip of the shaft,

clutching my deck and my bergen. Far below, a city slumbers. A city of power and light and communication and energy. A city like this used to be my home.

But not any more. They taught me things. How to kill and eat things without puking, how to navigate where there are no roads and no signs, how to live and survive in the worst of elements, and finally, inadvertently, how to plant the biggest virus bomb the electronic world has ever seen right in the cold cold heart of their administration and security system. They'll feel the shockwave of this one all the way to Washington. Maybe I'll come back to this spot, later tonight, just to see what happens when darkness falls, and all the teevees and all the lights don't come back on.

The War Diary of Conolly Troon

ILLUSTRATION BY NIGEL DOBBYN

1st of Samhan
Dear Diary,

Dear Diary? What sort of opening is that? Isn't that what little girls write in little red books about virginity loss, broken hearts and first kisses? Don't know. Never kept a diary before. Never needed to. But this is the first day of Conolly Troon's war. I think that needs commemorating somehow, even in this pithy little way. Conolly Troon, lifelong pacifist, Mister Nothing-To-Do-With-Me, Mister Live-And-Let-Live, finally gets one kick in the teeth too many, and decides to fight back. It's been a long time coming, let me tell you. I better gather all my scraps of paper and nubs of pencils - all they let you have in the human zoo they call the z-blocks - and tell it like it is.

I think it's going to be a long war.

Resume of day one (very tired, very sore, want to sleep) : got up, kissed Gennifer goodbye, went to work at the Jinnar Independent Chronicle where I am the Interplanetary Trade Desk Correspondent (every bit as dull as it sounds). Z-squad kick in the doors of the office mid morning (don't think they'll be having me back there, no matter the outcome of the 'trial' - mud sticks) and arrest me under the Justified Detention of Terrorist Suspects Act 22-something. Surprised? You don't get further from the terrorist profile than me. You could almost accuse me of sleeping with the enemy (Gennifer is a card-holding Imperial citizen) - and believe me, many have. Doesn't stop the z-paras bundling me into the z-wagon and flying me north across the city, nap of the earth and at high speed, in case a homemade Jinnie missile is launched from a barrio roof to bring us down, which is highly likely. I sit in the back, in a full body restraint suit. Mirror-visored z-boys take turns to prod me with their shock batons. Unconscious by the time I get to the z-blocks. Woken by hyperinjection in an interrogation cell, cold and dark, Room

1001 the Jinnies call it. Interrogated by invasive brain probe. cold steel in the base of the skull. Pulls a memory from my childhood, Imperial military recruiters with their drums pressganging us in a school play ground. I kick the shins of one and run away, unaware that my single 'terrorist act' will be dragged from my subconscious fifteen years later and used as evidence of my affiliations. I am tagged Jinnie by birth, I've spent half my life fighting that tag. Today, it takes the other side to show me who I really am. Sharing a cell with Divid, the Mad Bomber. Grins with steel teeth when I ask him to teach me all he knows. Gives me the secret handshake that's no secret at all. Grip his missing-fingered right hand like he's dragging me up a cliff-face. Welcome to the war, Conolly Troon.

4th of Culthan
Receive a communication from Gennifer. Single page, time lapse air-degradable paper, dissolving in my hands even as I read it. Can't bear to recall the exact wording now, even though I know Genni didn't write it. Denounces me as a hardened Jinni terrorist who kept her a slave for years, suffering in silence under pain of death. Signing my death warrant. What has happened to Gennifer? Will I ever see her again?
More beatings today. Chemical torture, too, hyperinjections to set you babbling and confessing to all sorts of heinous crimes. Wish I *had* done some of them. Later, when my body stops shaking, Divid shows me how to make lock-blowing explosive out of office stationery products. Our war continues.

37th of Asai
Divid isn't exactly a favoured son in the z-block. His last bomb-making escapade accidentally killed several Green Republic senators along with his intended target, an Imperial

patrol. But he's an old timer, a running dog with the Jinnie warlord Mackenzie when all the Imperial troops had to worry about was banners and drums and shouts of *"Imps out!"* and the odd shaken fist. Now its snipers and bombers and chemical weapons, and has been since I can remember. Divid uses the old school tie - crossed bombs and respirators - to get me an audience with Mackenzie. Should I be grateful?

Must admit, despite my new found revolutionary streak, don't exactly fit in here. Die hard cradle terrorists with parades and salutes and Orders and Meetings and Lectures. On the Settler side of the Z they're just the same, only they swear allegiance to the Imperial throne. The Imperial Throne throws them in here with the rest of us. A terrorist is a terrorist. They may not receive the kind of individual attention that we do, as their efforts are primarily directed against Jinnie civilians as opposed to Imperial targets, but the Imperial troops have little time or support for them.

There, I said it. *'We'*. I may think *'we'*, but what about Mackenzie? Will he look into my eyes and see an Imperial stooge or a waverer, caught in no man's land, and order me thrown off the highest slammer balcony? He can do that. Divid tells me as much. Mackenzie's a general, inside or out. And if I am to be a footsoldier, it will be Mackenzie that will attest me. I have the pedigree - Jinnie through and through, I've cursed it enough times - but will he look at me and see a heart of stone or one of a turncoat?

19th of Nogheda

Z-blocks aren't towers or forts. They're pits, dug deep into the ground, hollow concrete cylinders burrowing to the core of Jinnar, where the little people who bother the might of Imperial rule are dumped like so much rubbish. Atmospheric pressure increases with depth, a form of slow torture all by itself. The hard men live at the bottom of the pit, down in the depths with permanent headaches. Men are murdered there over spilt drinks or odd glances.

Divid leads me down the spiral, through the flapping Jinnie flags and the murals painted on cell doors and cylinder walls : JINNARI FREEDOM FIGHTERS - WE WILL NEVER SURRENDER; SONS OF JINNAR, FIGHTING FOR ONE GREEN REPUBLIC; REMEMBER BLACK NIGHT 2297 - WE WILL NEVER FORGET, NOT WHILE ONE JINNARI VOLUNTEER IS ALIVE TO TELL THE TALE. Fists and masks and crossed guns and rippling pennants and the deep deep green of the Green Republic. Surrounded by all this all my life, meant nothing. Seeing it here with three hundred metres of rock over my head, trapping me, it stirs my soul, like the beat of the drummer-boys on a Black Night parade.

Mumbles and handshakes and catcalls as we descend into Mackenzie's lair, down where the Imp guards don't dare go. Hands reach out from between bars.

"Hey, Divid, how many fingers you got left?"

"Fuck you, gunrunner. At least I'm a fightin' volunteer."

"Don't listen to him, freshface. You'll end up just as ugly and useless."

"Hey, shortfuse! Blow up any Greenies lately? I hear they got a price on your head - in the Green Republic!"

"Who's killed more Jinnies than the z-paras? Divid Donnell! Ha ha!"

Divid takes it all with good nature. I see the embers of flame in his eyes. Once this man had been a living legend, the Mad Bomber. On the outside, these men who jeer him would have paid for their taunts with their legs - the dull thud from the ignition key of their air flyers one morning signalling a Triple D - a Divid Donnell Device - under their seats, planted in the dead of night. Divid tells me these stories when the lights go out. I believe him. But now, half-blinded and maimed, the best he can do is pass his knowledge on to me.

And introduce me to the Network.

Down in the dungeon. Rank smell of caged man, heavier than air, collecting and polluting in the bottom of the pit. No wonder these bastards are so mad. Smells like an opened grave.

Divid guides me through corridors of pneumatic gym equipment, injection molded into the walls to prevent spars and pulleys and cables being used as weapons. Big chemically-assisted guys sweating in sickly yellow low light, intimidating. No need for weapons - these jacked-up superheroes could tear you limb from limb.

Mackenzie, Grand Chieftain of the JLA - Jinnari Liberation Army, by far the oldest and strongest Jinnie organisation, and most-feared amongst the Settlers and Imperials - sits behind this wall of muscle reading political texts from an omniviewer. His cell is a library, walls lined with hard plastic cassettes. He has small pebble glasses mounted on a small nose, small features on a small face; a small man. But a Big Man. He turns to face me as Divid mumbles an introduction, and retreats. I am a rabbit fixed by the stare of the hawk.

How many men has this man killed? How many more has he ordered to their deaths? Does it keep him awake at night, here in the stink of the z-block? He looks at ease with himself. He takes off his glasses - a cosmetic affection, even Jinnies can afford Imperial medical care, retinal implants are commonplace - and rubs the bridge of his nose. An incline of his birdlike head indicates that I should sit down.

How many men has this man killed? Probably none, at least personally. Men like Mackenzie kill with whispers, orders and circles on maps, flips of coins. I may be a convert to the Glorious Jinnari Cause, a fledgling Warrior of the Green, but that doesn't mean I have to *like* this man. I am chilled in his presence. Serious doubts enter my mind that I could carry a gun for these people. What am I doing here?

Mackenzie doesn't do small talk. Asks me where I was born. I tell him - the moon of Jinnar, only satellite of the Green Republic, under centuries-long occupation by troops and Settlers of the Imperial Homeworld. Father and Mother? Alyssa and Brendan Troon, both Jinnari of four generations plus. Married? Ah, a stumbling block. Gennifer Auley, Imperial Citizen. Settler. Hands across the divide. Surely...?

Drops bombshell into my hands. Thick permanent paper, will sit and stare its bald facts at me until I rip it to shreds. Cold, hard words. JLA intelligence report. Headed with my surname and prison number. No *'We regret to inform you...'*, just a scene of crime description from an Imperial Police investigation. *ConApt 1138 burnt out. Gennifer Troon found dead in ruins by emergency personnel.* The phraseology of people numbed to death. But even that's not enough for Mackenzie. He goes on to say how a suppressed coroner's report revealed that she was raped and shot by z-paras before being set on fire, *Jinnie-Lover* spray painted on the conapt door. I grip the paper, ball it in my fist. Mackenzie grips my shoulder like a vice, a confusingly touching and at the same time aggressive gesture. Tells me that I am moving cells. Divid has taught me all I need to know. Do I still want to learn how to kill Imps?

Yes, yes I do. Fucking yes I do.

42nd of Lahne

Divid moves out. Orders from Mackenzie - Divid barely registers annoyance. In comes Furgal, two years younger than me, two hundred years older. Tough young streetfighter from the Barra Project, an area of Jinnar where Imperial troops don't go without space weapon platform support. I shit you not. In the last months of his sentence for possession of weapons and an extension for the savage beating a Settler prisoner during a cell allocation fuckup. Hatred runs through him like bone marrow. Brought up on

Jinni revolutionary songs, drum beats, parades and martyrs. Knows nothing else. Doesn't *want* to know anything else. Is he my political or military teacher? Maybe both. Shows me marksmanship techniques with a make-believe rifle carved from plastic piping, hardens my resolve with stories of rapes, beatings and executions. Has a grudging respect for Imperial troops, but hates z-paras, and foams at the mouth when he mentions Settler paramilitaries. He could let an Imperial patrol walk by. Settler civilians he has to kill. I'm sharing a cell with a stone cold predator.

7th of Liobhan

Trial by fire. Whispers spread, orders to riot to cover a breakout attempt, nine JLA volunteers needed on the outside for a special operation, twenty five will stage an attack to spring them. The 'volunteers' are hand-picked by Mackenzie - snipers, gunmen, pilots, sappers. No room for a rookie of dubious political persuasion, even one burning blood-hot with revenge. This time I must set fire to the bedding in my cell, wrestle with my neighbours and punch Imp guards. Next time, maybe it'll be me that gets to flee to the Green Republic, to regroup and tell war stories in spaceport bars.

But things don't always go to plan in such unpredictable schemes as z-block riots. It starts carefully enough - fighting in the gym lures in a small squad of riot officers who are ambushed and disarmed. Fire of mattress pads and bedding on level thirty meant to stop reinforcements reaching the trapped guards gets out of control, over-zealous arsonists having a field day. The escape party are trapped, prevented from reaching the planned route out to the surface where a stealth-cloaked air transport awaits, but we are in a position to go, to run, to freedom. Us, the little people. Divid and Furgal and Shawn and Cam and me and the others, not the elite, not the special blue-eyed boys. But the golden rule is to exploit every opportunity. So we go, running for the surface like drowning men trying to stop from going under for the last time. *Air!*

3rd of Neaveigh
Freedom!
Writing this in the attic of a safe house in Magreggan, capital of Jinnar. Looking out of the skylight at Imp z-flyers, their active sensors probing the shit out of the city, probably giving half the population tumors, looking for little old me. Remembering the look on the faces of the boys in the back of the flyer as we streamed across the wasteland toward them, half-expecting them to take off and leave us there. But they didn't. We weren't what they came here for, but we were all they were going to get. And they were intending to make us pay for our freedom. But then, doesn't freedom always come with a hefty price tag?

Magreggan and the barrios and the z-blocks locked down tighter than drumskins, Imp reinforcements pouring in from Homeworld. Permanent air patrols, roadblocks, searches, dawn raids, all in the name of protecting Imperial democracy. I sit and watch it all from my lofty perch, untouchable.

The leader of the Magreggan Active Service Unit is a dour-faced man called McArdle, cheeks and forehead pitted like old acne with the scars of faulty bombs. He is mightily aggrieved that he has been landed with ten rookies, crazies, rejects and dropouts rather than the nine steely-eyed killers he wanted. Crazily, he still intends to carry out his plan. When the heat dies down, we are to be smuggled through the Imperial Naval cordon, over the border into the Green Republic. As to the mission, McArdle operates what he calls NTK - *need to know*. If we are caught by the Imps, they cannot beat the information out of us, no matter how much it hurts. Should I be comforted by this fact?

33rd of Samhan

Still on Jinnar. It is Green Republic Day, when all Jinnaris and Greenies celebrate the throwing off of the Imperial shackles and the declaration of the Green Republic's independence. For Greenies, this means a day off work or school, parties in the park, all day wine and song. For Jinnaris it means riots and fires and Imp curfews, attempting to batter all the deep-seated pride of a generation. We sit in our attic, my comrades and I, and share a few dusty bottles of Green's Finest, and as night falls watch the streets below explode, and Jinnar comes alive. I remember cursing this night as a teenager and then as a law-abiding young man seeking Imp citizenship with my lovely young Imp bride *(did I really call Gennifer an Imp?)*. I spit on their citizenship now. I spit on it and burn it and stamp it into the ground. Take me to the Green Republic, learn me how to kill Imps, teach me your rebel songs.

> *Take me to the Green Republic*
> *O you wild colonial boys*
> *Away from guns and bombs and death rays*
> *To my sweetheart's home*
>
> *Though the Imps may chain and beat me*
> *Nothing will I tell of you*
> *All our brave deeds and our secrets*
> *Take them to my grave I do*
>
> *Now the time has come for me*
> *Brave Volunteers, to say farewell*
> *I took up arms against the Impies*
> *Served the Green Republic well.*

Served the Green Republic well... words ringing in my ears as we board a freighter in the dead of night, strap into g-

couches hidden inside carbonfibre cabinets in the hold.   In
these coffins, bound for training camps in the Green Republic.
If the Imps don't shoot us out of the sky first.

1st of Culthan
Successfully evade Imp naval squadron cruising in low
orbit, testing Green Republic territorial space.   Half-hearted
efforts by Republican Aerospace Control to get us to identify
ourselves (by now we are out of our coffins and have the run
of the ship. I go on the bridge, like a big kid). Pilot puts her
down in a forest clearing to the north of the capital, Dun
Leach. First time I've been on the Republican soil in twenty
years - last time was a school trip. Feels good to be here
again. But does it feel like home?
Incident on landing makes me think *no*. Ship is
surrounded by Republican panzers and troopers before we
have a chance to disembark. I wasn't expecting flags and
cheering crowds and kisses from pretty girls, but a little
courtesy, no, *gratitude*, fuck it, wouldn't go amiss. The
Republican troops are hostile and nervous. I look into their
faces and see the same fresh youngsters that the Imps draft
into the z-paras. Are we really all so different?
Itchy stand-off for several hours. Hot and sweaty
inside the freighter, nervous youngsters with loaded guns
outside. McArdle negotiates with their commander. Money
changes hands. Panzers withdraw, standoff over. Our
transports emerge from the woods, completely undetected by
the 'professional' Green Republic troopers, and we disembark
for Dun Leach. Feels good to have the sun on my face again
after the z-block, the dusty lofts of Magreggan, and the
coffins.

42nd of Asai
Quartered across the port city of Dun Leach in the
houses of sympathisers, we await McArdle's instructions. We

are told not to go into the city alone. I am bunked with Shawn, a fervent youngster with an appetite for the skirt and the sauce. Against my better judgement he persuades me down to the port side bars to drink in some summer evening sunshine and watch pale young things play on plastic boats and behave like free people. There are no weapons here, apart from the not-too scary black plastic stunners carried by the cheerful cops. No patrols dashing from doorway to doorway, no roadblocks from opposing sides harassing the innocents, no holographic multimedia sectarian murals bullying the mind and scaring the children. *This* is what we are fighting for. *This* is the way *I* want it to be.

Shawn gets lubricated and gets louder and louder, drawing attention. Our harsh Jinnar accents stand out amid the soft brogues of the Greenies. Disapproving looks from nearby tables, two girls at the bar giggling at Shawn's curses and his - luckily, unintelligible - attempts to sing our battle songs. I try to restrain him but he insists on approaching them. Lots of drunken banter, hands on arms and linked elbows and (I've never done this before) what seems like minutes later we're up some alley that smells of rotting fish-things and her clothes are around her ankles and mine are fumbled and oh god, it's been so long, Genni forgive me, and I go off like a z-para sniper. Then she's calling me all sorts of names and pummeling my chest and telling me I'm a dirty Jinni bastard and why don't I fuck off home, they don't want our kind here, don't want our troubles. I run home, back to the lodging house, find Shawn face down on his bed, snoring. Try to sleep, but her words ring in my ears. Don't know whether she really meant them, or whether she was just angry at me for coming too soon.

3rd of Nogheda
Spirited out of Dun Leach at night by lifter to the forests and lakes to the north of the city. No sign of McArdle

or Divid or Furgal - rumour is they have been seconded to another operation. Borrow a crewman's night vision glasses as we pan over a mirrorlake than reflects the silver-blue orb of Jinnar above us. Lifter's jets shatter the reflection as it vectors. Bad omen?

JLA has purpose-built training facility, buried deep in these woods. ranges and assault courses, accommodation, vehicles and training areas. Instructors are spook-types in unorthodox semi-uniform. Rumours are that some of them are moonlighting Greenie army officers. Some are mercenaries, ex-Imp troops. They won't fight for Jinnar, but they'll take our hard earned cash and teach us how to shoot and bomb and burn. We are issued with fatigues and a hotch-potch of personal weapons, some lasers, some percussion guns. I feel like a soldier now, fighting a war, not a bandit on the streets of Magreggan. We do drill, like real soldiers, call the instructors 'sir', get up before the sun rises to run and train and go to bed long after Jinnar sets over the horizon. Slowly - painfully - we learn the trade of death. Many nights I sit on a rock overlooking the lake and watch Jinnar slip into the hills, watching over it with my weapon in my hand and my diary on my lap, until it is gone. Then I go to bed.

17th of Lahne

Regime in the camp is locked-down, no teevee, no interspace radio - torture for this media-hungry freedom fighter. They justify it by explaining that our military training requires focus that would be disturbed by outside influences - particularly insidious Imp propaganda, poisoning our hearts and minds. So that's how we nearly miss the Imperial-Jinnari Agreement Declaration.

One of the boys has a little set that he smuggled in with him. We huddle around it in the darkness of our bunk hut, faces blued with the teevee light, passing around the earpiece and listening with incredulity as the suits stand and sell us all neatly up the river. No one was going to accept this, not the JLA, not the Settlers. Not the people that mattered. The war was about to move up a gear. The gloves were coming off.

7th of Liobhan
Mission briefing. It seems like we've only been in this camp for such a short time, but the JLA has suffered heavy losses recently due to spectacular successes by Imp undercover special forces units and we're badly needed, as undertrained as we are. I'm expecting to go back to Jinnar. Instead, we're going to the Imperial Homeworld.

We listen with open mouths and fast beating hearts as an intelligence officer that we hadn't met before outlines the plan, or at least our little part in it. We are to fly into the heart of the Empire and assassinate its cabinet on Resurrection Day, when the Imperial Throne celebrates its war dead. A massive attack, snipers and bombers combined, to make sure that the Agreement Declaration is thoroughly derailed, with a surgical strike at the most important people. Must be careful not to kill any members of the Imperial Family who may be present - God knows why, it's a JLA taboo.

Stunned silence when the int officer leaves. Murmurs of *suicide mission*, people scared. We haven't been fully trained for this, of that I am sure. Shawn is more upset that now we've been briefed, we're fully locked down within the camp. He was hoping for a final night on the town. Is it really so different here to the z-blocks? I am a prisoner if I am imprisoned.

14th of Neaveigh
No coffins this time, but smart haircuts, trimmed beards, falsified travel and identification discs and expensive looking civilian clothing. I am Walther Jones, a representative of Hanlan Transgalactic, a huge Settler trading company. I'm visiting the Imperial Homeworld to attend a

conference at the vast *Glory of the Empire* concourse complex, a celebratory temple dedicated to the Empire's might. As a writer, it's not hard to lie and play a part. Comes second nature.

So we fly in from Dun Leach on a scheduled Imperial Spaceways flight, twelve hours of high-g in cushioned couches, watching bad movies and drinking through tubes. There are nine of our number on this flight - I don't even recognise some of the others, the disguises are that good. We have no equipment, that would be stupid - all guns and explosives will be provided by agents and safe houses on the Imp Homeworld. It should be as smooth as this - arrive, travel to safe house, check equipment, carry out mission. I am a bomber - the skills I was taught by the much-maligned Divid Donnell far outweigh my prowess with a laser or percussion gun. I will plant my undetectable biological bomb close to the rostrum of the Resurrection Day monument the night before the event, and be on the shuttle back to the Green Republic before it is detonated. Simple. So why, as I watch the vast, bloated blue disc of the superplanet Homeworld fill the shuttle's viewports, does my stomach turn flips and try to climb out of my throat?

This is all for Gennifer.

16th of Samhan

First foot on the Imperial soil. Try to resist the temptation to spit on the spaceport floor, that would give the game away. Glance around at the faces of the departing passengers, see Shawn and some others disappear into the crowds, get the odd wink or knowing incline of the head. Now, we are on our own.

Out on to the streets of Albia, the Imperial Capital. The scale is so vast, ostentatious architecture dedicated to the Empire's dead generals, scientists, poets. The impression is of an incredibly well-preserved ancient city, but the majority of this capital has been built in the last twenty years, funded by taxes from the conquests across the galaxy as the Imperial war machine has pushed out the borders, reclaiming lost colony worlds. People throng these gilded boulevards lined with alien tree species - the enemy, I must keep reminding myself, even though they carry no weapons and pose no immediate threat to me. They are enjoying the warm sunshine, oblivious to the angels of death walking in their midst. I can feel no animosity toward these people, wish them no harm, only the butchers who are their leaders. But maybe, just maybe, blood and violence on the streets of Albia rather than the streets of Magreggan will make them question the policies of those rulers.

Find the safe house, nondescript conapt overlooking the river. The sympathiser, a middle aged man, doesn't have a Greenie or Jinnie accent, doesn't speak much at all. Shows me to my room, where a strongbox waits under the bunk. I wait until he is gone before I open it. Familiar contents - timers, initiators, and the biological packages that are undetectable as explosives by any known means, combinations of elements that in their unmixed state are innocuous. The Greenie bombmaker who constructed this one and showed me its prototype in the Republic told me that it also carried a trace element that is DNA coded to typical Imperial chemical profiles. It would seek out those first to deliver harm to, in a sense a true *smart* bomb, targeting enemies only. I didn't get a chance to question him further, but the concept struck me as flawed. What was it targeting? Blue eyes instead of green? Tall people instead of short? An accent, a turn of the palette? I wasn't aware that there were DNA differences between us, just ideological ones. All the same, I will be back in the Green Republic before this bomb explodes, and resist the temptation to stand beside it and test the bomber's theory.

This is for you, Gennifer.

Watching the streets of Albia, light rain softening the harsh light from the aerial adverts and the holographic subliminals. News reports ten metres high on cloudscrapers show rioters on the streets of Magreggan. Feeling guilty, here in borrowed clothes, drinking beer from wax cups bought from pavement stalls as family and friends fight on back home. A strange war, this one - a home front with a higher casualty rate than the theatres of conflict. Tonight, we do our bit to even the balance.

The *Monument to the Unknown Imperial Trooper* is ringed by a cordon of steel, z-paras on their home turf, panzers and z-wagons providing armoured back-up. No way to get near the rostrum. But that will not stop me planting my bomb. The biological package has a built in, limited lifespan sentience. In addition to its dubious ability to correctly target, its actual target location is chemically pre-programmed. If delivered short, it will develop prehensile limbs and execute evasive manoeuvres that will enable it to reach its intended location. Confident of this facet of its abilities, I let it fall from my coat into the gutter. It flickers for a few seconds, chameleon skin testing the surrounding environment, then assumes a low-visibility earthy dun colour. Then it begins to move, toward a gritted drain, very slowly, suckered feet feeling the way. It reassembles its form in order for it to fit through the grid, then vanishes, hitting the water below with a plop. It may take many hours for it negotiate the sewers to the target, but get there it will. I hurry from the scene, the grey man, drawing the attention of no one.

That night, I sleep the sleep of the dead. No conscience, no guilt. This is how Conolly Troon fights his war.

17th of Samhan
Woken in the early hours by explosions and sirens in the city. Rush to the window, watch Albia on fire like

something from a cheap movie. Even from the window I can tell that more than one of the bombs have detonated early. Columns of smoke rise from the square where I left my package, and further north, near the cabinet offices. It has all gone horribly wrong. I slump back on my bunk. Was it our fault, were the devices assembled wrong, or have we been used as scapegoats? So many possibilities. I switch on the teevee. Instant access to the scenes - torn bodies, massive loss of civilian life. My own bomb exploded as an unofficial delegation of war wounded and widows, banned from the state-sponsored parade, lay their tokens in a pre-Resurrection Day service. Most are now dead. This wasn't how it was supposed to be. These weapons were supposed to smart, clean, accurate, intended to maximise their tactical use, *minimise* civilian casualties, not to maim indiscriminately and harden resolve against Jinnie independence. I don't know if I have been used as a patsy. I guess I may never know.

Door explodes inward, black-garbed and masked z-para rushes in and empties full magazine from a wicked-looking percussion weapon into my legs. The pain is indescribable. I pass out.

Here ends the war of Conolly Troon.

1st of Nogheda - Epilogue

This my first diary entry since I was shot and captured by z-paras after the (as it swiftly became known) Resurrection Day massacre. Myself and my team were responsible for the loss of seventy eight lives that night. Seventy eight Imperial citizens. No soldiers, no troopers, no policemen, no z-paras. Seventy eight *people*.

I was lucky to live through that night. After the z-paras found traces of the biological package on me, they wanted to throw me from the conapt balcony. Their commander stopped them, administered first aid to my shattered legs, and ordered me removed in their convoy. On the way to the hospital the panzers were caught in the blast of another device, this time deliberately triggered by one of my panicking colleagues. In the mayhem I was spirited away from the z-paras by a man I recognised as the quietly-spoken custodian of the safe house. He ensured that my wounds were tended to by a discreet doctor, and I was smuggled back to the Green Republic where my legs were amputated and I was given cybernetic replacements.

The events of the Resurrection Day Massacre polarised opinion across the galaxy. Initially a ferocious crackdown on Jinnar led to further loss of life on both sides. Then the Green Republic made the shock announcement that it was withdrawing its constitutional claim to Jinnar. the cornerstone of its fight removed, the JLA fell into disarray and in-fighting. Mackenzie was murdered by one of his own pumped-up bodyguards in the z-block. No one seemed willing to step forward and take his place. Then, a move no could have predicted - the Imperial Senate vowed to remove all troops from Jinnar by the end of the year, hold free and democratic elections, and appeared ready to grant independence to Jinnar. The Settlers weren't too happy, of course. So it isn't over yet. And this isn't what we wanted, isn't what we fought for - we wanted to be part of the Green Republic once again, to fly the green green flag. But the Green Republic doesn't want a group of butchers and bombers. That's what we've become. Brutalised, criminalised. *I* wouldn't want me as a citizen either.

I have also learned that the story told to me of Gennifer's death was a lie, concocted by Mackenzie to harden my attitude. Gennifer moved back to the Homeworld, away from Jinnar. I have thought long and hard and decided in the end not to contact her. She belongs to my previous life, the one that ended at the gates of the z-block. How could I ever explain to her some of the things I have done?

This will be my final diary entry. All I have is on my

back in an old Imp trooper's pack, and I'm about to see if these cybernetic legs are really as good as the old flesh and blood ones, and if they'll carry me over the Green Republic's mountains and valleys, an old volunteer trying to find a place of peace to see out his days.

Here ends the war diary of Conolly Troon.

The Fugazi Virus

ILLUSTRATION BY ALWYN TALBOT

I have been killed nine times. Ritual nine, beloved of the occult, three times three. Luckily, I take regular backups. That is why I am here to tell the tale Well, sort of. And what a tale it is.

Perhaps I should start by telling you who I am and why I am so important that someone would deem it necessary to have me killed nine times in nine spectacular fashions (which I will detail at length later). I *would* tell you who I am, if I knew, but to be perfectly honest I don't. All I can tell you is who I was when I woke up on the morning that this whole sorry episode began. Or rather, when I didn't wake up.

I'm not making much sense. Of course I woke up that morning - how else could I be writing this? What I mean to say is that when I went to bed the previous night, fully backed-up as usual, I was President Ludwig Mandala Holgerstein, democratically elected leader of the tiny principality of Magdebourg, a statelet within the island nation (former continent, before the Siberian Underground Planet Eater Disaster - *scheissenkopfen Russians!* - and the creation of the only planet-bound Event Horizon in the known Universe) of Greater Europe. While I slept, Magdebourg was subjected to a violent military coup by some of my - in retrospect, rather naively - most trusted officers, and I was ritually beheaded with one of my own ceremonial swords, gifts from the Emperor of NeoNippon. Ah well, at least I didn't suffer. And even if I did, I wouldn't have remembered. So when I woke again in the deep blue depths of a suspension tank with a freshly grown body, I was ex-President Holgerstein of the renamed New Republic of Gainsberg, with absolutely no knowledge of the previous night's events, until my small band of loyal staff, who had escaped into Free Europe with my data and my head while the renegade generals publicly defiled the remains of my body, briefed me on the shocking events. I was upset, to say the least. But as I wandered, wet and naked, unashamed amongst my closest aides, I realised that my newly cloned body had a number of subtle improvements, most notably the absence of a fencing scar I had sustained in a university tournament, and the limp that had cursed me during my lifetime, sustained as a hip injury during my birth. For some reason, my reactivated brain was unable to remember the name of the first man on Mars until Ygor, my aide-de-camp, pointed out that it had been my brother in law, Sebastian. He also gently informed me that I had been dead for seven weeks before they had had a chance to revive me safely, and during that time Magdebourg-Gainsberg had suffered several more coups, changed names as many times, then vanished completely as Greater Europe and PanAsia had engaged in a particularly destructive bout of tectonic plate warfare which had destroyed our dear little country and several others, and had drastically rewritten the geographical map. I was particularly shocked at this news, not so much at the loss of Magdebourg but at the notion that tectonic plate warfare was anything other than a crazy science fiction idea. Ygor assured me that it was hard fact.

Seven weeks can be a long time to be dead.

And so we set about forming a government in exile, from a base of operations in the old artists' quarter of Paris, now a squalid barrio of renegade software, hardware, nanoware, bioware and ready-to-ware jockeys. To be in with a chance of further survival, I needed to be in close proximity at all times to as many highly skilled technicians as possible.

The second attack came while we were enjoying a rare night out, watching from a canopied street bar as teams of young lycra clad girls speed-hockeyed on the ominously luminous glassed-over Seine. I was leaning forward to talk to Ygor, pointing out a particularly athletic young speed-hockeyer who I would have liked on my personal staff - even from that distance, I could see that she would have a fine dictation style - when I saw the motorised rickshaw bearing down the Left Bank at us with unnerving speed. Ygor drew his needle laser and set the thing on fire while I fumbled with my belt and the small unit there that would flash-transmit a highly compressed version of my memory into safekeeping. And that was the last thing I remember.

When I finally awoke again, a horribly disfigured Ygor described to me the events of that day, filling in the gaps, manually repairing the missing files. The kamikaze rickshaw had exploded and tore apart the river front. I had been virtually incinerated as the attack had homed in on a microscopic beacon that had been covertly attached to me by an agent at some point earlier that day. Ygor, terribly injured, had grovelled around in the broken glass and spilt guts until he had gathered enough of my biological remains to effect a reincarnation, then escaped across the river, witnessing the terrible sight of the nubile speed-hockeyers boiling and dissolving in the toxic Seine as the protective glass sheeting cracked and split in the explosion. Insane, in Seine. I was fortunate that I had been spared that particular visual memory.

Seven months had passed by since that episode. During that time Ygor and my loyal followers had survived as best they could in a Europe that was increasingly deteriorating; politically, socially, militarily and geographically. A confederation of states from the east of the Urals were unleashing weapons of unprecedented technological fury, armaments at the edge of physics, biology and biochemistry, bending the very nature of the landscape and its unfortunate inhabitants. The Earth to which the deposed President Holgerstein was reborn this time was a very different place from one he left so suddenly and violently seven months before.

You will notice that I slipped into referring to myself in the third person. I can only think that this is a manifestation of the utter desolation I felt in this, my third body. It now sported a number of birthmarks and slight skin disorders due a fault in the reincarnation module. The passage of time between each death only served to accentuate this mood. The world seemed to be changing on a daily basis while my flesh rotted in a vacuum jar, my memories deteriorating in a hard drive. And we had yet to discover why I, the holder of a defunct office in a dead country, could be so important as to be assassinated twice. And now, by whom?

The next attack came as we sheltered in a bunker far beneath the old city of Sarajevo, razed to the ground above us, flamebombers finishing the job that the Serbians had started a hundred years earlier. We thought we were safe, plotting and planning our return to power. We were wrong.

I discovered later that the great shaggy thing that dug its way through ten metres of reinforced concrete with its bare paws was a *skilloth*, a hybrid of some Balkan folk-devil and the overractive imagination of a biotech programmer. I remember seeing it tear Ygor limb from limb and scatter his entrails all over the steel walls, until they were slick with his blood. Then it chased the rest of my staff through the corridors and shafts of the bunker complex, hunting them down like a level of a computer game, playing with them, torturing them, tearing them to bits. It appeared to save me to last. When it finally came for me, I gladly placed my head in its stinking maw, thumbing the flash-send on my belt, not knowing if this time there would be anyone left to revive me. At least I never ever remember the suffering.

I awoke in a glass tube on the command bridge of a Land Leviathan crawling over a blasted and desolate wasteland. It belonged to a group of renegade Magdebourgans, perhaps the only members of my clan left alive on the face of this doomed Earth. I had - I was told by a fresh-faced Leviathan

Commander, who stood rigidly to attention and seemed about to burst with pride - been dead for thirty five years. During this time, the mission that he (and his father before him) had been entrusted with had been the protection of my memory (a rather more literal protection than the majority of personality-based religions and cults could muster, I wager) and the search for the required technological equipment to make my reincarnation a reality. They had ranged far and wide over the face of Hell in their quest. And here I was, thirty five years later.

I examined myself, naked as usual, in the reflective surface of the bridge's canopy. Young girl operators seated to either side giggled at my morning glory. How long had it been since I had made love to a woman? The face and body that looked back at me from the smooth glass were as alien as the young face of the Leviathan Commander. Then I saw the missile over his shoulder.

Across the blasted landscape it came, a horizontal tower block, flying nap-of-the-earth, dodging craters and petrified forests, homing in on whatever genetic code or tagged data corrupted my body. The pretty girls screamed , the young Leviathan Commander froze and wet himself rather than attempt some sort of evasive action. I reached for my belt. Of course, I wasn't wearing it.

"It's automatic," said the Leviathan Commander, which were pitiful last words, and we all died.

Seventy years later I awoke in the cold steel laboratory of a space platform geosynchronously orbiting above long abandoned Europe. My saviours were fervent Holgersteiners, cultists of many generations, and they worshipped me in robes and with blazing lasers as I stepped - naked, of course - from the metal womb that they had prepared for me. Again I pondered on the importance of myself, that I was being killed and resurrected so many times over a period of that was now stretching into centuries. The Holgersteiners prostrated themselves at my feet, calling me their Immortal Lord. Immortality, I could have told them, was getting a little wearing. But that isn't what cult worshippers want to hear. I had to be careful and try to be everything they wanted. Fallen idols have a very short life expectancy.

I was assigned a new aide de camp, Raoul, a young man whose fervour matched that of any of his fellow worshippers, and who had dedicated his life to the study of mine. I was eager for him to fill in some of the gaps in my knowledge of my own lives, and also to find out if he had discovered any clues as to the reason for my unexpected importance in global schemes. Sitting with him in an arboreal dome looking down on the desertified continent that had once been my home, I listened intently to his nervous reports, acutely aware that he regarded me as a living deity. I tried to calm and reassure him as best I could. It crossed my mind that I was an albatross, the ancient harbinger of doom, and to be close to me was to court death as the hawks descended, as surely they would for a fifth time. But Raoul and the Holgersteiners had no thought of their inevitable fate. Most interestingly, Raoul's research had uncovered references to a phenomenon known as the Fugazi Virus, which had turned up on his database searches cross-referenced with my name no less than nine times. But Raoul did not know what the Fugazi Virus was, nor could he find information about it anywhere else. Was it a metaphor? Was it a disease? Was it a software agent? What had it all to do with me?

All questions unanswered, of course, as the freighter drone ploughed into the station and knocked us into a fast decaying orbit. I uploaded before suffering the horrific burning death that surely awaited me and my loyal acolytes.

A dream, then? Or maybe a stray record from a long lost

database hidden deep in the worldnet. But information, nonetheless:

Fugazi Virus : Trans-spatial self replicating reality reconfiguring biochemical entity (TSSR-RRBE). Registered product of the Minsk Exotic Weapons Cadre, People's Republic of Northern Slavonika, Baltic Bloc. Unleashed as field test upon the strategically neutral European principality of Magdebourg, virus taking up host body in the form of President Ludwig Mandala Holgerstein. Order to terminate with extreme prejudice by all FreeWorld forces, in order to prevent massive and irretrievable reality reconfiguration. (NB MEWC closed in 2052 due to health and safety documentational infringements)

Early indications - rains of fishes, blood lakes in Negev Desert, Israel, spectral panzer battalions attacking Moscow and Berlin.

Intermediate - drop in light and heat emission from the Sun by 10%, permanent discolouration of the moon, sea levels dropping, massive ecological disturbances.

Advanced - tectonic plate warfare, mutation of species, exodus from Earth of all surviving lifeforms. Termination order on President Ludwig Mandala Holgerstein extended, bounty of starship fleet offered by unknown sponsor. Termination estimate - Holgerstein will need to be killed nine times.

Nine times nine times nine.

Date from nowhere. True? False? Know or care? The virus, calling to me across space, telling me what I am - what we are. Fugazi Virus in human form, tearing the Universe asunder, reversing the law of physics. pulling together the expanding limits, back, back, back, into the Big Crunch.

I had never visited Mars before. I woke in the encampment of desert nomads, red zuaregs, a subcult of Holgerstein worship

(I had served as a tank commander in a desert war in my youth), their bodies and their pack animals mutated into forms able to metabolise CO_2 and withstand Mars' extremes of temperature and radiation. Shivering in rug-strewn gompa dome, frosting on my naked body, I caught site of myself in the curved surface of a highly polished metal jug. Slitted, heavily lidded eyes, broad nostrils on a shallow nose, leathery skin. Like all messiahs, I had been recreated in the image of my worshippers.

Travelling with the red zuareg caravan in the highlands around Mons Olympus, I experienced a calm that I had not felt since my childhood. I understood why the prophets of the preFall - Jesus, Mohammed, Buddha - had come to the wilderness to meditate. Adapted as were to desert survival, the environment was still a daily challenge and a source of constant danger. It was a thing of fatal beauty, and to stare too long would mean the end of you. I learned a great deal about myself and my condition.   I took a zuareg lover, an androgynous desert rose called Lila.

Lila turned the cold desert nights alive with her passion for me. I wished my time with her and my ferocious zuareg followers would never end. Together we raided encampments of weak colonists from an Earth dead two hundred years, and hijacked the great hundred wheelers that hauled freight along the Roman-straight desert roads. But of course, it would all come to an end.

They - whoever they were or are - found us one night, all asleep, guards too, after a hard day digging ice from a permafrost oasis. A lone gossamer-light attack craft sprayed the camp with a retrovirus that attacked our oxygen-enriched systems and caused massive internal haemorrhaging and fits. I held sweet Lila and watch her die in my arms, deliberately holding on for the memory, joining her gladly, but I knew that it was not my place to be at her side for eternity. So die I did for the sixth time.

* * *

It was becoming difficult to tell how much time had passed between resurrections. The human race - what was left of it - had obviously colonised much of the galaxy, terraforming and mutating as it went. The Cult of Holgerstein travelled with it, being driven underground then overground, becoming the basis of vast empires in one century, then being outlawed and persecuted in another. I began to realise how Jesus must have felt.

My sixth resurrection coincided with an upsurge in my personal popularity (or at least, in the popularity of the cult founded in my name, about which I knew so little and which bore scant resemblance to any philosophies or strategies I had ever espoused), and on the colony planet of Endora, far out on the galactic rim, I stepped from a formless metal egg into the antechamber of a vast cathedral erected in my honour, a cathedral with a vaulted holographic ceiling where planets collided and black holes sucked whole galaxies into oblivion. A multitude of worshippers spread out in a vast carpet before me, and hurled themselves to their knees as I stepped, naked and dripping, on to a balcony of purple-veined marble high above them. High priests wearing robes and carrying wicked looking daggers whispered instructions to me, and I obeyed lest their daggers be the sudden tool of my next death. They draped me in a voluminous white robe and told me to hold my hands up to the crowd, who rose to their feet as one and roared their appreciation, a wall of sound that actually caused me to stagger. I felt incredibly vulnerable, buffeted by their adoration and open to any opportunist sniper who might have been hiding amongst them. And paradoxically, therein lay my fate.

It became apparent later, as I was left alone in a mosaic tiled cell of repeating fractals - torture by interior design - that I had been resurrected this time only to die again, by the ritual of assassination that had been popularised during the latter half of the twentieth century. As the *Kennedy*, I would be paraded in front of the crowd much as I had been earlier. The *oswald* would then shoot me using a high powered bullet with a seeker head matched to my retinal pattern. The *oswald* would then be torn apart by the crazed, baying mob. I would then be resurrected, exactly one month later (which was apparently equal to about an Earth month on this small, fast spinning planet) for the ritual to be re-enacted. So, that was my fate. A monthly execution to satisfy the perverse personality cult desires of my 'followers'. By now I did not fear death in the least, but the thought of multiple executions and resurrections in such a short time frame made me exceedingly weary.

Morning came. The planet assembled on the cathedral plain below me. This place is so vast, I remember thinking, it seems to have its own ecosystem. Was it a Dyson Sphere, enclosing this planet and its satellites, with the fictional dramas of the cosmos projected on to it, or were we really in constant imminent danger of being sucked into a black hole?

The warrior-priests led me out on to the execution platform. The crowd bayed for my blood, and I gazed up into the dilated eye of the black hole, seeking salvation. A flash and puff of smoke from far away, a master sniper attending to his art.

I was out of there.

He was the first alien I had ever met. He was tall and pinky-grey and smelled vaguely of aniseed as he bent over me in my coffin-womb, adjusting and arranging the myriad of pipes and cables that penetrated my body. I was suspended in a vat of molten gold, translucent and ephemeral, and I coolly appraised my new form, scratch-built by this being. I was humanoid, that much was evident, but there was something wrong, something missing. Something not quite right about my genitals, something a little strange about my nipples. The alien disconnected all the umbilicals as I regained consciousness, and stepped back as I sat up and examined myself.

He explained that he had saved me from a cataclysm that had engulfed the civilisation built in my name, the one that had intended to execute me for all eternity. While manoeuvring his ship (a fine beast) through what he took to be a particularly dense asteroid field, his sensors alerted him to a tiny floating module containing a few terabytes of data and some DNA samples. Filling in the gaps as best he could, he built me in the cellular regenerator his ship carried to deal with his own combat wounds. It turned out that he was an advanced scout for an alien empire that was intent on domination of the universe. As soon as I heard this, I knew what I had to do, and the seed of an idea was sown in my brain. I began to cast around his ship for the necessary equipment with which he might be able to further my plan. He was quite naive, and most obliging.

A cybernetic body is so practical, I wish I had embraced the concept centuries ago. I feel neither pain nor anguish in the cold of space, as I drive my bodycraft over the event horizon, down to the bottom of the black hole. There will be no coming back this time. The virus knows this. Like any intelligent organism, it has a survival instinct, and it will know that my time as it host has come to an end. It must find a new one if it is to destroy the universe before the alien invasion comes.

If I can't have it, no one can.

Small rocket detaches from cyberhost, fires away from event horizon, negative acceleration but transmitting, transmitting, before host vehicle destroyed by pressure.

Virus successfully transmitted. Seeking new host.........

Bad Jihad

ILLUSTRATION BY DAVID STEPHENSON

1

Honourable Patrons,

I beg the forgiveness of Allah and, more specifically, of the Covert Projects Committee of the Revolutionary Council, for the failure of the B.A.D. JIHAD project. As Project Director and Military Commander of the Masshad Research Village, it is with me that sole responsibility lies. I accept this responsibility, and ask only that your punishment be just, merciful and (above all) swift, and that you spare my comrades and brothers any retaliatory action. They were, after all, only following my orders.

You have requested a detailed breakdown of the project stages and some indication, in my opinion, of where the project went wrong. I stress again that where I may appear to blame other members of my team, I personally oversaw all major phase decisions and completions. The project was executed as follows:

PHASE ONE – Selection of the candidate

There was much debate among the teams as whether to use a live or deceased volunteer, or to attempt the construction of an undetectable cyborg (an option favoured by the robotics and artificial intelligence teams, always eager to justify their budgets), and in the early stages a number of variants were completed and tested. My own choice would have been the cloning of an Olympic athlete and training the child from its earliest years in the skills of a warrior, however the time scale imposed upon the project precluded this. After several disastrous attempts with live subjects and some promising but ultimately fruitless androids, a hybrid was suggested and although initially dismissed by all concerned, proved to be the best compromise.

Our subject was Private Hanan Bashir of the Islamic Guards.

He was gloriously killed in action at Shiraz on January 7th, 1987. As per our request to the forward field hospitals, his body was identified as conforming to our template and had all major organs intact –he had been suffocated in a collapsed bunker during an assault by Iraqi forces. His body was delivered to us on February 1st.

At this stage we had settled on the preferred method of advance on the project and had pre-cast the hydraulic limbs, optical devices, sensors, weapon systems, heart/lung units and neural enhancements, hence the need for a physical type that lay within narrow parameters. Appropriately, Private Bashir was officially re-animated on February 24th, Martyrs Day, when a blood supply was restored to his brain.

It was at this point that I feel the project first floundered. While my teams were attempting to test and develop the unit's combat prowess and the largely experimental software, an increasing amount of operational time was being taken up by the mullahs assigned to the military village, with the express remit of investigating the after-death experiences of the subject individual. I understand that they were reporting directly to the Revolutionary Council. While I appreciate the importance of their Holy Work, I feel I must faithfully report that their presence hindered our advance and was also, I feel, instrumental in altering the mental state of the individual beyond the stable condition that we had worked hard to maintain. In my opinion, this was the main cause of failure in Phase One.

PHASE TWO – Advanced Training and Combat Orientation
The Biological Attack Djinn proved extremely receptive to military and covert operations training. Our choice of a combat veteran was thoroughly vindicated, it showed little or no fear during live fire exercises – perhaps because it had already gazed on the face of Allah, and returned? As the war drew to a close we were able to recruit

many highly skilled advisors as well as those who had experience of the 'dirty operations' as taught to the Palestinian groups, the kind of environment that the B.A.D. would encounter on the missions that it became apparent it was being earmarked for, as large scale offensives became a thing of the past. It proved as capable in the face of an assault by a captured Iraqi tank as it did assassinating the sentries on a mock-up embassy. I am satisfied that this phase was carried out to the best, if not beyond, of our abilities, however the approach of the end of the war with Iraq and the marked change of emphasis from overt to covert operations sowed a degree of confusion in the subject's mind. Paradoxically, it is the intensity of the covert operations training undertaken that currently makes the B.A.D. so elusive for our agents to recapture.

PHASE THREE – The Field Test

I am on record as stating that I was opposed to the planned field test. I felt that it was an unnecessary risk of an invaluable resource, for minimal research gains. At this point in the project, the emphasis had changed completely, even the enemy was different. I have no doubt that the objective was political. Forgive my candidness, but the order *was* carried out without question.

The B.A.D. was inserted into the battlefield during the final week of the long war that we had waged against the aggressor Iraq. I had absolute faith in the B.A.D.'s abilities but it could not win a war single handed and besides, it has primarily been designed as a prototype for the manufacture of hundreds of thousands of such units. The B.A.D.'s heroic exploits in those seven days before the ceasefire are the stuff of legends, and are well documented elsewhere. Less well known, of course, is the failure of the unit to return to base and its current whereabouts, some six months later. There have been numerous suspected sightings across the Gulf region and the Islamic world, but as yet our agents have not positively identified the unit's movements and above all, its motives.

Of course, its re-assigned primary mission remains unfulfilled. Rushdie still lives, under heavy guard by British intelligence at an unknown location. Whether or not the B.A.D. retains enough programming or human desire to carry outs its primary function remains to be seen. If reports of its appearance alongside Mujahideen in Afghanistan are accurate, then it appears to be fighting a wider Jihad than we first envisaged for it. The fatwa remains unresolved, and I did not get the opportunity to implement the revised Phase Four, the assassination of the Heretic Writer.

I have of course received your order to purge this site. The order is at the moment being carried out by the unit of the Revolutionary Guard that hand-delivered it. My teams were take away by bus into the desert earlier today, I trust you saw fit to relocate them in a place suitable for such keen minds in the service of Allah and the Revolution. Would that I join them, but the Guards ordered me to stay. It seems I must go down with my 'ship'.

The flames lick at the door even as I feed this, my report, into the fax machine. Please forgive the bloodstains at the foot of the page.

Yours in the service of Allah
Professor Menez
Director of Operations
Masshad Military Research Village.

2

Report X22331, October 17th 1989, CIA Field Operative

Howard Ringmeyer, Operation Iguana, Afghanistan
(Note : this report has been written by a highly regarded operative, a veteran of several Middle Eastern covert operations, who holds a Masters Degree in Psychology. After filing this report, the agent was withdrawn from the field and given a full medical examination and psychiatric evaluation. Analysts are convinced that the report is accurate, however the validity of some of the agent's observations cannot be independently confirmed)

The incident took place on October 9th 1989. I was on my fifth and final assignment in Afghanistan, accompanying a party of Mujihadeen fighters, who I had been in contact with since my first visit in 1982. Then, I was supplying and training them with Stinger missiles to bring down the MIL-24 Hind helicopter gunships. Now, I was observing their tactics and conduct as they pushed the hastily withdrawing Russians north, and out of their troubled country.

We had been in sporadic combat for three days. The Muj were stalking a Russian armoured column that had got separated from its mother unit after developing mechanical problems, and was having trouble navigating its way out of a narrow valley. The column consisted of two T-72 main battle tanks and two BTR-70 PB wheeled armoured personnel carriers, about 16 airborne infantry soldiers, around twenty six Russian soldiers in all. Over the three days of the contact, snipers (including, contrary to orders, myself – Marine Corps training proving just as effective with a Dragunov as a M16) and the odd skirmish had whittled these numbers down to about fifteen souls. One of the BTRs had been disabled by a RPG, and abandoned.

The Muj, as usual on foot, were in danger of losing their quarry if they managed to make it over the pass and on to the main metalled highway to Kabul. The lead tank was cresting the ridge and making a dash across open ground to the north, when something hit it and sheared its turret straight off. I have no idea where the weapon came from or indeed what nature of weapon it was. My best assessment, given that there was no flash, hear, smoke or signature of any kind, was that it was an extremely powerful and sophisticated laser. When we inspected the vehicle and its crew later, they had all been neatly decapitated or cut in two.

However, I did not at any time observe a vehicle or any other kind of installation that would have been required to mount a weapon of this nature. What I did see was a man in a black outfit that appeared among the remaining Russian vehicles (by now debussing their crews and paratroopers in blind panic at the fate of the lead vehicle). I thought I saw him look at an attacking Russian infantryman who then exploded. Of course, I realise how absurd this sounds, but I feel it is my duty to relate these impressions as well as harder observations. It is highly likely that the Russian's grenades exploded prematurely while trying to attack the man in black. However, I did observe this phenomenon at least three more times as the Russians scattered and the Muj fighters moved in to take advantage of their mysterious ally's actions. I tried to get in close to see who this man was, but other than to confirm he was of Arabic origin, I can provide no further information. One of the Muj fighters did manage to exchange a few words with him before he vanished. When I questioned the fighter later, he said that he had thanked the man and asked him his name. The man replied *"Bad Jihad"*. The talk around the campfire that night was of a djinn sent to expel the Russians from their country, to kill as many of them as possible even as they retreated, to make sure that they never, ever returned. The fighter who had talked to the man, a hardened veteran of their ten year war and as cold blooded a killer as you were ever likely to meet, was visibly shaken by his experience.

I can offer no rational explanation for what I saw that

day. The damage to the Russian vehicle was conducive with
that which you would expect from advanced heavy weaponry,
perhaps chemical laser or supercharged plasma, of a type that
is not, to the best of my knowledge, in production even in the
United States. I know of no country capable of producing
such weaponry. Nor did I see this weapon or its vehicle. All I
saw was one man, who the Muj called *djinn*. We would call
him a *devil*.

3

Excerpt from *Weekend In-Depth* magazine, October 1990.
Reporter – Don McDonald

I first met Ali Hussein earlier this year when I was researching
a piece on Iranian mural painters for the *Observer*. Ali had
been an officer in a tank regiment during the Iran-Iraq war and
had fought for five long years, leading by all accounts a
charmed life that endeared him to his men and earned him the
nickname the Lucky Lieutenant. Ali's luck ran out in the high
passes of the Zagros Mountains during the Battle of Ahwaz,
when he was ambushed by an Iraqi Sagger antitank missile
team, and his British-made Chieftain tank was blown out from
under him, along with both his legs.

"Thank Allah, they left me my hands," says Ali with
characteristic pragmatism. "I cannot walk, but at least I can
still paint."

The murals celebrating the heroics of the those
martyred in the struggle with Iraq began to appear all over
Tehran and the larger Iranian cities soon after the end of the
war, depictions of muscular, clear-skinned Arabian warriors
that would not have looked out of place on the covers of
romantic novels. They splashed their Technicolor exploits
across canvases hundreds of feet high, with the blessing and

support of Khomeini's successors, eager to commemorate the horrific losses of a campaign of trench warfare and poison gas that had drawn parallels with World War One. And who better to lend authenticity to the paintings than a war hero, a live martyr like Ali, still making sacrifices for his country, for Allah, and for the memory of the fallen.

I was led back to Tehran recently by a photograph that had appeared in National Geographic of a particular mural in downtown Tehran. I recognised it immediately as the work of Ali – while he conformed to the ideal of the homogenous mural painters, his work had enough stylistic originality for it to be identifiable. I was extremely intrigued by this painting. It depicted a figure that had begun to crop up in soldiers' reports from the front line, on both Iranian and Iraqi sides, that of a lone warrior dressed in black, fighting for the Iranian side but apparently under no one's direct command. Certainly, there is no official confirmation of the individual's existence, and I have even experienced hostility when investigating the story through official channels. Of course, in a society as secret and secular as post-revolutionary Iran, hostility to enquiries of a sensitive military nature is to be expected. But the stories of this individual's exploits read more like the adventures of a comic book hero. A comic book hero brought to life by the brush of Ali Hussein.

Ali had begun work on a third mural when I visited him for the second time. Alone, I visited his second mural first, the one I had seen in National Geographic. The hero's jaw, the rippling dark hair, the laser-light stabbing from the eyes, the black cape cracking in the desert wind. Bullets bouncing off a manly chest and dead Iraqi soldiers flying in all directions. How much truth was there in these paintings, and how much was simply propaganda? And if it was just propaganda, what drove a legless war veteran to give up his life to spend eighteen months or more on each canvas, devoting himself to a single enigmatic subject, starting a new one scant days after finishing the previous?

I found Ali fifty feet in the air, sitting in the battered, paint-smeared metal bucket that was his means of transport up and down the array of scaffolding that had been erected – by government hands? – for his express use on the drab grey flank of an office block that he had chosen as his new canvas. His painting was only partially completed but already I could see the form of what was taking place. The hero of his previous mural had taken shape as full-blown superhero, flying over the battlefield knocking Iraqi MIG fighters out of the sky with his fists. All that was missing were the *kpow!* and *splat!*

I made myself known to Ali. He acknowledged me and I waited while he finished a portion of the painting and laboriously let himself down the system of scaffolding by ropes and pulleys. Remaining in his basket, we shook hands – his were rough and callused from many hours hauling his battle-scarred body up and down the ropes. We shared a cigarette and I asked him about the subject of his most recent painting. Surely, this was a figment of the artist's imagination, an idealised Persian warrior, a metaphor for a dream victory over the Iraqis that never came? Or, maybe, Ali was working under the instructions of the mullahs, perpetrating a mythic reasoning for the madness that had engulfed their country for eight years.

"He is called Bad Jihad, and he is real. I have heard many reports about him, from many different soldiers, and I would not believe them if I had not witnessed him with my own eyes. I met Bad Jihad during the Battle of Ahwaz, shortly before I lost my legs."

I asked him did he think that the man had supernatural powers. This seemed the most common presumption that I had read from other reports.

"I do not know. I felt no evil from him, so if was a creature not of this earth, then surely, he was sent by Allah.

Certainly, he was on our side, on Allah's side, that day."

Ali told me a story. The story of the Battle of Ahwaz. How a black-garbed man attacked an Iraqi tank column with no visible weapons, bending gun barrels and slicing of turrets with blasts of terrible light from his eyes. I looked deeply into Ali's own eyes as he told me this, a most familiar story. In there I saw no lies, nor madness. If the story is not true, it does not matter to Ali. He believes it is the truth.

His voice wavered as he finished his tale with details of his own fate, then without another word – I think he did not want me to see him cry – he dragged himself back up his rope to the painting and restarted his work. He had told me, in answer to my question, that he denied his memory of Bad Jihad until he started his paintings, and that it was a chance meeting with other veterans of the battle that had reactivated his recollections, and they had urged him to use his skill to commemorate the incident.

Ali died two months after I returned from Tehran, the brush strokes on his last completed painting still drying in the wind. I do not know what he saw that day at Ahwaz, and my further research has come to nothing. Lies, propaganda, myths. I do not know which, if any, are true. But Ali's belief was fundamental in its totality. Bad Jihad exists. And he's still out there.

4

Video tape supplied by French Secret Service (GIGN). Classification – Tres Confidential.

(Quality 8mm video footage from tripod mounted camera in corner of hotel room. PRISONER tied to chair in centre of room, facing camera. Arabic origin, dressed smartly in a black linen suit, no tie, barefoot. Bruise on right cheek.

Four other men in room, all in light summer suits or shirtsleeves. Identification badges on pockets mark them as GIGN AGENTS. The man in the chair has his hands secured behind his back, but appears relaxed. The agents rotate around him, either standing or sitting astride a chair to one side of him, firing questions in rapido French. Occasionally one strikes his face, but the prisoner does not appear overtly concerned at this treatment)

AGENT ONE – Do you know why you have been brought here?

PRISONER – I know that you are agents of the French government. I presume that I am accused of some crime under French law.

AGENT TWO – That is very perceptive of you. Let us show you a photograph.

(Agent Two brandishes a large glossy print in front of the prisoner's face. Prisoner scans it, unmoved. Agent Two approaches the camera and allows the lens to record the picture. It is a high quality print of a photograph from a desert war incident. An armoured vehicle is on its side, smoking, with several soldiers lying around it, some dismembered, in French desert camouflage uniform)

AGENT TWO – Would you like to tell us what you see in the photograph?

PRISONER – It appears to be the aftermath of a successful attack on a VBL armoured vehicle of the French Foreign Legion 2nd Regiment Etranger d'Infanterie, during operations conducted during the liberation of Kuwait.

AGENT THREE – That is an extremely accurate observation. Would you like to tell us how your intelligence is so accurate?

PRISONER – Of course. I was there. I retaliated against an unprovoked attack by the Legionnaires.

AGENT FOUR – This 'unprovoked attack' was a direct hit by a MILAN antitank missile on your person. Would you like to explain to us how you survived such an attack?

PRISONER – That is classified information.

(AGENT ONE jumps up and strikes the prisoner across the face)

AGENT ONE – We just de-classified it! What the fuck are you? A fucking freak? Don't fuck us about, *cochon*, we don't play by the rules. Ever heard of 'Rainbow Warrior', eh? You are in some very serious shit.

(The agents pace the room. They take off their jackets, sweat is marking their shirts. The prisoner remains calm and unexpressive)

AGENT TWO – Why did you kill the legionnaires?

PRISONER – I was conducted operations against Iraqi forces on behalf of the personal orders of the Great One, the Ayatollah Khomeini. The legionnaires wrongly identified me as an Iraqi soldier and opened fire, impeding my mission. I was forced to defend myself.

AGENT FOUR – I will ask you again, how are you able to survive the impact of a MILAN missile? And what weapons did you use against the Legion unit?

PRISONER – That is classified information.

(AGENT TWO straddles the prisoner and begins to beat him around the face. Suddenly, he takes his hand away, screams, and brandishes his hand at the camera. His hand is on fire)

(PRISONER sits passive in the chair as AGENT TWO falls screaming to the floor. The other agents attempt to put out the flames with their jackets. AGENT ONE abruptly spontaneously combusts. PRISONER sits passive in the centre of the room, unmoved, as the remaining agents and the whole room is engulfed in flame. Free of his bonds, he reaches forward and picks up the video camera, holding it up to his face. Film ends)

(Tape was retrieved by intelligence sources from the ruins of the Hotel Libre, Paris, destroyed by fire on January 17th 1993)

5

(Extract from the personal diary of Major Rupert Hockedy, Company Commander, 'A' Coy 1st Battalion The Queen's Own Yorkshire Rifles, attached to UNPROFOR, Bosnia-Herzegovina)

I've been dreading writing this entry. God alone knows how it will sound when I read it as a wizened old lieutenant colonel (retd.) sipping my g&t in the Savoy. One thing is certain – unless a Chetnik sniper takes me down and this is sent home to my nearest and dearest along with my dog tags and lucky pewter hip flask, no one is going to read it. If they did, I would be declared insane and thrown out of the service. Or maybe they would put it down to battle shock, or traumatic stress disorder, or whatever they call it these days, and give me a nice desk job. Sitting here, in a portacabin with a wooden pallet floor awash with mud, that sounds pretty good to me.

Anyway, onward and upward. This is roughly how, where, when and what. The observations are outlandish, I know. But they are the observations of a trained military officer who has been shot at by people of three different nationalities over the past five years, and who is unlikely to find himself hallucinating about Bosnian super-partisans when the first crack-thump is heard.

I had received orders to mount an armoured patrol eastwards from our base in the old school at Drbac, to monitor an apparent Serbian withdrawal from a factory complex that they had been zealously guarding for over a year. It was rumoured to contain a POW camp full of Bosnian civilians, but the Serbs had defied UN and Red Cross requests for access. To be honest, as our white painted Warrior armoured vehicles thundered down the single metalled road toward the Jinska factory, all I was expecting to find were bodies. I had come to know the Serbs, and their methods, very well.

Taking the high ground above the factory complex, we consolidated our position, sent out flanking teams of heavy machine guns and antitank weapons, and generally got ourselves into a good position in case the Serbs had decided to set a trap for us. I sent a rifle section of experienced Toms in to check for mines around the factory's huge iron gates, and they came back safely to report that there were none. But they had observed – and been observed by – unarmed civilians within the compound. The rifle platoon sergeant told me that the men had looked too emaciated to react or follow them. So, the intelligence reports about this place had been true. Leaving behind a sizeable rearguard and reserve element, I personally took two our Warriors into the heart of the complex.

I will never forget the sight that met me that afternoon. Perhaps this is what our fathers and grandfathers saw as they knocked down the gates of Bergen-Belsen and Auschwitz. Thank God that a Serbian never entered my gunsight from that day onwards, otherwise I would have been as guilty of murder myself, my hatred of them was that strong.

The Serbs had used Jinska as a holding camp for Bosnian civilians, mainly Muslims with a few out of favour Christians. But it was much, much more than that. As I took my men through its dusty interior wary of tripwires and with shemaghs pulled up over our faces to keep out the stench of human decay, it became evident that experimentation had been taking place here. There were rooms that had been given over for the express and evil purpose of torture, hung with meat hooks and shackles imbedded in the wall, bare electrical connections and pools of stagnant water dripping from rusty faucets. Survivors – aided from the building by my medics and some UN personnel that had joined us – were horribly disfigured, with wounds and sores reminiscent of the biological and chemical warfare training videos I had been shown at Porton Down. There had been rumours that the Serbs had stocks of nerve agent, the hallucinogen BZ and 'dirty nukes', conventional explosives laced with plutonium waste, and here was evidence that they were planning to turn Bosnia into apocalypse now. I began to withdraw my men in an orderly fashion, fearing that the whole complex might be contaminated, clearing rooms and collecting survivors as we went. I became separated from my close protection team, and found myself in a wing of the factory that had been hastily transformed into a makeshift hospital ward by thin wooden walls. It was completely silent, but on and in the dusty beds there were shapes. I stood frozen in the doorway. Facing me at the other end of the ward was a man in black. He was bent over the last bed on the row on the right. Its occupant was still alive – he lifted a hand as the man in black laid his hand on the patient's arm. But the patient's hand was like a lobster claw, a gnarled mass of bone and muscle. The man in black looked up at me, and the – God forgive me – *thing* in the bed turned too. Words fail me to describe it, I can only allude to the worst Lovecraftian nightmare, a face turned inside out, an external brain pulsing with wet life. The man in black placed his palm on this horror and I heard a brief *fzzt* like a fuse blowing, and the creature went limp in the bed. A whiff of ozone stung my nostrils. Then the man in black spoke. I remember his words, they were spoken loud and clear and in good English, with a cultured Middle Eastern accent:

"Stay your hand, Christian soldier. We fight on the same side. These men are beyond your help. I am sending them to stand at the right hand of Allah."

I watched, my weapon hanging forgotten from its sling around my neck, as he moved from bed to bed, responding to the movements of the hideously mutated forms there, placing his hands on them, and apparently killing them with the slightest of touches. Before his work was over, I retreated from the room, ran through the factory and linked up with my men, who informed me that they had found stocks of Russian-labelled nerve agents and unidentified, possibly biological agents in a factory storeroom. I ordered a full withdrawal and we took the UN team and the survivors of Jinska back to Drbac. Later, after the agents had been safely removed, Jinska was purged for good measure by fuel-air explosives delivered by RAF Harriers, in a spectacular fireworks display that the Toms appreciated.

I did not report my meeting with the man in black, nor the things that I saw in that room. Certainly, the dubious looking UNSCOM team that took over Jinska before its destruction brought its own armed protection and I heard no more about the place once they had left. Perhaps, as with the Nazis in World War Two, they took away secrets that we

ourselves will one day use.
  Remembering what I saw in Jinska that day, I pray God
that we do not.

*(Major Hockedy was killed by a Serbian sniper in Sarajevo
several days after completing this diary entry)*

6

*(Extract from Final Solution, article in Spartan 2000 – The
Magazine of the Modern International Military Man, by
Warren Grant, Balkan Correspondent)*

I sit with him on a hillside overlooking the refugee camp at
Mace. Behind us is Albania, a country honour-bound to
welcome those who call it an ancestral home and who are
fleeing persecution, but whose faltering steps into the modern
world after fifty years under the surreal grip of Hoxha have
been knocked flat by the human wave of misery that has
engulfed them. NATO forces stationed here, expecting to
launch an onslaught against the JNA, have found themselves
on riot duty in Tirana. They call this phenomena 'mission
creep'. Such is the fluid nature of millennium global politics.
  He calls himself Hanan. It is his given name, he says,
and he only remembered it recently. His comrades in the
UCK, of which he is a new member, call him Jihad, and are
proud to have him here as one of their warriors. His claims
are enormous and entirely unsubstantiated, but in the myth-
ridden world of the guerrilla fighter and career partisan –
some of these men have been fighters since pre-teens – only
one thing is undeniable : the number of enemy you have slain.
Crossing the mountainous border time and time again to
terrorise hidden bands of Serbian paramilitaries, Hanan has
proved himself worthy of the title Jihad – Holy War. A one

man Holy War.

Hanan's claim is that he is the product of an ill-fated military experiment in Iran during their desperate war with Iraq. That he saw action there, and was subsequently tasked to kill the heretic writer, Salman Rushdie. It was at this point that his brainwashing, or programming, began to malfunction, and it was a mission that he never completed. On the death of the Ayatollah Khomeini, architect of the fatwa, he considered his mission cancelled. Since then, he has fought on almost every front where Muslim soldiers or civilians have been imperilled – Afghanistan, Iraq during Desert Storm, Beirut, Bosnia, Algeria, Somalia, Libya, Chechnya. The claims are incredible, and he performs a trick for me to prove his story, burning a piece of notepaper on the palm of his hand by apparently raising his skin temperature, a skill he claims was responsible for the deaths of four GIGN agents in a Paris hotel room after he had 'allowed' them to capture him, for his amusement. It is a clever trick, and I do not know how he did it. I ask him what is his purpose. His answer is forthright.

"To wage holy war on the infidel. I was created to serve Allah, to do his Holy Will. That is why I broke from my controllers and disobeyed the Iranian state. They may have created me, but often Allah's will and the will of the Iranian government, are two different things. Now, I serve only Allah."

I asked him what his plans were.

"When I have aided the UCK in their mission, I will return to my home in Iran. I have read that a Pan-Arabic Mars Mission is being prepared. I am an ideal candidate, a prototype if you will, for spaceflight. With a little oxygen, I could survive on Mars. I have breathed raw nerve agent with no ill effect. Allah willing, they will forgive me and welcome me back."

Did he think this would happen? Would he not be shot as a deserter?

"I am an expensive investment. I am sure they will be pleased to have me back. Allah willing!"

He takes his leave. Dressed in the battle fatigues of a UCK soldier, but carrying no weapon, he walks back down the hill to the camp. Thorn bushes crackle and burst into flames in his wake. The hairs on the back of my neck prickle, as they do when you see something that you know is not right. I don't know if Hanan, or Jihad, is telling the truth. All I know is, he will kill many Serbs before he decides to go home.

I hope he makes it to Mars. Because he is far too dangerous to keep on Earth.

Who *Is* Noel K Hannan?

Noel K Hannan was born in 1967, learnt to read at age four, and has been writing ever since. He graduated through science fiction fandom as a teenager, writing and publishing his own fanzines and comics, and after a brief sabbatical in which an attempt was made to mature to adulthood, burst upon the active small press scene in the early 1990s as the editor and publisher of *NIGHTFALL*, an unusual anthology magazine that mixed text stories and comics. A brief but fruitful diversion into the world of American independent comics brought scripting credits on *NIGHT OF THE LIVING DEAD, AIR WARRIORS* and *WEIRD WEST*, and led to a resurgence of comics self-publishing that culminated in the critically acclaimed *STREETMEAT* graphic novel. In recent years Noel has concentrated on prose and has had short fiction published in *NEW WORLDS* and *ALBEDO ONE*, and he has four (tragically) unpublished novels awaiting loving homes. His occasional series of self-published story pamphlets (from which several of the stories in this collection are taken), expertly illustrated by collaborators from his comics imprint *BAD TO THE BONE*, brighten up many a dreary junkmail postbox. In 1999 Noel was a guest at the Break 21 Young Artists Festival in Ljubljana, Slovenia, despite being old enough to remember Apollo missions.

Noel's interests (okay, obsessions) include science fiction, detective stories, pulp culture of all kinds, cocker spaniels, the Boer War, military history, travel, kebabs, thrash metal, computers and manga. He is never bored unless he is being forced to do something boring, and happy when he has a blank piece of paper and a new pen in his hand. He thinks that writer's block is for wimps.

Noel lives in Crewe, Cheshire, with his ever-patient wife Helen and sometimes-patient son Alex, who has visited more military museums than any other toddler in history. Noel is currently working on the final draft of his latest novel, *THE CHILDREN*, a supernatural techno-thriller set in Beirut, the Brecon Beacons and Manchester, and *THE RAILWAY VOLUNTEERS*, a non-fiction book concerning a locally-raised volunteer unit in the Boer War.

You are welcome to visit his web site at: http://www.nhannan.freeeserve.co.uk, or comment on his work via email at: noel@nhannan.freeserve.co.uk

Also Available

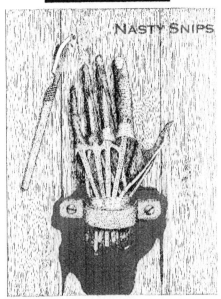

NASTY *Snips*

EDITED BY CHRISTOPHER C TEAGUE

An anthology of over thirty short, sharp and shocking
horror stories, from some the best new names in horror
Fiction, including: Simon Clark, Tim Lebbon, D F Lewis,
Mark McLaughlin, Steve Lockley, Edo van Belkom,
Paul Bradshaw, Darren Floyd, and many more.

"... the book works... it will shock, disturb and amuse you"
M J Simpson, SFX Magazine #63

"... stories... billed as short, sharp, shocks... achieve their aim in
spectacular style" *Lesley Beedal, Terror Tales #1*

£5.99   ISBN 0 9536833 0 3

Coming Soon in 2001

The Ice Maiden
by
Steve Lockley and Paul Lewis

A tale of supernatural retribution, set in the modern-day city of Swansea, Wales, written by the editors of the critically-acclaimed *Cold Cuts* series of horror anthologies.

To be published as a limited edition novella.

Tourniquet Heart
edited by
Christopher C Teague

An anthology of love stories, with a nasty and twisted edge, featuring fiction by Ramsey Campbell, Christopher Fowler and many more.

If you would like to know more, or to keep posted on any future publications from Pendragon Press, then please browse our website at:
www.pendragonpress.co.uk